剑桥英语等级考试系列·原版影印
北京英语水平考试(BETS)共享题库

Cambridge FCE Practice Tests 2
Teacher's Book

剑桥第一证书英语考试教程 2
（教师用书）

Nicholas Stephens
尼古拉斯·斯蒂芬斯

北京大学出版社
PEKING UNIVERSITY PRESS

CENGAGE
Learning™

Contents

Introduction   4

Test One

Paper 1: Reading
An in-depth look   6
Exam technique   7
Hints on answering the multiple-choice
   questions (Part 1)   7
Test   8

Paper 2: Writing
An in-depth look   14
Exam technique   14
Hints on writing a letter/email (Part 1)   15
Test   16

Paper 3: Use of English
An in-depth look   18
Exam technique   18
Hints on answering the multiple-choice
   cloze passage (Part 1)   19
Test   20
Vocabulary Extension   24

Paper 4: Listening
An in-depth look   26
Exam technique   26
Hints on answering the multiple-choice
   questions (Part 1)   26
Test   27

Paper 5: Speaking
An in-depth look   31
Exam technique   31
Hints on answering personal
   questions (Part 1)   31
Test   32

Test Two

Paper 1: Reading
Hints on working with a gapped text
   (Part 2)   33
Test   34

Paper 2: Writing
Hints on writing an informal
   letter (Part 2)   40
Test   41

Paper 3: Use of English
Hints on how to gap-fill (Part 2)   43
Test   44
Vocabulary Extension   48

Paper 4: Listening
Hints on sentence completion (Part 2)   50
Test   51

Paper 5: Speaking
Hints on comparing pictures (Part 2)   55
Test   56

Test Three

Paper 1: Reading
Hints on answering the multiple
   matching task (Part 3)   57
Test   58

Paper 2: Writing
Hints on writing an article   64
Test   65

Paper 3: Use of English
Hints on word formation (Part 3)   67
Test   68
Vocabulary Extension   72

Paper 4: Listening
Hints on multiple matching (Part 3)   74
Test   75

Paper 5: Speaking
Hints on speaking with a partner using visual
   prompts (Part 3)   79
Test   80

Test Four

Paper 1: Reading

    Hints on answering questions   81

    Test   82

Paper 2: Writing

    Hints on writing an essay   88

    Test   89

Paper 3: Use of English

    Hints on 'key' word transformations

      (Part 4)   91

    Test   92

    Vocabulary Extension   96

Paper 4: Listening

    Hints on answering multiple-choice

      questions (Part 4)   98

    Test   99

Paper 5: Speaking

    Hints on speaking with a partner and

      the interlocutor (Part 4)   103

    Test   104

Test Five

Paper 1: Reading

    Hints on improving your reading skills I   105

    Test   106

Paper 2: Writing

    Hints on writing a short story   112

    Test   113

Paper 3: Use of English

    Hints on answering questions   115

    Test   116

    Vocabulary Extension   120

Paper 4: Listening

    Hints on improving your listening skills I   122

    Test   123

Paper 5: Speaking

    Hints on improving your speaking skills I   127

    Test   128

Test Six

Paper 1: Reading

    Hints on improving your reading skills II   129

    Test   130

Paper 2: Writing

    Hints on writing a report   136

    Hints on answering the task for the

      set books   136

    Test   137

Paper 3: Use of English

    Hints on improving your Use of

      English skills   139

    Test   140

    Vocabulary Extension   144

Paper 4: Listening

    Hints on improving your listening skills II   146

    Test   147

Paper 5: Speaking

    Hints on improving your speaking skills II   151

    Test   152

Photographs and Visuals for Tests   153

Glossary   165

Tapescript   170

What makes this Practice Test Book different from other test books available?

This book is different because it is more than just a book of practice tests. It has been designed not only to give students ample and realistic practice of the format and content of each part of the Cambridge First Certificate in English Examination (FCE), but also to provide useful vocabulary expansion and relevant advice on how to acquire the skills required in the examination.

Cambridge First Certificate Practice Tests 2 contains:

- six complete practice tests for the Cambridge First Certificate in English

- full information about each paper

- exam technique sections – hints and tips for the student on how to approach each paper

- hints on how to approach each of the composition question types

- extra vocabulary practice for the Use of English paper

- high quality photographs for the Speaking paper

- listening practice containing a variety of accents, recorded by professional actors

- a wide range of topics in all papers to cover all the themes likely to be encountered at this level

The first four tests in *Cambridge First Certificate Practice Tests* can be completed by students at home as homework and then checked in class. The last two tests can be carried out under timed conditions prior to the final examination, in order to give students a realistic expectation of the time available. It is suggested that all unknown vocabulary is given due attention in the classroom – students should be encouraged to write down the new words and expressions in their notebooks, along with any collocations or derivatives. Certain vocabulary can be selected for the students to practice, either in writing or as a basis of any spoken activities. Students who use new vocabulary in realistic activities in the classroom are more likely to retain such items and to incorporate them effectively into their spoken and written work at a later date.

Cambridge First Certificate in English (FCE): A brief outline of each paper

PAPER 1: READING (1 hour)
Students are asked to carry out a variety of comprehension tasks based on passages varying in length. The paper contains three parts, one of which may contain two or more shorter, related texts. There is a total of 30 questions. All answers are written in pencil on a separate answer sheet.

PAPER 2: WRITING (1 hour 20 minutes)
Two compositions to be written. The first question in Part 1 is compulsory for all candidates and includes material of up to 160 words (with the possible addition of graphic or pictorial material) that students are expected to manipulate in an appropriate manner. In Part 2, students choose one question from a range of task types, including a question on the optional set book. Compositions have to be written in blue or black pen and NOT in pencil.

Note: The set books are changed frequently and it is, therefore, unrealistic to provide specific questions related to any particular book. However, based on experience and previous examination questions, we have provided a wide range of questions that can be applied to whichever set book the student is reading and studying.

PAPER 3: USE of ENGLISH (45 minutes)
The paper contains four parts. Questions for Parts 1 (multiple-choice cloze), 2 (open cloze), and 3 (word formation) are based on short texts. Part 4 consists of 8 gapped sentences and a lead-in sentence for students to perform "key" word transformations. There is a total of 42 questions. All answers for Parts 2, 3 and 4 should be written in pencil using capital letters.

PAPER 4: LISTENING (approximately 40 minutes)
A cassette recording for the four parts of the paper, each of which is heard twice. Pieces include a wide range of items that a student would be expected to encounter on a visit to an English-speaking country. Students will be expected to complete a range of comprehension tasks including multiple choice, sentence completion and multiple matching. Answers are marked directly on the question paper. Students have five minutes at the end of the test to transfer their answers onto a separate answer sheet. All answers for Part 2 should be written in pencil using capital letters.

PAPER 5: SPEAKING (14 minutes)
Students are interviewed in pairs in the presence of two examiners. One examiner takes the role of interlocutor and asks questions or provides written or spoken stimuli for the candidates. The other examiner does not contribute to the conversation but observes and assesses each candidate. There are four parts in this paper.

Part 1   Students are encouraged to give information about themselves.
Part 2   Students take turns to talk about colour photographs they are given and to comment briefly on their partner's photographs.
Part 3   Students work with each other, using visual and written prompts, to generate a discussion that might involve tasks such as problem solving, prioritising, etc.
Part 4   Students are invited to discuss themes related to Part 3 with each other and the interlocutor.

Marking System
The overall grade is based on the aggregate score for all five papers. In other words, if you fail one paper, it is still possible to pass. Pass grades are A, B and C. Fail grades are D and E. The results slips of students indicate areas in which a high level of performance has been achieved (for those candidates who achieve a pass grade) or where performance is particularly weak (for candidates with fail grades).

Paper 1 : Reading

An in-depth look

In this paper, you have 1 hour to complete three parts. Each part contains one or more texts with a comprehension task.

Part	Number of Questions	Marks per Question	Task
1	8	2	Four-option multiple-choice questions based on a text **Tests**: understanding of gist, detail, what is implied and lexical reference
2	7	2	7 sentences which have been removed from a text must be replaced **Tests:** understanding of how a text is structured in English
3	15	1	15 multiple-matching questions based on one or more texts **Tests:** ability to locate specific information quickly

You are required to mark your answers on a separate answer sheet in pencil. This must be done during the 1 hour given. You will not be allowed extra time to transfer your answers to the answer sheet.

Exam technique

In the Reading Paper of the FCE examination, the ability to manage the time available is an essential skill. It is not enough just to be able to understand written English and complete comprehension tasks correctly.

You have 1 hour to complete all three parts of the paper and complete the separate answer sheet. It is important to time yourself well before the examination so you can adjust your technique according to the time available. As the different parts of the Reading Paper test different reading skills, it is more than likely that you will be better at, or able to complete more quickly, one or more parts of the paper. You must also leave sufficient time to transfer your answers to the answer sheet in an unrushed manner. Be careful not to fill in any answers in the wrong place, which may then make the following answers incorrect.

Hints on answering the multiple-choice questions (Part 1)

This part of the Reading Paper tests your detailed understanding, global understanding (eg The purpose of this text is ...), inference (eg What does the writer mean when ...?) and lexical reference (eg What does 'they' in line X refer to?).

This part of the paper can be approached in two ways:

a   Read the text fairly quickly and then read the questions one by one. Hopefully, you will have some idea of where to return to in the text when you read the questions. Identify the correct place in the text and work through the four options until you find the one supported by the text.
b   Read the question stems first so that when you start reading the text, points relating to the questions will sound familiar. You can then go back to the relevant question and look at the options available, working through them until you find the one supported by the text.

Have confidence in your decisions. If you can support your answer with something from the text, it is probably correct. Do not choose an answer based on what you think or know, but which is not mentioned in the text.

Answer all the questions.

Part 1

You are going to read part of an instruction manual for an iron. For questions **1–8**, choose the answer **A, B, C** or **D** which you think fits best according to the text.

Instructions

Filling with water (for steam–ironing and spraying)
◆ You can fill this iron with normal tap water.
◆ Remove the mains plug from the wall socket before filling the iron. Set the steam control (B) (fig. 2) to position 0 (=no steam).
◆ Stand the iron upright and open the slide valve. Pour no more than 170 ml of water into the filling aperture (F). Otherwise there will be a problem with steam ironing and spraying.

Ironing temperature
◆ Sort the laundry out according to ironing temperature first: wool with wool, cotton with cotton, etc.
◆ The iron heats up faster than it cools down. Therefore, start ironing the articles requiring the lowest temperature such as those made of synthetic fibres.
◆ If the fabric consists of various kinds of fibres, you must always select the lowest ironing temperature of the composition of those fibres. (Eg, an article consisting of 60% polyester and 40% cotton should be ironed at the temperature indicated for polyester [•] and without steam.)

Setting the temperature
◆ Stand the iron upright.
◆ Set the temperature control (A) to the correct ironing temperature as indicated in the ironing instructions or in the table. (See fig. 1.)
◆ Insert the mains plug into the wall socket.
◆ After the temperature indicator light (G) has gone out and come on again, you may start ironing. The indicator light will go out from time to time during ironing.

If you set the temperature control to a lower setting after ironing at a high temperature, do not begin again before the indicator light comes on.

fig.1

Instructions on label	Textrle	Temperature control	Steam control
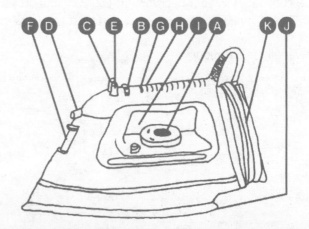	**synthetics** eg, acetate, acrylic, viscose, polyamide (nylon), polyester **silk**	Low •	no steam
	wool	Medium••	low steam
	cotton linen	High •••	high steam

Note: ✕ on label means:"This article cannot be ironed!"

Steam ironing
◆ As indicated on the temperature control (A) and the table, steam-ironing is only possible at higher ironing temperatures:

•• or••• for moderate steam.
••• for maximum steam.

With conventional steam irons, water may leak from the sole-plate if a too low temperature has been selected. This will then cause stains. However, your new steam iron features 'Drip Stop' steam shut-off: the iron will automatically stop steaming at too low temperatures. When this happens, you can hear a click. Set the temperature control to the advised position. Steaming will recommence as soon as the appropriate temperature has been reached.

◆ Ensure that there is enough water in the water reservoir.
◆ Stand the iron on its rear side.

◆ Set the temperature control (A) at the required position within the 'steam area' (•• or•••).
◆ Insert the mains plug into the wall socket.
◆ Wait a little while for the green indicator light (G) to go out and to come on again.
◆ Set the steam control (B) to the required position.

Auto stop
If the iron is left in a motionless horizontal position for more than 30 seconds, or in a vertical position for more than 8 minutes, the red pilot light (H) will come on blinking and the heating element will switch off automatically. You will also hear a sound signal.

When picking up the iron again, the red light will go out and the green temperature indicator light (G) will come on. This indicates that the iron has begun heating up again.

When the green light has gone out you can recommence ironing.

General description (fig. 2)

A	Temperature control (variable)	G	Temperature indicator light
B	Steam control (variable)	H	'Auto Stop' pilot light
C	Spray button (press)	I	'Self Clean' button (press)
D	Spray	J	Type plate
E	'Shot of steam' button (press)	K	Cord storage
F	Filling aperture with slide valve		

1 Why should you put no more than 170 ml of water in the iron?
    A   That's all the iron can hold.
    B   The measuring beaker can only hold 170 ml.
    Ⓒ   The steam-ironing and spraying features won't work properly.
    D   Tap water contains a lot of salt.

2 What is the advantage of ironing clothes made of a synthetic material first?
    A   It is impossible to damage clothes if you do.
    Ⓑ   It won't take as long to do the ironing.
    C   The iron won't leave so many stains.
    D   There are bound to be more of them to iron.

3 How should an article consisting of 80% cotton and 20% wool be ironed?
    A   at a low temperature with no steam
    B   at a high temperature with no steam
    C   at a high temperature with high steam
    Ⓓ   at a medium temperature with low steam

4 What would you do if the indicator light went on and off while you were ironing?
    Ⓐ   Ignore it because it is normal.
    B   Stop ironing immediately.
    C   Let the iron cool down.
    D   Use the spray when the light is on.

5 What special feature for steam ironing does the iron have?
    A   It prevents too much spray from going onto clothes.
    B   It removes stains causes by steam.
    C   It warns the person ironing that it is dripping.
    Ⓓ   It stops steaming when the temperature is too low.

6 When can you start using steam while ironing?
    A   only when you press button E
    B   after you hear a clicking noise
    Ⓒ   when the temperature is medium or high
    D   when the green light goes out

7 What does the 'auto stop' feature do?
    A   It starts working when you press button H.
    B   It switches off the iron 30 seconds after the green light comes on.
    C   It switches off the iron if it is moved for more than 30 seconds.
    Ⓓ   It acts as a safety shut-off for the iron.

8 How can you tell if the 'auto stop' feature has been activated?
    A   The green light will go out.
    Ⓑ   You will hear a sound and see a red light.
    C   The iron will be in a vertical position.
    D   The iron is heating up.

Part 2

You are going to read a newspaper article about an art exhibition. Seven sentences have been removed from the article. Choose from the sentences **A–H** the one which fits each gap (**9–15**). There is one extra sentence which you do not need to use.

Pick up a painting at the academy

Art lovers are streaming into the Royal Academy and they are not going in empty-handed. They are armed with their cheque books and they are ready to use them. The attraction is the 231st annual summer exhibition and within the first two weeks, enthusiasts have purchased almost everything on the walls.

'We have been coming here for four years and are amazed at the number of paintings that have already been sold. This is much faster than last year,' said Ruth Plain of Essex, who has visited the show with her husband, Richard. **9** C

'We have just the place for it in our cottage,' said Mr Plain. **10** H So the Plains will have to make their minds up quickly if they are going to add some colour to that space over the stairs.

Cuffe is one of the 383 exhibitors in this year's festival who are not members of the Academy. Each of the 100 academicians has the right to show up to six pieces, which accounts for 442 of the works in the show. **11** B

The original number was reduced to a short list of about 2,000. Then each of the 13 committee members was assigned one of the gallery's rooms and told to fill it with fine art. **12** G

'This blend of works by obscure artists and well-established names is unique,' said committee member, Norman Ackroyd. 'Where else would you see an unknown artist's work like this hanging between pieces by two internationally-recognised people like Jasper Johns and Jim Dine? **13** F

This disregard for commercial valuation is demonstrated by a £95 print by Barbara Hermann surrounded by pieces worth thousands of pounds. Ms Hermann's dry point etching of a woman lying in bed is apparently benefiting from this prime location as her edition of 20 prints is close to selling out. **14** A

At the other end of the price range but just one room away is a Kitaj offering called Sandra Five, a Magazine at £500,000, framed. Actually, there are three frames, one for each of the sections that stretch side-by-side for five feet. However, you can't buy the most valuable paintings in the show. **15** D

Despite this, Mr Ackroyd says buyers are assured of a good purchase from the summer exhibition because each of the pieces has been chosen by a panel of top artists who certainly know their stuff.

A   Her work is among the more affordable at the show.

B   The other 540 pieces were chosen by a committee from the 9,000 submitted by artists from around the world.

C   After looking at the 982 works on offer, they decided that Irish artist Grainne Cuffe had produced what they were looking for in the form of a huge etching of a bold, red flower.

D   David Hockney's colourful vistas of the Grand Canyon, for example, are not for sale.

E   It doesn't really matter which painting you take home with you.

F   The answer, quite simply, is nowhere.

G   The left-over pieces were sent back to the artists with a 'thank you' note.

H   They are not absolutely sure whether they are going to make the purchase but, at £435 for each print in the run of 65, the pieces are going quickly.

Part 3

You are going to read a newspaper article about buying a house. For questions **16–30**, choose from the people (**A–D**). The people may be chosen more than once. When more than one answer is required, these may be given in any order.

Which of the people suggest the following?

A	Lorna Vestley	**C**	Kim Bailey
B	Mark Watts	**D**	Jim Keene

Personal contact with the agent is vital.	**16**	B
I made a new friend while looking for a house.	**17**	B
I didn't get on with an agent.	**18**	D
I wanted to get everything done quickly.	**19**	C
I felt like calling the agent all the time.	**20**	B
Agents appreciate honesty.	**21** A	**22** C
I lost money because of a delay.	**23**	D
Changing your mind can cause a delay.	**24**	A
I shouldn't have spoken to anyone about my affairs.	**25**	D
I told my agent the maximum price I could afford.	**26**	C
I made my agent work hard.	**27**	C
If you can't make a meeting, let the agent know immediately.	**28**	B
The agent is not employed by the buyer.	**29**	A
Looking for a house can be very tiring.	**30**	A

Buying a House

How do you get the best properties first? **Lonta Vestley** *gives some good advice.*

Finding and buying a house can be an exhausting and emotional experience at the best of times and when there are few properties available, there are always people richer than you who keep pushing the prices up. However, there are things you can do to improve your chances of being the one who actually finds and buys the perfect property.

First of all, you should know your own mind – not just on what your ideal home looks like but on what you are prepared to accept. It is a waste of time if you refuse to consider a home which is less than ideal at first but then change your requirements and price range at a later date.

You should always choose an agent you feel comfortable with. Remember, they are human, too, and will make an extra effort for those people they trust, like and find responsive. You should also be straightforward with them. This will gain you valuable points since they are under pressure and have dozens of buyers to satisfy. Although the agent has a duty to be honest with you, you should bear in mind that you are not his client. The client is the person who pays the agent's bill and this is the seller.

At the moment, sellers are in short supply so they are the ones that are likely to be known to the agent. **Mark Watts**, a computer programmer, realised this from the start. "Normally, buyers are just names on a card or on file in a computer. This means that the agent has no personal relationship with buyers," he says. "Fortunately, I made an appointment to see the agent who had been recommended to me. I found it much better to talk face to face than to send a letter. I also resisted the temptation to ring him every day but I did call him twice a week to see if there was anything new and demonstrate my keenness. It's also best if you show the agent that you are a serious buyer so if you are running late or can't make an appointment, let the agent know as soon as possible. I built up quite a good relationship with my agent and now he is a welcome guest in my home nearly every weekend."

Another person who had no real difficulty in finding a property to her liking was **Kim Bailey**, a business executive. "I had planned everything from the start. I set my budget at the highest possible figure and searched furiously for the right property. I had to get things done quickly because prices seemed to be rising all the time and my budget was at its limit," she says. "I might have put my agent under pressure, but she certainly got the message that I was serious and that turned out to be good. We worked well as a team and the whole thing was over in about a month. I think she appreciated the fact that I didn't underestimate the amount I was prepared to spend. Buying a house is a team effort so you shouldn't do it alone!"

However, not everyone can work towards a goal with others. **Jim Keene**, a mechanical engineer, says: "Buying a house turned out to be a nightmare for me. I thought I could do nearly everything by myself but I was wrong. It took me a while to realise that what I was doing was foolish and by the time I did, prices had risen – not by too much, but by enough to put financial pressure on me. I was told to get to know the agent personally and not to be a faceless name on file. I did that but I found that the agent was too busy. He also had an air of self-importance that I found irritating. Perhaps it was just that the property market was slow for the buyer. Anyway, I got another agent who found a property for me quite quickly but I went and told a friend about it. Before I could seal the deal, my friend had let someone else in on the secret and I'd lost my ideal home. I think there are lessons to be learnt from my experience."

An in-depth look

In this paper, you have 1 hour 20 minutes to complete **two** tasks. The first task is compulsory for all students and the second task is chosen from four optional questions, one of which is based on the optional set text.

Part	Type of Task	Length
1	Letter or email (formal/informal)	120–150 words
2	One task from four (article, letter, report, review, essay or story)	120–180 words

Each composition is given a mark out of 20 based on the student's ability to produce writing that is well organised within a suitable format, interesting, appropriate in terms of vocabulary and register and that answers the task set fully.

You must write your composition in the answer booklet provided in either black or blue ink, and not in pencil.

Exam technique

1 hour 20 minutes is sufficient time for you to complete both tasks. It is important to spend an equal amount of time on both compositions rather than a particularly long time on one and then have to rush the second task.

Spend a few minutes at the beginning of the Writing Paper choosing the question in Part 2 which you feel you can answer best. Remember that Part 1 is compulsory and all students must answer it.

When you have decided on the questions to be answered, take some time to plan each one. You will not be able to write a well-organised composition without writing your thoughts down on paper first and then arranging them into paragraphs. This should take about 10 minutes and you should make sure at this stage that your plan is relevant to the question and has answered it completely.

Then spend about 20 minutes writing the composition, which will leave you about 10 minutes at the end for checking.

Make sure you write the correct number of words. A short answer will often mean that a student has not answered fully whereas a long answer obviously takes more time to write, may contain more errors and will not receive the best mark from the examiner.

Take two or three pens with you and make sure your writing is clear and easy to read. If you make a mistake, put a neat line through the word or phrase and continue writing. The examiner will not mind your making mistakes if your composition looks neat and tidy.

Hints on writing a letter/email (Part 1)

When answering this task, it is important to spend adequate time reading and understanding the information provided. This information is provided in the form of text and notes and may include pictures.

To achieve a good mark in this type of question, you must utilise the information fully, being careful not to miss any points out. The examiners are also looking for evidence that you can express the information in your own words and expand on it. You must think about who your target reader is and choose a suitable style and register accordingly.

The following types of letter or email may be required:

- letters/emails giving/requesting information
- letters/emails of complaint
- letters/emails giving advice
- letters/emails of apology
- letters/emails accepting/declining an invitation
- letters/emails of invitation
- letters/emails of recommendation
- letters/emails of application (i.e. for a job)

Although addresses are not required for letters in the FCE examination, a correct layout is required. Paragraphs need to be well thought out and salutations and closing phrases must be appropriate.

Try to vary your vocabulary and phrases to avoid sounding repetitive. For example, in a letter or email giving advice, don't keep using the phrase: 'If I were you,...'. You could also use other expressions such as 'It would be a good idea ...', 'Have you considered ...?' or even 'Why don't you ...?' for an informal letter or email. See the section below on style for some helpful vocabulary.

You may include your own ideas in this type of writing task, but make sure you cover all the points mentioned in the question first and that you don't write a letter or email which is overlong.

HELPFUL PHRASES:

Giving/requesting information
- *In answer to your request for information ...*
- *I hope this information is of use to you.*
- *I would be grateful if you could tell me ...*
- *I'm writing to enquire about ...*

Letters accepting/declining an invitation
- *It's with great pleasure that we accept your kind invitation.*
- *Unfortunately, we are unable to attend.*
- *Thank you so much. We'd love to come.*
- *I'm afraid I already have plans for that particular day.*

Making a complaint
- *I am writing to express my dissatisfaction with ...*
- *I wish to complain about ...*
- *...did not live up to my expectations/your advertisement.*

Making an invitation
- *I'd be delighted if you could join us at ...*
- *I was thinking how nice it would be if ...*
- *Would you like to ...?*

Giving advice
- *In my opinion, you should ...*
- *Have you considered ...?*
- *If I were you, I would ...*

Making recommendations
- *It really is the best cinema/restaurant/hotel around.*
- *I don't hesitate in recommending it to you.*
- *I'm sure you will be more than happy there.*

Apologising
- *I regret to inform you ...*
- *Please accept my apologies.*
- *I'm very sorry about ...*

Making an application
- *I am writing to apply for ...*
- *As far as my qualifications are concerned, ...*
- *As regards work experience, ...*

Part 1

You **must** answer this question.

1   You are interested in science, technology and the future. One day, you see the following advertisement for a new magazine.

Read the advertisement carefully and the notes you have made for yourself. Then write a letter to the publisher of the magazine asking for the information covered in your notes.

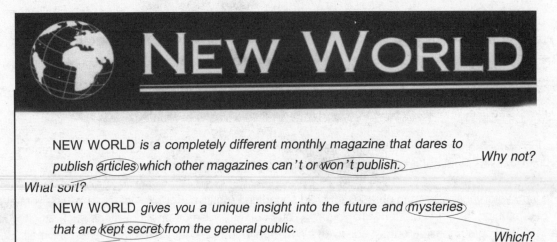

NEW WORLD *is a completely different monthly magazine that dares to publish articles which other magazines can't or won't publish.* — Why not?

What sort?

NEW WORLD *gives you a unique insight into the future and mysteries that are kept secret from the general public.* — Which?

Why?

NEW WORLD *offers subscribers unique benefits through its membership card, such as membership to other clubs and cheaper subscription rates for other magazines.* — Which ones?

Order your first copy now by completing the coupon below.

Also: Information for articles–new?
                     where from?
                     proof?

Write a **letter** of between 120 and 150 words in an appropriate style. Do not write any addresses.

This model is provided as an example of the standard expected for FCE and to show how the notes can be expanded.

Dear Sir/Madam,

I read your advertisement about 'New World' in yesterday's newspaper. I am very interested in this magazine, but before I subscribe to it, I would like to know more.

I would like to know exactly what sort of articles you publish and why you say other magazines refuse to publish them. Could you tell me which mysteries you refer to in the advertisement and why they are kept secret? I would like to know where your information for the articles comes from, whether it is new and what proof you have to support it.

The advertisement also mentions membership to other clubs and cheaper subscription to other magazines. I would be grateful if you could give me the names of these clubs and magazines.

I look forward to your reply and, hopefully, to subscribing to your magazine.

Yours faithfully,

Marios Economou

Part 2

Write an answer to **one** of the questions **2–5** in this part. Write your answer in **120–180** words in an appropriate style.

2 A letter criticising tattoos, earrings and modern hairstyles has provoked a storm of protest in an international student magazine. The magazine has announced that it is looking for articles entitled:

"Personal appearance–a matter of freedom."

Write your **article.**

3 You see this advertisement in a local newspaper.

Restaurant reviewers needed!

Have you been to a restaurant recently? Fancy the idea of a free meal?

Send us a review of a restaurant you have visited recently, including your views on the food, service and atmosphere. Say whether you would recommend the restaurant to anyone else. The best reviews will receive a voucher for a meal at a top restaurant!

Write your **review.**

4 You work for a travel agency that has decided to publish an entertainment guide for tourists. The manager wants you to visit a restaurant and write a report, covering every aspect of it and saying what makes it different from other restaurants.

Write your **report.**

5 Background reading texts
Answer **one** of the following two questions based on your reading of **one** of the set books. Your answer should contain enough detail to make it clear to someone who may not have read the book.

Either (a) A college is going to put on a play based on the book or a short story you have read. They have invited students from other colleges to describe how the most important scene should be performed. Write a **letter**, giving your suggestions for the scene you have chosen.

or (b) How well do you think you would get on with the main characters in the book you have read? Write an **essay**, saying why you would or wouldn't get on with one of the main characters, and why.

An in-depth look

In this paper, you have 45 minutes to complete **four** parts.

Part	Number of Questions	Marks per Question	Task
1	12	1	Four-option multiple-choice cloze passage containing 12 gaps. **Tests:** mainly vocabulary
2	12	1	Open cloze – a text with 12 gaps. **Tests:** grammar and vocabulary
3	10	1	Word formation. A short text containing 10 gaps. From a given word, students make a new word which fits the gap in the text. **Tests:** vocabulary
4	8	2	'Key' word transformations. Students are required to complete a second sentence using a given word without changing the meaning. **Tests:** grammar and vocabulary

Exam technique

As techniques for the different tasks vary, we will look at each task independently.

Remember that you will need to complete the separate answer sheet in pencil. As you are not given extra time to do this, it is advisable to complete the answer sheet as you go through the Use of English Paper.

Hints on answering the multiple-choice cloze passage (Part 1)

In this part of the paper, you need to choose one word or phrase from a set of four (**A, B, C** or **D**) to fill a gap in the text.

It is a good idea to read the text through quickly first to get an idea of what it is about.

When deciding which option is correct, you must remember that the correct meaning of the word is not always enough. Very often you need to look at the structure of the sentence or look for fixed phrases and collocations as well as phrasal verbs and linking words.

Answer all questions. Even if you guess, you have a 25% chance of success.

Here are a number of examples of multiple-choice cloze questions and what to look out for:

1 Meaning

It may involve choosing a word according to meaning only. For example:

It is common for................ to visit Delphi during the summer.

A observers   **B** spectators   **C** sightseers   **D** passers-by

The answer is 'sightseers' because it fits in terms of meaning.

2 Grammar

It may involve choosing a word that fits in with the grammar of the sentence. For example:

He never .... in reaching the source of the river.

A managed   **B** achieved   **C** arranged   **D** succeeded

The answer is 'succeeded', not because it fits in with the meaning but because it is the only one that is followed by 'in' and a gerund.

3 Fixed phrase

It may involve choosing a word that fits in a set phrase. For example:

Students rarely .... any notice of their landlords.

A paid   **B** took   **C** got   **D** brought

The answer is 'took' because it is part of the phrase 'take notice of'.

4 Collocation

It may involve choosing a word that usually goes together with another word. For example:

The .... road was once used by smugglers.

A curling   **B** rolling   **C** winding   **D** waving

The answer is 'winding' because it is the only one that goes with 'road'.

5 Phrasal verbs

It may involve choosing a word that forms a phrasal verb with the correct meaning. For example:

Scientists have been quick to .... out the problems with the new theory.

A point   **B** give   **C** let   **D** come

The answer is 'point', not because the other words do not form phrasal verbs with the word 'out', but because 'point out' fits in with the meaning of the sentence.

Part 1

For questions **1–12**, read the text below and decide which answer **A, B, C** or **D** best fits each space. There is an example at the beginning (**0**).

Example:

0 **A** latter   **B** recent   **C** current   **D** former

0	A	B	C	D
	▭	▬	▭	▭

Changing History

In (0) .... years, it has become fashionable to explain sudden changes in the past by (1).............. them to a natural disaster. Now (2).............. has been uncovered which suggests that the Dark Age were also caused by a catastrophe. In 535 AD, a volcano, Krakatoa, (3).............. with a force equal to 2,000 million Hiroshima bombs. This (4)............ to a natural nuclear winter which, in turn, had dramatic (5)............ on global history. In many parts of the world, there was a lack of rainfall. The resulting (6).............. and famine forced people to migrate and invade areas where there was food. In other parts, a massive increase in rainfall meant that rats thrived and (7) ....a disease, the plague, into Europe. This disease (8).............. rapidly and killed up to 80% of the populations of some cities.

Although some experts have (9).............. this theory, science and historical records have supported it. Scientists have discovered that tree rings in wood from all (10).............. the world indicate there was low growth in the years following the disaster due to a decrease in temperature. As regards history, the Roman historian, Procupius, reported that the sun didn't shine (11) .... for about a year.

This new theory supports the idea that a natural disaster can be responsible for the disappearance of a (12).............. civilisation. It should also warn us about what global warming might do to our own civili-sation.

1	A	bonding	B	combining	C	joining	D	linking
2	A	testimony	B	evidence	C	fact	D	proof
3	A	collided	B	erupted	C	burst	D	blasted
4	A	resulted	B	caused	C	led	D	created
5	A	effects	B	conclusions	C	meanings	D	circumstances
6	A	draught	B	flood	C	current	D	drought
7	A	transported	B	located	C	carried	D	transferred
8	A	spread	B	scattered	C	distributed	D	moved
9	A	denied	B	refused	C	rejected	D	turned
10	A	through	B	along	C	across	D	over
11	A	usually	B	regularly	C	typically	D	normally
12	A	total	B	whole	C	complete	D	full

Part 2

For questions **13–24**, read the text below and think of the word which best fits each space. Use only **one** word in each space. There is an example at the beginning (**0**).

Example:

| 0 | CAN |

CYCLING FOR HEALTH

Nobody doubts that cycling (0) ...can...... lead to better health, but it seems that people need to see figures before they actually (13)...do....... something positive. Now, these figures have been made available through the charity, *Going for Green*. The charity claims that (14)....an..... increase of ten per cent in the (15).number. of people cycling regularly to work would mean four per cent fewer people developing heart disease. This would happen because people could get their heart beating and avoid the stress that comes with sitting in traffic jams.

In the long term, (16)....there..... would also be benefits for the non-cyclist. Provided enough people started cycling, it would reduce the fumes blamed for causing as (17)..many.... as 20,000 premature deaths per year. From these figures, it can (18)....be..... seen that cycling not (19)..only..... benefits the cyclist but also patients who could be treated as a (20)..result..... of the money saved from not having to treat so many heart patients.

Cycling makes sense, especially for journeys of (21).....less..... than five miles. This is because pollution-reducing catalytic converters in cars are least effective (22)...on....... short journeys and five miles (23) .....is....... a distance that people of nearly (24)....all....... ages can manage.

Part 3

For questions **25–34**, read the text below. Use the word given in capitals at the end of each line to form a word that fits in the space **in the same line.** There is an example at the beginning (**0**).

Example:

0	SALES

Selling more

It has long been known that the (0)……sales…… of any	SELL
particular (25).product… can be affected by its appearance in a	PRODUCE
shop or store. The appearance of an item is (26)…basically…… affected	BASE
by the (27)…lighting… and colour in the shop and its position relative	LIGHT
to other items. This is perhaps most (28) .apparent.in supermarkets,	APPEAR
where it has been found that the most (29).effective… place for gum	EFFECT
and batteries is (30).directly… before the check-out. Supermarkets	DIRECT
also persuade customers to buy by (31)…brightening…. some areas and	BRIGHT
pumping the smell of fresh bread into the (32).bakery…. section.	BAKE
This sounds perfectly (33)…reasonable…, but it has also been found that	REASON
smells that have absolutely no (34) …connection.. with the items on sale	CONNECT
can encourage people to buy these items.	

Part 4

For questions **35–42**, complete the second sentence so that it has a similar meaning to the first sentence, using the word given. **Do not change the word given.** You must use between **two** and **five** words including the word given. Here is an example (**0**).

Example:

0 We got to the island at midnight.
   REACH
   We didn't ....midnight.

The gap can be filled by the words "reach the island until", so you write:

0	REACH THE ISLAND UNTIL

35 You really shouldn't enter the laboratory without permission.
   SUPPOSED
   You ....*are not supposed to enter*.............. the laboratory without permission.

36 It would have been impossible for me to do it without you.
   HAVE
   I ....*could not/never have done*........... it without you.

37 She had no intention of insulting Jack.
   MEAN
   She ....*did not mean to insult*.............. Jack.

38 Carol didn't listen to what her teacher said.
   ATTENTION
   Carol didn't ....*pay (any) attention to*................. what her teacher said.

39 The party was rather disappointing.
   TIME
   We didn't ....*have a (very) good/great etc. time*............. at the party.

40 He only arrived on time because he didn't wait for you.
   LATE
   He would have............*arrived/been late if he had*............. waited for you.

41 Most of the men wore black clothes.
   DRESSED
   Most of the men............*were dressed in*.........................black.

42 Mark had nothing in his bank account.
   MONEY
   There............*was no money (left)/(at all)*...........in Mark's bank account.

Vocabulary Extension

A Vocabulary Building

Complete the unfinished words in the following sentences. The words are all related to sports and hobbies.

1 Some spectators shouted at the refe r e e as the footballers left the pit c h.

2 We found boxing gl o v e s, golf cl u b s, table tennis b a t s and some old track s u i t s in the attic.

3 She usually plays tennis on the co u r t near the golf co u r s e.

4 Stamp co l l e c t i n g was a popular pas t i m e among my classmates.

5 The school has no gy m n a s i u m and very little sports equ i p m e n t.

6 He enjoys making mo d e l aeroplanes from k i t s he buys at a local toy shop.

7 Ka r a t e and k u n g f u are two widely-practised martial a r t s.

8 She's been interested in photography since she was given a ca m e r a for her birthday. She even develops her own photos.

9 If you don't come to tra i n i n g sessions, you won't be in the t e a m.

10 Top sporting figures spend hours practising their sk i l l s and tech n i q u e.

B Word Use

Use the words on the left to complete the sentences on the right. Make sure the word is in the correct form. Use each word once.

1	collide	a	A water mains .....burst...... outside my house yesterday.
	erupt	b	If the train had ..collided... with the lorry, the driver would have been killed.
	burst	c	Scientists believe that the volcano will ...erupt..... very soon.

2	result	a	What ...caused.... the outbreak of food poisoning?
	cause	b	These technological changes will certainly ....lead...... to higher unemployment.
	lead	c	Our close cooperation can only ....result.... in better understanding.
	create	d	Her presence ..created.... a great deal of tension at the meeting.

3	draught	a	Don't sit over there because there's a ..draught... coming from under the door.
	flood	b	The ..current.... was too strong for the yacht to sail against.
	current	c	Heavy rain led to .....floods/flooding.... throughout the south.
	drought	d	Water is in very short supply because of the ..drought... .

4	deny	a	I flatly ..refuse..... to lend him any more money!
	refuse	b	Why did you ...reject.... their offer for your car?
	reject	c	I would never ....turn..... down a job like that.
	turn	d	They all ..denied/deny... writing on the classroom wall.

5	total	a	We've got a .....full...... tank of petrol.
	whole	b	When the investigation is ..complete... , the police will make an arrest.
	complete	c	The ...whole.... class had to stay behind after school.
	full	d	Competitors have to carry a ....total...... weight of over 50 kilos.

C Use of Prepositions

Use the prepositions below to complete the sentences.

in (x2)	of	on (x2)	to (x2)	with

1 At that time £1 was equal ......to...... about $2.

2 As far as I know, he's going ......on......... a long journey to do some research for his next book.

3 She has no intention ......of....... giving up her job.

4 This robbery has no connection ....with...... those that occurred in the capital last month.

5 I wish you would pay attention ......to........ what I say.

6 She arrived at the party dressed ......in......... salmon pink.

7 Despite her injury, she decided to run ......in....... the race.

8 These decisions will have no effect .....on........ you, so don't worry.

D Word Formation

I Use the word in capitals at the end of each sentence to form a word that fits in the space in the sentence.

1 It's not easy to fight crime ......effectively.... with so little money.   EFFECT

2 Fortunately, it ......brightened...... up in the afternoon and we went for a picnic.   BRIGHT

3 It was totally ......unreasonable.. of you to lose your temper like that. Don't do it again!   REASON

4 ......Sales........ have gone up since the summer.   SELL

5 ...Apparently.... , he's quite a famous architect.   APPEAR

II Choose the odd word out from the following groups of words according to how they form nouns.

For example: achieve   employ   ~~refuse~~   entertain

The odd word out is 'refuse' because it forms its noun with the suffix '-al', while all the others change into a noun by adding the suffix '-ment'.

1	survive	appear	enter	accept
2	depend	refer	employ	interfere
3	divide	confuse	conclude	tired
4	long	deep	strong	famous
5	belong	explore	save	surround

An in-depth look

In this paper, you have about 40 minutes to complete **four** parts, each of which is heard twice.

Part	Number of Questions	Marks per Question	Task
1	8	1	Three-option multiple choice. Eight unrelated extracts are heard, with one question based on each extract. **Tests:** understanding gist, main points, detail, mood, relationships, etc.
2	10	1	A monologue or text with interacting speakers is heard. Students must fill in missing information. **Tests:** understanding detail, specific information, stated opinion.
3	5	1	Multiple-matching task where students must match the correct option to a short extract. **Tests:** as Part 1
4	7	1	A monologue or text with interacting speakers. Students must answer multiple-choice questions. **Tests:** as Part 2

Exam technique

Before you hear each part of the test, you are given time to read the questions through. Make use of this time to familiarise yourself with the questions and to predict what type of information you are likely to hear.

Try to find as many answers on the first listening as possible, so that you can check them and complete the others on the second listening. Do not panic about unknown vocabulary or if you miss an answer. There is nothing you can do, so concentrate on hearing the next answer coming up.

You have time at the end of the Listening Paper to transfer your answers to the separate answer sheet. Do this carefully, making sure that you write your answers next to the correct question numbers.

Hints on answering the multiple-choice questions (Part 1)

In this part of the Listening Paper, you have to answer eight unrelated multiple-choice questions. Each question has three options to choose from. This part of the Listening Paper tests your ability to understand the general idea or main points of what you hear and questions may ask about location, mood, relationships and so on.

As with all parts of the Listening Paper, you are given time at the beginning of Part 1 to read through the questions. Don't waste this time. It gives you the opportunity to become familiar with the questions and to be able to predict what you are likely to hear.

Try to identify the correct answer the first time you listen and then check it the second time. Remember that all three options may be referred to in some way, but only one is correct. Try to identity a phrase or some items of vocabulary which justify your answer.

If you are unable to answer one question, don't worry and move on to the next. Answer all questions, even if this means guessing. You never know – you might be lucky!

Part 1

You will hear people talking in eight different situations. For questions **1–8**, choose the best answer, **A, B** or **C**.

1 Listen to a commentator describing a race on the radio. What kind of race is being described?
   A   a motorbike race   B 1
   B   a horse race
   C   a cycling race

2 You hear two people talking. How does the man feel about his cousin's haircut?
   A   He is shocked by it.   C 2
   B   He disapproves of it.
   C   He thinks it suits her.

3 You hear a person telling a story. Where did the story take place?
   A   in a jeweller's   B 3
   B   in a bank
   C   in a bus station

4 Listen to this radio advertisement. What is being advertised?
   A   a car breakdown service   A 4
   B   a car insurance company
   C   a car manufacturer

5 Listen to a woman talking about her home town. What is her profession?
   A   She is an artist.   C 5
   B   She is a sociologist.
   C   She is an architect.

6 You hear a conversation about a shopping trip. What does the woman say about it?
   A   The shopping trip didn't cost as much as expected.   A 6
   B   The shopping trip was unusual.
   C   It was an awful shopping trip.

7 You hear two university students talking about some reading they have to do. What subject are they talking about?
   A   history   B 7
   B   psychology
   C   chemistry

8 You hear two people talking in a hotel. What are they talking about?
   A   a mobile phone   C 8
   B   a DVD player
   C   a camera

Part 2

You will hear part of a radio interview about banking. For questions **9–18**, complete the sentences.

Banking – Cashpoint Cards

In order to get them to open accounts, gifts are given to   **students**   **9**

Using a cashpoint card at a branch of your own bank is normally   **free**   **10**

All customers have to pay £ 1 if they use a Kaspa's cash machine at a store or   **petrol stations**   **11**

The normal fee for using another bank's machine is between 60p and   **£ 1.50**   **12**

You won't be charged anything if you use one of Herd's Bank's   **25,000**   **13** cashpoint machines in Britain.

If you use another bank's cash machine, there is a chance that you will be charged   **twice**   **14**

You might even pay a fee of up to   **12.5**   **15** percent.

If there are any changes in charges, you will be warned   **30 days**   **16** in advance.

If there are extra charges, some machines will   **warn**   **17** you.

It can sometimes be cheaper to use a card abroad than to get currency   **before you leave**   **18**

Part 3

You will hear five different people talking about experiences they have had while driving. For questions **19–23**, choose from the list **A–F** what happened in each case. Use the letters only once. There is one extra letter which you do not need to use.

A This driver was driving without a licence.

B This driver nearly had a crash because of a technical problem.

C This driver failed to see a traffic sign.

D This driver's car developed a fault.

E This driver resisted the temptation to do something dangerous.

F This driver wasn't carrying all the right documents.

Speaker 1	E	19
Speaker 2	C	20
Speaker 3	F	21
Speaker 4	D	22
Speaker 5	B	23

Part 4

You will hear a radio interview with a policeman who was successful in tracking some burglars.   For questions **24–30**, choose the best answer, **A, B** or **C**.

24 How does Police Constable Walters feel about his experience last week?
   A   He found it thrilling.
   B   He found it tiring.
   C   He found it worthwhile.

   B 24

25 How did PC Walters track the burglars?
   A   He saw them running away.
   B   He could smell them.
   C   He saw their footprints in the snow.

   C 25

26 Where were the stolen goods found?
   A   in a private park
   B   in the local high school
   C   in the Duke's park

   C 26

27 Why didn't PC Walters give up when he found the goods?
   A   His dog was still tracking the burglars.
   B   Some of the goods were missing.
   C   He wasn't tired yet.

   A 27

28 What was PC Walters thinking about while he was chasing the burglars?
   A   about how cold it was
   B   about the physical effort
   C   about catching the burglars

   C 28

29 Where did PC Walters eventually catch up with the suspects?
   A   at the River Aln
   B   in Morpeth
   C   at a train station

   C 29

30 Why were the burglars huddled together?
   A   They were hiding.
   B   They were astonished.
   C   They were freezing.

   C 30

An in-depth look

You will be interviewed with another candidate for about 14 minutes. This paper consists of **four** parts. There will also be two examiners. One examiner acts as the interlocutor and provides you with questions and photographs, while the second examiner acts as an assessor and does not take part in the conversation.

Part	Type of Task
1	The interlocutor asks personal questions. The candidates talk about themselves, their family, etc. **Tests:** responding to questions, giving information
2	The interlocutor provides pictures and asks the candidates to talk about them. **Tests:** ability to talk at length, vocabulary and grammar, expressing opinion through comparing
3	Candidates have to complete a task together. Visual stimuli is provided. **Tests:** expressing opinion, agreeing/disagreeing, suggesting, speculating
4	Extension of Part 3 in a three-way conversation between the candidates and the interlocutor. **Tests:** developing themes, responding, expressing and justifying opinions

Exam technique

Students often feel very nervous about their speaking examination and the best way to overcome this nervousness is to practise speaking English as often as possible. Take advantage of opportunities both in class and outside it.

When you are actually in the examination, do not be afraid of speaking. The examiner cannot give you marks if you give one-word answers.   Try to be as natural as possible and don't be tempted to learn sentences off by heart before you go in.

The examiner is there to guide the conversation and the photographs and pictures are for you to use.   You do not need to describe them in detail. Rather, refer to situations and your reactions to them.

Do not worry if the other candidate seems a lot better or worse than you are. The examiner will mark you individually and the other candidate's performance will not affect your mark. Most importantly, relax and treat the examination as a conversation.

Hints on answering personal questions (Part 1)

In this part of the Speaking Paper, you must give answers to questions asked by the interlocutor (the person interviewing you). He or she will ask for personal information about yourself, your family, your hobbies, your studies/job and so on.

It can be tempting to learn a little speech about yourself to tell the interlocutor.   You should avoid doing this as you will not sound natural.   It is far better to make the most of any opportunities to talk to foreigners about yourself.   In this way, you will be practising the first part of the Speaking Paper.

Part 1 (about 3 minutes)

Ask and answer the following questions with a partner.

- Where do you live?
- How long have you lived there?
- What's the place like?
- What do you think of it?
- What is there for people of your age to do there?

Part 2 (about 4 minutes)

Practise speaking about the photographs. The photographs for Test One are on page 153.

Candidate A, here are your two photographs. They show different kinds of relationships. Please let Candidate B see them. Candidate A, I'd like you to compare these photographs, saying what you think about the kinds of relationships shown. (approximately one minute)

Candidate B, could you please tell us whether you think it is more important to have one really close friend or several good friends? (approximately 20 seconds)

Candidate B, here are your two photographs. They show different places. Please let Candidate A see them. Candidate B, I'd like you to compare these photographs, saying where you would like to live and why. (approximately one minute)

Candidate A, could you please tell us which neighbourhood, if any, is closest in appearance to yours? (approximately 20 seconds)

Part 3 (about 3 minutes)

Discuss the following with a partner.

A wealthy businessman has donated a large sum of money to your school and several suggestions have been made as to how to spend it. Talk to each other about which two suggestions from page 154 would be most useful to the school and its pupils. It is not necessary to agree with each other.

Part 4 (about 4 minutes)

Give each other your opinions about the following questions.

- What do you think of the school you attend or attended?
- What do you think is the maximum number of pupils that there should be in a class?
- Do you believe that your schooldays are the best ones of your life?
- Apart from the subjects you are taught at school, what else can you learn there?
- How important do you think it is to go to university?

Hints on working with a gapped text (Part 2)

This part of the Reading Paper tests your understanding of the way a text is structured in English.   This is often thought of as the most difficult part of the Reading examination because you are asked to complete a task you may not have had much experience of.

This part is best approached in the following way:

a   Read through the whole text first, looking for words or phrases before and after each gap which will help you to identify the missing sentence.

b   Read through the sentences which have been removed, identifying words or phrases which will help you to understand where in the text the sentence was removed from.

c   Begin to make decisions about which sentence goes in which gap,   making sure that tenses and reference words fit logically.

Do not be afraid to change your mind as you complete more gaps.

Finally, read the whole text through carefully to see if it "flows".

Answer all the questions.

Part 1

You are going to read an article about a cookbook author. For questions **1–8**, choose the answer **A**, **B**, **C** or **D** which you think fits best according to the text.

No more food fights

Annabel Karmel, *the bestselling author of cookbooks for children, is bringing new harmony to mealtimes.*

Annabel Karmel is Britain's second most successful cookbook author. Her *The Complete Baby and Toddler Meal Planner* is an
5 authoritative work known to, if not actually used by, virtually every middle-class mother of a child under 10. Even those who have rejected it, feeling life's too short
10 to cut out starfish salmon cakes and make chicken and cherry tomato caterpillars to tempt their fussy two-year-olds, appreciated the reason for it being written.

15 When her eldest child, Nicholas, got to the stage when he could eat solid food and she had difficulty in getting him to eat, she became anxious. "I was particularly concerned that
20 Nicholas should have good food – and eat it. But all I could find in the bookshops to help me was recipes for party food or boring dishes such as liver poached in milk, so I
25 started experimenting."

The professional musician turned herself into a career playgroup leader so that she could do some research. "There was nowhere nice
30 for mothers and children to meet in this area, so I started a group called *Babes in the Wood*, expecting two people to turn up. We ended up with 75. I experimented on small
35 groups with my recipes. The rule was that 15 out of 20 children had to like a dish. I still have a big testing table in my kitchen, where mothers come with their children." Annabel
40 also sought expert opinion and approval from nutritionists at Great Ormond Street Hospital. The success of the resulting book, *The Complete Baby and Toddler Meal*
45 *Planner,* was both massive and worldwide – it has been translated into everything from Hebrew to Slovenian and she has already
100 been on three promotional trips to
50 America this year alone. In fact, it was the Americans who first recognised how good the book was. It was turned down in Britain –
105 "Nobody believed there would be
55 any interest in a cookbook for babies, because parents would just buy their food in jars" – but it was accepted by Simon and Schuster
110 at the Frankfurt Book Fair.

60 Annabel believes her secret is as simple as discovering that toddlers actually prefer tasty food. "It had
115 always been believed that children only liked food without a strong
65 flavour. But I discovered they didn't like it at all, which is why so many mothers have difficulty in getting their children to eat. In fact, you
120 have no problem getting them to
70 eat vegetables if you make them tastier. I make a salad dressing so delicious that no child can resist it. It's got vinegar, ginger, celery,
125 tomato puree and a little bit of
75 sugar, and it comes out pink. Without salt or sugar in the first year, it's hard, so I had to find other ways of making the food
130 tasty, such as putting chicken
80 together with apples. If you give children a variety of foods at an early age, they are much more likely to accept them."

Annabel also urges mothers to
85 experiment with more exotic ideas. "Children are stereotyped as wanting only burgers when, in reality, they'll eat food from all over the world, like yakitori chicken and crunchy
90 seaweed." She defends the fancy presentation of many of her dishes such as the peach and yoghurt
95 arranged to look like a fried egg as "fun to make with your child and appealing to a difficult eater." The Karmel children have developed their own specialities. Nicholas, now 11, crushes together meringues, raspberries and cream. Lara, nine, has her own onion soup and seven-year-old Scarlett a pasta sauce. All of them feature in her new book, *The Family Meal Planner*, which is aimed at older children. Although she speaks about the dangers of fragmented family life, she admits that in the Karmel household, where both she and her husband Simon, an oil executive, work late, they are unable to spend much time together. In fact, her feet hardly have time to touch the ground. She is next off to a "tomato ketchup" plantation in Spain for a children's book on where processed food comes from and will then decide whether to accept an offer to license her ready-made foods to Marks & Spencer or go it alone.

120 The dishes include a Japanese bento box with special foolproof children's chopsticks and a kit including a half-made dish to be finished off by the child. 'When it's
125 finished, it looks like a snake.' Anyone who thinks this sounds like hard work should remember that this is Annabel's idea of convenience food. "There will always be people
130 who won't be bothered to cook" is the critical comment of the woman who only that morning had made not one, but eight shepherd's pies for the family freezer. She
135 confesses: "I plan my day down to the last five minutes. It's the only way I can do it all."

1 Why have some mothers rejected Annabel's book?
A They don't think the recipes are very good.
B They don't think it is well written.
C They are too busy to use it.
D They believe junk food is better.

2 What was the main reason for Annabel starting *Babes in the Wood*?
A She wanted to test her recipes.
B She thought it would help her children make friends.
C She needed to make some money.
D She wanted to open a restaurant for children.

3 Why did British publishers reject Annabel's book?
A They knew American publishers wanted it.
B They thought mothers were only interested in buying ready-made food.
C The cost of translation would be too high.
D They thought the recipes were too difficult to follow.

4 What did Annabel discover about children's taste in food?
A They prefer colourful food.
B They hate fruit.
C They develop their likes and dislikes when they are young.
D They don't really like salty food.

5 What does "it's hard" refer to in line 77?
A the salad dressing
B working
C making interesting recipes
D the food

6 What does Annabel imply about the presentation of food?
A It's important that it should look nice.
B It is difficult to come up with new ideas.
C Most food doesn't look very nice.
D Exotic food always looks better to children.

7 What is meant by "fragmented family life" in lines 106?
A spending little time with the rest of the family
B having a lifestyle which is much too expensive
C working so hard that every member of the family is always tired
D making family life so routine that it is boring

8 What does "it" in line 125 refer to?
A the kit
B the bento box
C a child
D the food

Part 2

You are going to read a newspaper article about golf balls. Seven sentences have been removed from the article. Choose from the sentences **A–H** the one which fits each gap (**9–15**). There is one extra sentence which you do not need to use.

Old golf balls can fetch big money

Big hitters always try to knock the stuffing out of the ball every time they tee up on a long hole, but the way balls are made these days, nobody succeeds. But 150 years ago, with an especially good hit, the ball would explode into a cloud of feathers. Featheries, as they were called, first rolled across Scottish courses 500 years ago. Their recipe was simple. A top hat full of goose feathers was mixed with water and boiled into a soft mash. A rawhide cover was cut and sewn to the size of a modern ball with a small gap left in the stitching.

The shell was filled with wet feathers and closed. The ball-to-be was then thoroughly soaked and hammered into a round shape. **9 B**

These were then painted white and sold for about five shillings each, a substantial sum in those days. Although their owners would have been keen to avoid losing them, few of these early balls have outlived the golfers who hit them. **10 F**

In golf's ancient days, the professionals' job was to make equipment by hand in their workshops. **11 G** He was one of the best ball makers in Fife and he was the first player to break 80 on the Old Course at St Andrews. He was also conservative. His refusal to accept change saw him fall out with his apprentice, Tom Morris, when gutta percha – also known as rubber – balls were introduced in 1848. **12 H** Early gutta perchas now sell for close to £1,000 in the collector's market.

Tom Morris turned out to be as fine a craftsman and golfer as Robertson. **13 D** They are still appreciated today. A hickory shaft Tom Morris hand-shaped wood sells for as much as £1,000.

The improvement in the construction of the balls added distance to the drive. **14 A** The early gutta perchas, struck with a heavier club, went about 200 yards.

Because anybody could pour liquid into a mould, countless ball makers hit the market with strange ideas in the early gutty days. The Henry Rifle company introduced a ball with the surface cut in swirls. The manufacturers promised extra yards, saying the ball would spin like a bullet out of a rifle. **15 E** One of these balls sold for £24,000 last year.

A   A well-hit featherie travelled about 170 yards.

B   As the concoction dried, the filling expanded and the cover shrank, making a hard golf ball.

C   It did not stay on the production line for long because golfers realised it wouldn't roll along the fairway either.

D   He won three Open championships and his clubs were among the best in the world.

E   However, the swirls swerved the ball wildly to the right or left.

F   The survivors are so rare that collectors sometimes pay as much as £8,000 for one of Alan Robertson's featheries.

G   Robertson had two claims to fame.

H   The solid rubber gutties were easier to make, more durable and about one-fifth the price of the featheries, allowing the less well-off to join the rich in appreciating the game of golf.

Part 3

You are going to read an article about places to visit in England and Scotland. For questions **16–30**, choose from the list (**A–E**). The places may be chosen more than once. When more than one answer is required, these may be given in any order.

Which of the places A–E

doesn't offer much for younger visitors?	**16**	D
is similar to another place?	**17**	A
used to be a family home?	**18**	E
used to be in a different location?	**19**	D
gives an idea of how people lived a long time ago?	**20**	C
has rides you have to wait a long time to get on?	**21**	A
has quiet places where you can get away from others?	**22**	E
has a weapon that is still in use?	**23**	B
is considered perfect for fanatics?	**24**	D
is best for younger schoolchildren?	**25**	A
have extremely valuable objects on show?	**26** B	**27** E
is an old tourist attraction?	**28**	C
provides a trip on a boat?	**29**	C
provides a change of footwear?	**30**	E

England and Scotland

Outlined below are just a few of the many interesting places you can visit there.

A Legoland, Surrey

Built in 1995, Legoland Windsor is the sister ship to the original Legoland in Denmark, but the days when kids were content to look at working models alone are long over. Now there are roller coasters, waterslides and hands-on activities alongside buildings constructed with lego units. There are various adventure playgrounds, an explorer's zone and both car and boat self-driving schools. The latter are very popular and along with the Dragon Ride and Pirate Falls, these can have queues of up to an hour. However, if you do not want to waste time, it is best to go on them very early or late in the day. Lego is trying to extend its age range appeal upwards but essentially it remains perfect for children up to the age of ten.

B Edinburgh Castle

Scotland's top visitor attraction is really several attractions in one. Go early and head straight to the top of the castle, then work your way down (everybody else does it the other way round), and you'll be able to take in the most interesting display – the crown jewels – first, before the worst of the queues forms. A gradual descent, taking in the various museums, prisons, the huge Mons Meg cannon and a couple of cakes in one of the cafés, should find you at the Mills Mount Battery in time for the firing of the 1pm gun. The castle has an excellent audio presentation on little digital machines that you pick up at the front gate. Spot a number, key it into the machine and you get a lively commentary complete with background sounds of battlefields and flutes. There are conventional guided tours as well.

C Shakespeare's Birthplace, Stratford-upon-Avon

Tourists have been flocking to Stratford-upon-Avon for more than 250 years to see where the most famous playwright of all time was born and spent his latter years. The Shakespeare Houses consist of five historic buildings in or near the town that are directly associated with the great dramatist and his family. Even if you only visit one or two, it will give you an insight into what life was like during this period of history. There's also a surprising amount to amuse toddlers in Stratford. The new Ragdoll Children's Cruise is ideal for children aged 2–4, as it gives you and them a break from touring and a chance to sing along to Rosie and Jim songs as you cruise down the pretty Avon River.

D Wisley Gardens, Surrey

The Royal Horticultural Society's garden was transplanted from Chiswick to Surrey in 1903 in order to be unaffected by London smoke. Its 240 acres are home to roses, rock gardens, Mediterranean blooms and vegetables, model gardens, glass houses and a plant centre with 10,000 varieties. There is also an extremely well-stocked bookshop. For keen gardeners, a visit to Wisley is essential as the Gardens are regarded as the centre of gardening knowledge and wisdom. There's little of specific interest for children, but they can play or walk on the grass (without balls or radios).

E Polesden Lacey, Surrey

The lavish estate of Polesden Lacey was once the home of the Hon Mrs Ronald Greville, heir to the McEwan distillery. As well as acquiring wonderful paintings by famous artists, silver, porcelain and furniture, she also threw amazing parties. Polesden Lacey is gloriously sited on the south-facing slope of the North Downs. Apart from its Edwardian garden, the estate has 1,385 acres, with interesting walks and quiet, lose-the-crowd spots. There is only one disadvantage in this marvellous place: neither prams nor pushchairs are allowed in the house, nor, indeed, are high-heeled or muddy shoes ("enjoy a pair of our fashionable plastic slippers", invites the brochure).

Hints on writing an informal letter (Part 2)

Question 2 on page 42 is an example of this type of letter. The question puts the letter in context by telling you who you are writing to and giving some background to your relationship with that person. In this case, you are writing to a friend you have regular written contact with.

Make sure you understand exactly what the question is asking you to do before you start writing your plan. In this question, you are writing a descriptive letter. Your description must include details about the concert itself and also some people you went with. If you make the mistake of describing the evening, the music and the singer/musicians at length without including descriptions of two or three people who went with you, the examiner will not be able to give you a good mark even if you use wonderful vocabulary and your letter is exactly right in terms of style.

Once you have completed your plan and organised your thoughts, you need to decide on a short opening paragraph for your letter. Think about what you would write in your own language if you were writing to a friend. The chances are that you would thank them for their letter, ask how they and their family are and so on. Do the same in this letter.

Finally you need to end the letter in an appropriate way. In this letter, you could say: "I'm looking forward to hearing your news soon." Sign off your letter in an appropriate, informal way, such as "Best wishes", "Regards", etc.

Style

The key to writing a good informal letter is making it sound friendly. You need to use idioms, phrasal verbs, expressions and lots of descriptive adjectives to achieve this.

The tenses used will depend very much on the question asked. For example, the question in this test, describing a concert you went to, would require use of the past tenses because you are describing one past event. Likewise, if you are writing a letter to invite a friend to stay, you will probably use the present continuous or the "going to" future for future arrangements, and also the future tenses to tempt him/her with the promise of fun to be had.

Part 1

You **must** answer this question.

1 You are responsible for advertising for a travel agency and you have just received a holiday magazine in which you have advertised. To your disappointment, there are a number of errors in the advertisement.

Read the advertisement from the magazine and the notes you made to indicate the errors. Then, using the information, write a letter to the publishers of the magazine, pointing out the errors and asking what they intend to do about the problem.

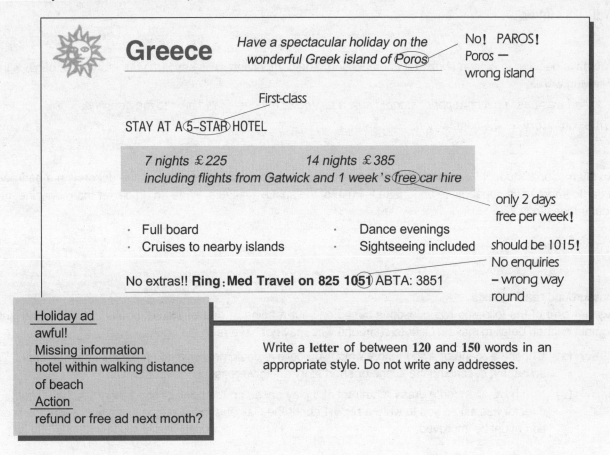

Write a **letter** of between **120** and **150** words in an appropriate style. Do not write any addresses.

This model is just an idea of the type of letter expected at this level.

Dear Sir/Madam,

I am writing in order to complain about the advertisement you published in your magazine for our travel agency. The advertisement contained many errors and some information was missing.

Firstly, the holiday destination was incorrect. The advertisement said Poros instead of Paros, which is a completely different island! The hotel the tourists would stay in is a first-class hotel and not a five-star hotel as you stated. There was also a mistake concerning the free car hire, which was for only two days rather than one week. Also, our phone number should have been 825 1015. Consequently, we received hardly any enquiries. Finally, the information about the hotel being within walking distance of the beach was missing.

I therefore suggest that you refund the money paid to you or place the correct ad in next month's edition for free.

I look forward to reaching a satisfactory agreement.

Your faithfully,

Georgia Thanou

Part 2

Write an answer to **one** of the questions **2–5** in this part. Write your answer in **120–180** words in an appropriate style.

2 You attended an English course at a college in Britain last summer. You write regularly to a friend you made while on the course. Write a letter to your friend, describing a concert you went to. Describe the whole evening and include some details about the people you went with. Do not write any addresses.

   Write your **letter.**

3 You have decided to enter a short story competition. The competition rules say that your story must begin with the following words:

   As I was passing a newspaper stand, I saw a picture of my best friend next to the headlines.
   Write your **story** for the competition.

4 An international student magazine has invited readers to suggest ways of designing and decorating a bedroom in order to improve its appearance and make full use of the space available. Write an article for the magazine, giving your suggestions.

   Write your **article.**

5 Background reading texts
   Answer **one** of the following two questions based on your reading of **one** of the set books. Your answer should contain enough detail to make it clear to someone who may not have read the book.

   Either (a) Choose a scene or a short story which you believe could not have taken place in your country. Write an **essay**, describing the scene or short story and give reasons for your choice.

   or   (b) You have attended a dress rehearsal of a play based on the book or short story you have read. The director has asked you to write a **report** about the play and make suggestions about how the production might be improved.

Hints on how to gap-fill (Part 2)

In this part of the Use of English Paper, you must fill in each of the 12 gaps in the text with one word. This part tests grammatical structure rather than vocabulary.

The best approach is as follows:

a   Read the title and the text fairly quickly to get an idea of what the text is about.   Think about whether it is using the past, present or future tenses.

b   Read the text a second time,   filling in the gaps which are fairly obvious.   Make sure any words you fill in fit the structure of the sentence as well as the meaning.

c   Go back to any gaps and try to identify what part of speech is needed, i.e. a verb, a noun, an adjective, etc. Then try to come up with a suitable word.

When you have finished, check that the text makes sense and that your answers are in the correct form.

Remember, spelling counts, so check it carefully. Also, words like *don't, won't*, etc, count as two words (although *cannot* is one word).

Answer all questions even if you are not sure about something. You will not lose marks for trying.

Part 1

For questions **1–12**, read the text below and decide which answer **A, B, C** or **D** best fits each space. There is an example at the beginning (**0**).

Example:

0   **A** disastrously   **B** particularly   **C** specially   **D** precisely

| 0 | A ▭ | **B** ▬ | C ▭ | D ▭ |

Driving in Delhi

Whenever a (0)..............terrible car (1) ....is reported on the news, people claim a lot more could be done to improve driving conditions. This may be true, but road (2).............. in Europe seems to be fairly good when compared to some cities in the world.

Delhi, the capital city of India, for example, has a (3).............. for being a terrifying and lethal place to drive and the figures which are released by the police confirm this. On average, about 180 people are killed and 750 are seriously (4).............. on its potholed roads every month. Although the police are trying to reduce the number of accidents, the job ahead of them will be very difficult, to (5).............. the least. As (6).............. as driving is concerned, Delhi is quite unlike anywhere else in the world.

India's capital has 48 registered means of (7).............., including tractors and camel carts. Of the three million car owners, few have legal (8).............. . Consequently, the roads are (9)............. of drivers who have had no formal instruction. Vehicles (10)..............on both sides, drivers rarely use indicators and truck owners drive in a drunken state. However, the drivers are not the only ones to blame. More than three-quarters of the city's (11) ....lights are constantly out of order and there are no road markings.

The authorities are now imposing (12)..............on drivers who break the law, but this is having little effect on the chaotic situation there.

1	**A** collision	**(B)** crash	**C** hit	**D** strike
2	**A** security	**(B)** safety	**C** protection	**D** defence
3	**A** gossip	**B** rumour	**C** fame	**(D)** reputation
4	**A** wounded	**B** damaged	**C** harmed	**(D)** injured
5	**A** tell	**B** mention	**(C)** say	**D** remark
6	**A** long	**B** soon	**(C)** far	**D** well
7	**(A)** transport	**B** vehicle	**C** movement	**D** traffic
8	**A** diplomas	**(B)** licences	**C** certificates	**D** degrees
9	**A** crowded	**B** packed	**(C)** full	**D** covered
10	**A** pass by	**B** cross	**C** go by	**(D)** overtake
11	**(A)** traffic	**B** vehicle	**C** signal	**D** sign
12	**(A)** fines	**B** tickets	**C** fares	**D** payments

Part 2

For questions **13–24,** read the text below and think of the word which best fits each space. Use only **one** word in each space. There is an example at the beginning (**0**).

Example:

0	CALLED

Balls of fire

One of the rarest weather phenomena is (0) ..called... ball lightning. Indeed, it is (13)....so...... rare that until fifty years ago scientists even doubted (14)....its...... existence, claiming that it could be an optical illusion caused by light from lightning being retained in the eye just (15)....like.... the light from a camera flash that temporarily blinds people in a room when a picture is (16)...taken.... .

On average, the phenomenon is reported twice (17).....a.......year in the UK. In most cases, there are only a (18)....few.....witnesses to each event, but when ball lightning entered a factory in Tewksbury earlier this year, it was seen by about forty people. (19)....At......first, it looked like a dazzling blue-white ball bouncing along the roof. Then, it passed through netting into the building, (20)..where... its colour was described as blue, white and orange and its size as that of a tennis ball. The glowing sphere moved rapidly around the factory for several seconds (21)..before.. hitting a window and vanishing with a very loud bang. The window was not broken.

The workers could not explain what they (22)....had....seen and they are not the only ones. Although there is (23)...still/some.... doubt about what causes ball lightning, there is (24).....no.....doubt that it exists.

Part 3

For questions **25–34**, read the text below. Use the word given in capitals at the end of each line to form a word that fits in the space **in the same line.** There is an example at the beginning (**0**).

Example:

0	SOCIOLOGISTS

MOVING HOUSE

(0).Sociologists.. always seem to come up with interesting	SOCIOLOGY
pieces of research which have surprising results. In one of these	
(25)investigations, people were asked where they would	INVESTIGATE
like to live. The (26).....choices..... that were made in the	CHOOSE
majority of cases were quite (27).....unexpected.... . Apparently,	EXPECT
most people were unwilling to move to a (28).....tropical.....	TROPICS
island with sandy beaches or a paradise for the wealthy like Monaco.	
They said they would not like to move (29)further/farther	FAR
than a few miles from their present home. (30)...Strangely....	STRANGE
enough, some people said they had no desire to move at all,	
(31).....adding..... that they were perfectly happy where they	ADD
were. Those who wanted to move selected a more (32)...luxurious.....	LUXURY
house nearby. One (33).explanation... for these answers to the	EXPLAIN
question was that moving house can be very(34)...stressful....	STRESS
if the move is accompanied by a loss of friends and familiar sights.	

Part 4

For questions **35–42**, complete the second sentence so that it has a similar meaning to the first sentence, using the word given. **Do not change the word given.** You must use between **two** and **five** words including the word given. Here is an example (**0**).

Example:

0 I can't possibly finish the work so quickly.
ENOUGH
There .... me to finish the work.

The gap can be filled by the words "isn't enough time for", so you write:

0	ISN'T ENOUGH TIME FOR

35 It was wrong of him to leave the child alone.
SHOULD
He ....should have asked/told/got someone....... to look after the child.

36 Sheila's not the sort of person who talks about other people's business.
HABIT
Sheila's not ....in the habit of talking.................about other people's business.

37 You must show your pass to the security guard.
BE
All ....passes must be shown.............. to the security guard.

38 Don't blame me for breaking the vase.
FAULT
It's not ....my fault the vase got/was............ broken.

39 When did Mark start making his own bread?
LONG
How ....long has Mark been making............. his own bread?

40 Their flat was much bigger than I thought it would be.
EXPECT
I didn't ....expect their flat to be............... so big.

41 The ferry couldn't sail because of strong winds.
TOO
It ....was too windy for............ the ferry to sail.

42 Henry has forgotten about the money you lent him.
REMEMBER
Henry ....can't/doesn't remember borrowing...... any money from you.

Vocabulary Extension

A Vocabulary Building

Complete the unfinished words in the following sentences. All the words and phrases are related to entertainment.

1 I never sit in one of the front r o w s in the cinema because I can't stand being too near the sc r e e n.
2 We could clearly see the ac t o r s on st a g e from our seats on the bal c o n y and we thought the play was marvellous.
3 There's an exh i b i t i o n of paintings by Monet at a private art ga l l e r y in town.
4 During the con c e r t, the pop gr o u p was supported by an orch e s t r a.
5 It was one of those restaurants with a piano player, but the ser v i c e was awful so I didn't leave a tip for the wa i t e r.
6 I prefer com e d i e s to hor r o r films.
7 The plot is so complicted that you won't understand the end i n g if you miss any part of the film.
8 The mus e u m contains a wide variety of scul p t u r e s from all over the world.
9 It was a great film, but I can't remember who dir e c t e d it or who com p o s e d the soundtrack!
10 Some of the street mus i c i a n s and jugg l e r s we saw while walking round London gave very good perf o r m a n c e s.

B Word Use

Use the words on the left to complete the sentences on the right. Make sure the word is in the correct form. Use each word once.

1	**gossip**	a	She has a ....reputation......for remaining calm under pressure.
	rumour	b	There is a ......rumour......... that you're leaving. Is it true?
	fame	c	Most of what you hear in this office is just ....gossip........ .
	reputation	d	His ....fame...... has spread far and wide and now he's an international film star.

2	**wound**	a	Fortunately, they weren't seriously ...injured.... in the crash.
	damage	b	Several buildings were..damaged.. during the floods.
	harm	c	He was ..wounded... during the war.
	injure	d	A gorilla won't .....harm...... you if you sit on the ground and look down.

3	**tell**	a	What did he .....say........ to you?
	mention	b	I have ......told...... you time and again not to shout.
	say	c	She didn't ...mention... you in her letter.
	remark	d	He .remarked.. that I didn't look a day older than when he'd last seen me.

4	**diploma**	a	Make sure you carry your driving ...licence..... at all times.
	licence	b	She's got a ...degree.... in physics from Surrey University.
	certificate	c	You can't have a passport unless you bring your birth ..certificate. to this office.
	degree	d	You get a ...diploma... when you complete the six-month course successfully.

5	**fine**	a	I couldn't afford the air .....fare......, so I went by coach.
	ticket	b	I had to pay a .....fine....... for parking in a restricted area.
	fare	c	Keep your ....ticket......in case you have to show it to an inspector.
	payment	d	I've bought a new television and the first ..payment...is due on the first of next month.

C Use of Prepositions

Use the prepositions below to complete the sentences.

> as   by   of (x2)   on (x2)   out of   to

1 She's not in the habit .....of....... spending a lot of money on clothes.
2 There's a good film .....on..... television tonight.
3 I'm afraid the photocopier is ...out of.... order at the moment.
4 We're all looking forward .....to...... seeing your family again.
5 ....On...... average, he scores about ten points a game.
6 Michael has been described .....as...... the best player the world has ever seen.
7 The minister arrived at the reception accompanied .....by...... his wife.
8 We finished the job one day ahead ....of........schedule.

D Word Formation

I Use the word in capitals at the end of each sentence to form a word that fits in the space in the sentence.

1 I hadn't prepared a meal for Karen because she arrived ...unexpectedly... . EXPECT
2 The ...explanations.... they gave for the delay were not very convincing. EXPLAIN
3 Do you think I made the right ....choice.......? CHOOSE
4 ....Scientists...... are working hard to find a vaccine for the disease. SCIENCE
5 Nobody has concrete proof of the .....existence...... of UFOs. EXIST

II Choose the odd word out from the following groups of words according to how they form <u>nouns</u>.

1	warm	wide	brave	grow
2	shy	except	describe	react
3	achieve	believe	relieve	grieve
4	rude	lonely	bright	original
5	disappoint	regular	excite	entertain

Hints on sentence completion (Part 2)

In this part of the Listening Paper, you have to complete sentences with gaps in them. Answers will require you to write up to three words or a number.

Make good use of the time given to you to read through the questions. You may be able to predict what type of information you need to fill in. For example, in this test, question 12 is obviously the quantity of bananas, so it will probably be a weight or a number. In the same way, question 16 also refers to quantity, and question 18 is more than likely a telephone number.

Try to complete the gaps on the first listening so that you can check your answers on the second listening. Do not hesitate if you hear an answer. Write it down. Do not panic if you miss an answer. Move on to the next question.

Part 1

You will hear people talking in eight different situations. For questions **1–8**, choose the best answer, **A**, **B** or **C**.

1 You hear two people talking. What was the cause of the problem?
   A   The woman's answerphone wasn't working.
   B   The woman didn't receive the message.
   C   The woman forgot about the message.

B 1

2 You hear two people talking about an electricity bill. Why does the woman think the man's bill is smaller than usual?
   A   It is a mistake.
   B   The man's family has been away.
   C   The electricity company doesn't charge as much now.

C 2

3 Listen to the following conversation. Who is Bob Turner?
   A   a private investigator
   B   a research scientist
   C   a police detective

A 3

4 You hear two people having a discussion. What are they talking about?
   A   a film
   B   a play
   C   a concert

B 4

5 Listen to two people talking about a friend's wedding preparations. In what way will the wedding be different?
   A   It will take place on another planet.
   B   It will take place under the sea.
   C   It will take place in the air.

C 5

6 Listen to a conversation between two people at home. Why can't they go shopping?
   A   The man has lost his credit card.
   B   The man has left his wallet at work.
   C   The man has no money in his bank account.

B 6

7 You hear two people talking about a friend who has moved to a village called Caldy. Where is Caldy?
   A   in England
   B   in Scotland
   C   in Wales

A 7

8 You hear two people talking. Who is the man?
   A   a doctor
   B   the woman's boss
   C   a friend

C 8

Part 2

You will hear a man ordering goods from a supermarket over the telephone. For questions **9–18**, complete the sentences.

☆☆☆☆☆☆STAR SUPERMARKET☆☆☆☆☆☆

ORDER FORM

The customer's name is   Coleman   **9**

The delivery address is   16,Neston Drive   **10** , Neston.

The delivery will take place between   half past four   **11** and five o'clock.

The customer would like   half a dozen   **12** bananas.

The chickens should be large and   frozen   **13**

A dozen   medium (sized)   **14** eggs were ordered.

The milk should be the   long-life   **15** variety.

The caller also needs   2 loaves   **16** of bread.

The lamb chops should have the   fat   **17** removed.

The contact telephone number is   982 4791   **18**

☆☆☆☆☆☆☆☆☆☆☆☆☆☆☆☆☆☆☆☆☆☆

Part 3

You will hear five different people taking about electrical items that they have had repaired. For questions **19–23**, choose from the list **A–F** which item is being described. Use the letters only once. There is one extra letter which you do not need to use.

A a vacuum cleaner

B an electric toothbrush

C an iron

D a dishwasher

E a clothes drier

F a washing machine

Speaker 1	F	19
Speaker 2	C	20
Speaker 3	A	21
Speaker 4	D	22
Speaker 5	B	23

Part 4

You will hear part of a radio programme about teenagers who have left home. For questions, **24–30**, choose the best answer, **A**, **B** or **C**.

24 How much time did Brian spend at his new flat at the beginning?

A weekends only

B week days only

C only four months

`A 24`

25 Why did Brian want to leave home?

A He felt his parents didn't understand him.

B He wanted somewhere peaceful to work.

C He wanted to be financially independent.

`B 25`

26 Why doesn't living away from his family and friends pose a problem for Brian?

A He can catch the bus to visit them.

B He has his own transport.

C His parents support him financially.

`B 26`

27 Why did Carolyn leave home?

A She disagreed with her parents.

B Her parents asked her to leave.

C She wasn't speaking to her younger brother.

`A 27`

28 How is Carolyn's relationship with her parents now?

A They are not speaking.

B They talk on the phone sometimes.

C They send messages through Carolyn's brother.

`B 28`

29 How has Carolyn changed since she moved out of home?

A She has lost her confidence.

B She feels more mature.

C She is grateful to her parents.

`B 29`

30 What advice does Brian have for teenagers thinking of moving out?

A Don't be miserable.

B Make sure you have a good reason for moving out.

C Make sure you have enough money first.

`C 30`

Hints on comparing pictures (Part 2)

In this part of the Speaking Paper, you must talk uninterrupted for about one minute about two colour photographs. You should not describe them in detail. Instead, comment on them and tell the interlocutor about your reaction to them.

Be methodical. Comment on the connection between the photographs first and then go on to compare them, making sure that you talk in a logical way. Finish with a comment or two about your own reaction to them.

Remember that you must also comment briefly on your fellow candidate's photographs, so pay attention during this part of the examination, too.

Try not to hesitate for too long while you are speaking or say "er...". If the interlocutor interrupts you while you are talking, don't worry. It probably just means that you have used up your time.

Part 1 (about 3 minutes)

Ask and answer the following questions with a partner.

- Do you have a large family or a small family?
- Do you wish you had a larger family?
- Can you tell me something about your family?
- Do you see your uncles, aunts and cousins very often?
- Where is your family from?

Part 2 (about 4 minutes)

Practise speaking about the photographs. The photographs for Test Two are on page 155.

Candidate A, here are your two photographs. They show different kinds of places to go shopping. Please let Candidate B see them. Candidate A, I'd like you to compare these photographs, saying what you think are the advantages of shopping at each of these places. (approximately one minute)

Candidate B, could you please tell us which of these places you would prefer to shop at? (approximately 20 seconds)

Candidate B, here are your two photographs. They have a connection with money. Please let Candidate A see them. Candidate B, I'd like you to compare these photographs, saying what you think of these ways of making money. (approximately one minute)

Candidate A, could you please tell us which of these ways of making money is more popular in your country? (approximately 20 seconds)

Part 3 (about 3 minutes)

Discuss the following with a partner.

Imagine that you have been given enough money to study at a well-known university. Talk to each other about which of the professions on page 156 you would like to enter after your studies. Say which you believe would offer the most job satisfaction and money. It is not necessary to agree with each other.

Part 4 (about 4 minutes)

Give each other your opinions about the following questions.

- Is it always a good idea to do the same job as one of the older members of your family?
- How easy is it to get the job you want nowadays?
- Is it necessary to go to university to get a good job?
- How can a person be very successful or reach the top of their profession?
- Would you be prepared to move abroad to get a better job?

Hints on answering the multiple matching task (Part 3)

This part of the Reading Paper tests your ability to identify specific information in a text. This type of task requires the skill of scanning, in other words, looking quickly through the text to focus on specific information.

The best approach for this part of this test is to:

a read the questions first to identify the type of information that is required.
b read the first paragraph or part of the text while bearing the questions in mind.
c answer any questions that you can.
d move on to the next paragraph in the same way.

At the end, go back to any questions you have not been able to answer and scan the text again to locate them.

Remember, the questions in this part of the examination carry only one mark each, so do not waste time searching for a difficult answer when you could be finding a more obvious one.

Answer all the questions.

Part 1

You are going to read an advertisement about a device for car owners. For questions **1–8,** choose the answer **A, B, C** or **D** which you think fits best according to the text.

The Problem
Every day 1200 cars are stolen. Even cars with the latest alarm or the best immobiliser still get stolen. 50% of stolen cars are never seen by their owners again.

The Solution
→ **RAC Trackstar**tm

The Problem
Your car is a necessary part of your life. You use it every day, you rely on it and you are proud of it. Of course, you want to hold on to it so you make sure it has the latest alarm and immobiliser. But despite all this, cars like yours are still stolen every day. In fact, in this country, one car is stolen almost every minute! And if your car is stolen, you only have a 50:50 chance of seeing it again.

Each year, car crime costs nearly £3 billion. Of course, if you're insured, you won't lose out or will you?

Firstly, you will have to pay extra insurance later on, then you may not be offered the full amount by the agent, you will probably have to hire a car and you will also lose the value of the contents and accessories in the car.

The Solution
An *RAC Trackstar* device, hidden in one of 47 possible secret locations in your car, is the key to the system. If your car is stolen, radio signals are sent at twenty-second intervals from the car to the *RAC Trackstar National Control Centre* via a satellite network. Then a computer gives the vehicle's exact location, speed and direction.

The *RAC Trackstar National Control Centre*, which operates 24 hours a day, 365 days a year, will immediately contact the police in the area where the car is located. Because the police receive information every twenty seconds, they will always know the vehicle's location. Once the thief has been arrested, your car will be returned to you.

Security
For peace of mind, you can choose *RAC Trackstar*'s optional Emergency Call and Breakdown Call features.

Both features use the *RAC Trackstar*'s unique transmitter, a hidden microphone and speaker fitted in your car and the ability to provide the emergency services with your exact location.

Emergency Call Benefits
Statistics show that if 90% of life-threatening emergency calls were reached within eight minutes, a further 3,000,000 patients could be treated within the 43 critical 'golden hour'.

If you have or witness an accident, you can have your details sent to the emergency services simply by pressing a button on the transmitter. With the microphone and speaker, you can remain in contact with an emergency operator.

Breakdown Call benefits
According to the RAC, half of those motorists who break down do not know exactly where they are. If

press the Breakdown Call button on the transmitter, the National Control Centre will know your exact location and even which side of the road you are on!

Protection
RAC Trackstar is unique in being able to provide the National Control Centre with details of the exact location of your car, its speed and direction.

Speed is the key to the successful recovery of a stolen vehicle. *RAC Trackstar Control* will immediately alert the police if you report your car stolen and under the 62 24-hour Guardian Option, they'll also tell you if your car has been stolen. *RAC Trackstar*'s constant updates mean the police are kept informed of the car's location. All this dramatically improves your chances of seeing your car again. In short, **RAC Trackstar**

- reduces crime and increases the number of arrests.
- increases the number of cars recovered with less damage.
- saves time and money.
- saves lives and makes you feel more secure.

For further information, please contact **RAC Trackstar** on **0808 100 9991** or visit our website **www.ractrackstar.com.**

1 What does the advertisement say about alarms and immobilisers?
   A   Cars should only be fitted with new ones.
   B   They can be very expensive.
   C   They are no guarantee against theft.
   D   Lots of people have had them fitted lately.

2 If your car is stolen, your insurance company
   A   will charge you more in the future.
   B   will lend you a hire car.
   C   will try to replace the accessories from the car.
   D   may refuse to insure your car again.

3 The Trackstar system can tell the police
   A   how the car was stolen.
   B   how many cars are stolen every hour.
   C   how many people are in the stolen car.
   D   how fast the stolen car is going.

4 The term 'golden hour' (line 43) means
   A   the time when most accidents are reported.
   B   the time it usually takes an ambulance to reach an accident.
   C   the time in which someone with serious injuries should receive medical attention.
   D   when it is best to drive in areas where accidents are often reported.

5 How does the National Control Centre locate a broken-down vehicle?
   A   The driver uses the microphone to tell them.
   B   The driver presses a special button.
   C   They send a breakdown vehicle to look for it.
   D   They transmit details to the police.

6 What is the main advantage of the Breakdown Call feature?
   A   The transmitter is hidden.
   B   The transmitter can tell the RAC exacly where your car is.
   C   You can use it to make telephone calls.
   D   It informs you if you are driving on the wrong side of the road.

7 Who does 'they' in line 62 refer to?
   A   the police
   B   the emergency services
   C   the insurance companies
   D   RAC Trackstar Control

8 According to the advertisement, people with *RAC Trackstar*
   A   have less chance of being in an accident.
   B   never get their vehicles damaged.
   C   usually get their car back if it is stolen.
   D   automatically pay less in insurance.

Part 2

You are going to read a newspaper article about finding a flat in central London. Seven sentences have been removed from the article. Choose from the sentences **A–H** the one which fits each gap (**9–15**). There is one extra sentence which you do not need to use.

SMALL FLATS WITH BIG ADDRESSES

Even on a tight budget, it is still possible to find a small flat in the most expensive areas of central London. Penny Johnson explores the possibilities and meets two successful buyers.

If you live in an area of the country where a comfortable three-bedroom house can cost less than £70,000, property prices in the capital seem to be ridiculously expensive. Yet for many people a central London location is vital to their lifestyle.

Michela Savorelli is a ballet dancer with the English National Ballet. Because of performances, tours and family in Italy, she needs to be close to airports and rail terminals. **9** **E** "I had been flat-hunting for four or five months and was beginning to get fed up. We were on tour at the time, which made it even more difficult, but I was determined not to give up."

10 **H** She paid £86,000 for the property on the fifth floor of a mansion block. "It has one big room which is naturally divided into living and sleeping areas. Some work had to be done on the heating system but apart from that, I was able to move straight in."

11 **D** "But buyers should look carefully into service charges and the management of mansion blocks and bear in mind that they are often on busy roads."

In Pimlico, the area between Victoria and the Tate Gallery, prices tend not to vary very much. **12** **G** Dauntons has just sold a studio flat in this area in a matter of days for more than the £100,000 asking price. It also has a ground-floor flat in the same street on the market for £140,000. "It needs some work on it, but if the same flat were outside the 'grid', it would be closer to £125,000," says Gubbins.

In a low-budget search in high-value areas of London, you are bound to come across some awful properties. Thirza Vallois, a writer who commutes between London and Paris, needed a central base, too. "I saw some really horrible places and I was not at all hopeful. **13** **F** It was an ex-council flat in a perfect location. For £75,000, I am close to all the shops, cinemas and restaurants that I could want."

Council flats in popular areas of London do not stay on the market for long and Thirza Vallois nearly lost this one. "It was in a really terrible state when I first saw it. **14** **A** It is a bright and spacious flat and it would have been a terrible mistake not to have bought it."

15 **B** Tom Trudgian, the Managing Director, is seeing something of a recovery in this kind of property that fell in value during the economic crisis. Now they have become popular again and are in great demand.

A This nearly put me off and I made the decision to take it just in time.

B The flat was found by Stern Studios, which regularly adds new flats to its lists.

C A flat on the sixth floor in a block where the lift goes no further than the fifth would not be easy to sell.

D According to James Gubbins of Dauntons Estate Agents in SW1, £86,000 is a reasonable price for such a convenient spot.

E When it came to buying a flat in London, she wanted to live in Chelsea, which is pretty central, but everything she looked at seemed to be closer to £200,000 than her £100,000 limit.

F But at the last minute this wonderful studio flat came on the market and I just had to have it.

G In the 'grid', however, – an area of about six tree-lined streets – they are higher than elsewhere.

H Her persistence paid off and she now owns a studio flat a few minutes' walk from Victoria Station.

Part 3

You are going to read a magazine article in which people describe their daily routines. For questions **16–30**, choose from the people (**A–F**).   The people may be chosen more than once.   When more than one answer is required, these may be given in any order.

Which person or people A–F

sometimes watches TV late at night?	16 C	
find it an advantage to get up early?	17 B	18 E
works part-time?	19 A	
uses two means of transport to reach work?	20 B	
doesn't get enough sleep?	21 F	
doesn't want to change working hours?	22 C	
changes routine from week to week?	23 A	
are very tired after a day at work?	24 B	25 F
can work at any time?	26 D	
never use public transport to reach work?	27 D	28 E
sleeps in the afternoon?	29 E	
rarely goes out after work?	30 B	

Does your routine put you under pressure?

Stress can cause serious health problems. Is it an unavoidable part of your life?
Julie Miles *asks people about their daily routines.*

A Marcie Graham, secretary

I work as a secretary in a law firm. I either work mornings or afternoons, depending on which week it is. This is because I decided to take advantage of the job sharing scheme the company operates. So, when I'm working mornings, I get up at about seven and catch the eight o'clock bus. When I have to start at one, I have a lie-in and get up at about ten. Again, what I do at night depends on the hours I have to work the next day. I'm normally in bed by eleven if I have to get up early.

B Tom Lawson, accountant

I have to commute quite a long way to work, so I like to get up early, say six o'clock, so that I can catch the early train. I drive to the station and I usually take the 6:40 which gets me in at ten past eight. This is a little earlier than necessary because I don't start work till nine o'clock but I hate traveling without being able to sit down. I am the chief accountant in a multinational so I don't leave work until about seven or eight o'clock. By the time I get home, I'm worn out so we don't get out much during the week. I normally have dinner, read the newspaper and listen to music.

C Brian Cairns, assembly worker

I live near the factory where I work. Most days I get the bus, but if the weather's fine and I'm not in a hurry, I walk to work. The shift starts at eight and finishes at four. I could work another shift, but I don't think I could get used to working nights. I put my feet up after work and watch a bit of telly. After tea, I got out with my mates – except on Monday. We normally go down to the club for a game of snooker. I get home at about eleven and go straight to bed unless there's a late night film worth watching.

D Barbara Hudson, designer

Fortunately, I can choose when I work so I decide when to get up in the morning and when to go to bed. You see, I make use of technology to work from home. Normally, though, I get up at around nine o'clock and go to the supermarket at about ten. When I return, I start work. I finish at about four in the afternoon and do another couple of hours in the evening. All this means that my social life is generally unaffected because I can fit in with other people's plans. Of course, when I'm working to a strict deadline, I spend more time working and my social life is restricted.

E Mike Briggs, baker

I'm a lark rather than an owl, so it's easy for me to get up at what others call an unearthly hour of the morning. I work in a bakery and I'm up at four. I drive to work, which is about ten minutes' drive away. It's great because there's hardly any traffic at that time of the morning. I finish at one or two and go home for a nap. In the evening, I go training or I serve in the bar at the football club. I'm normally in bed by ten, or 10:30 at the latest.

F Philip Owen, shop assistant

My day begins far too early for my liking. I'm up at 7:30 – usually after a late night. This means that I really need my coffee in the morning. I catch a bus to work. It's not very far so I don't get a chance to sleep on the way to the store where I work. That's a pity because most mornings I really need to catch up on my sleep. I work from eight to five with a lunch break in between. When I get home, I'm dead on my feet. I keep saying I'll have an early night, but I don't often manage to get one.

Hints on writing an article

Articles are usually written to be included in magazines or newsletters. You will be writing either for someone who has similar interests to you or for someone who is of a similar age to you.

Question 2 in this test is an article for an international young people's magazine, so you will probably be writing for people of your own age group.

After reading the question carefully, make a plan of your ideas, including any examples you can use to support your opinion and make your article more interesting.

Spending time reading magazine articles in English will give you a good idea of how they are written. It will help your own writing if you can read a few articles, concentrating on how the writer links their ideas and holds the reader's attention.

Style
Very often a question of this type is asking for your views on something. For example, environmental problems (Test 3, question 2) or appearances (Test 1, question 2). This means that your answer will involve the use of the present tenses as you are writing about the opinions you have at present.

Alternatively, you may be asked for your opinion of what is likely to happen in the future. For example, Test 4, question 3 asks about what the future holds for you. In this article, future tenses will be used to good effect.

In Test 2 question 4, you will need to use hypothetical tenses as you are asked for suggestions about ways of improving the appearance of a bedroom. For example, "It would be a good idea to ..." or "I would ...".

Make sure you read the question carefully to check whether you will use a formal or an informal style. Very often you will use a semi-formal style, which is polite but not too impersonal.

Part 1

You **must** answer this question.

1   You entered a competition in a music magazine and you have just received the email below, on which you have written some notes.

---

email

From: Nick James

Sent: 17th July

Subject: '**Meet the Band**' competition

Dear George,

We would like to congratulate you on being one of the lucky winners of our 'Meet the Band' competition. You and a friend of your choice will receive backstage passes for the three-day Wembley concert on one of the following days (see enclosed programme):

Friday 19th August
Saturday 20th August   *which one?*
Sunday 21st August   *where exactly?*

which
nightclub?
Your prize includes return flights,   two nights in a top London hotel and an evening at one of London's top nightclubs. You will also be a guest of the group or singer for lunch.

Could you please let us know which of the dates above you would like a backstage pass for and the name of the group or singer you would like to have lunch with (give two choices).
We would also like to know your friend's name and the name of your nearest international airport.

We look forward to hearing from you.

Best wishes,   *Ask about: travel in UK*
                                                        free time to do shopping

Nick James

Read the email carefully.   Then write a reply giving the information requested and making enquiries as indicated in your notes.

Write an **email** of between **120** and **150** words in an appropriate style. Do not write any addresses.

Here is an example of the type of email expected at this level.

Dear Mr James,

Thank you very much for your email informing me about my winning a prize in your "Meet the Band" competition.

I will be travelling with my friend Eleni Dimitriou from Athens International Airport. We would like a backstage pass for Saturday 20th August if possible, and we would prefer to have lunch with either The Corrs or Ricki Martin.

There are also some questions I would like to ask.   I would like to know which hotel we will be staying at and exactly where it is.   You also mention an evening at a nightclub.   Could you please tell me which one?   Finally,   I would appreciate some details about our travel arrangements in England and I would like to know whether there will be any free time to do some shopping.

Thank you once again.

Best wishes,

George Papaionnou

Part 2

Write an answer to **one** of the questions **2–5** in this part. Write your answer in **120–180** words in an appropriate style.

2 An international young people's magazine is investigating the question:

Is enough being done to protect the environment in your country?

Write an **article** for the magazine on this topic, based on your own experience and anything else you have heard about.

3 You see this advertisement in an English-language magazine for young people.

> So, do you think you can write? Send us a short story beginning with this sentence:
>
> *It was a dangerous game to play but I knew I had no choice but to play it.*
>
> We will publish the best story in our next issue. The winner will also receive a cash prize of 500 Euros.

Write your **story**.

4 You are attending a course at a college. As part of the course you have been asked to write a review. A very large supermarket has just opened in your area and you have been asked to write a review after visiting it.

Write your **review**, describing the supermarket, what it has to offer shoppers, its facilities and commenting on its good and bad points.

5 Background reading texts

Answer **one** of the following two questions based on your reading of **one** of the set books. Your answer should contain enough detail to make it clear to someone who may not have read the book.

Either (a) Describe one of the main characters in the book or short story you have read and say whether the character could be a good friend of yours or not. Give reasons for your choice. Write your **essay**.

or (b) A good book is full of surprises. Write an **essay**, describing one part of the book which surprised you and say what you thought would happen.

Hints on word formation (Part 3)

In this part of the Use of English Paper, you must complete a text with ten gaps, You are given a word at the end of a line in the text which has a gap. You must make a new word from the word given which fits both the grammatical structure and the meaning of the sentence. For example, look at the following sentence:

The .... who was responsible for this machine died a rich man. INVENT

Both the words "inventor" and "invention" fit grammatically, but only "inventor" is correct because it is the person.

Apart from identifying what part of speech is needed, you must also bear in mind whether nouns are plural, what tense of a verb is required and so on.

When you have completed the task, read the whole text through carefully to make sure that it sounds right.

Part 1

For questions **1–12**, read the text below and decide which answer **A, B, C** or **D** best fits each space. There is an example at the beginning (**0**).

Example:

| 0 | **A** statements | **B** reports | **C** notices | **D** announcements |

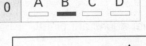

 Saving a Monument

After reading (0).............from archaeological experts that India's most famous tourist attraction is slowly being destroyed, the Indian Government has been forced to (1).............emergency measures to save the Taj Mahal, which is in (2).............of collapse from pollution. The Supreme Court has ordered the closure of 53 (3).............iron foundries. It has also ordered trees to be grown in a 500-yard area (4).............the site.

The decay of the monument has been blamed on the (5).............industries that have moved into the Agra area. In addition to these factories, illegal quarrying in the Aravalli mountains, which once formed a protective barrier around the Taj Manal, has (6).............the soft white marble exposed to sandy winds. The main result of these changes in the area has been that the Taj manal, built in 1632, has lost its (7) ....colour and is now yellow (8).............than white. The semi-precious stones set in the marble have also been damaged.

In a desperate (9).............to save the building, India's Archaeological Survey is replacing the original white marble blocks with new stones. This, however, has not been welcomed by everyone. A group of historians have claimed that if all the marble is replaced, there will be a (10).............new building – not the Taj Mahal. Other experts (11).............that old blocks of marble are being used to make (12)............. antiques. These groups undoubtedly feel that the Taj Mahal would be safer if it was left the way it is.

1	**A** take	**B** place	**C** put	**D** get
2	**A** hazard	**B** risk	**C** danger	**D** jeopardy
3	**A** close	**B** neighbourly	**C** nearby	**D** near
4	**A** through	**B** across	**C** above	**D** around
5	**A** dense	**B** heavy	**C** vast	**D** massive
6	**A** opened	**B** sent	**C** let	**D** left
7	**A** physical	**B** usual	**C** natural	**D** right
8	**A** rather	**B** except	**C** instead	**D** other
9	**A** attempt	**B** try	**C** work	**D** test
10	**A** completely	**B** terribly	**C** strangely	**D** truly
11	**A** accuse	**B** suspect	**C** blame	**D** charge
12	**A** forged	**B** false	**C** imitation	**D** fake

Part 2

For questions **13–24,** read the text below and think of the word which best fits each space. Use only **one** word in each space. There is an example at the beginning (**0**).

Example:

0	TO

Healthy Clothes

Up (0)........to........now, clothes have been worn either to protect the wearer (13).......or.........to make the wearer look attractive. Today, designers (14)......all.........over the world are developing what are known (15).......as......... "smart" clothes which provide a range of health-giving benefits. These garments can, for (16) ...example...., feed the body with essential nutrients, stop body odour, relieve back pains and reduce stress. Scientists in Japan (17) .....have.......already produced tights with vitamin C, which can be absorbed by the legs, and are in (18) ....the........ last stages of developing a material that stops embarrassing smells leaving the wearer. In Britain, there are some clothes covered with a secret chemical formula which keep (19).....out.........the harmful rays from the sun and others which let maximum sunlight pass through (20).....them...... and allow the wearer to get a tan. As regards exercising, there are socks that guarantee 1,000 miles of painless walking and there (21)......will........ soon be training shoes able to measure how many calories are burnt off during exercise.

There are not only healthy clothes but healthy accessories, (22).......too......... . A lipstick that can prevent depression is now on the market, together with spectacles that can be worn in (23)....order........ to prevent eye-strain and headaches that occur as a result of spending too much (24)....time.........in front of a computer screen or under fluorescent lighting.

Part 3

For questions **25–34**, read the text below. Use the word given in capitals at the end of each line to form a word that fits in the space **in the same line**. There is an example at the beginning (**0**).

Example:

0	KNOWN

URBAN FOXES

It is well (0)......known......... that humans have played a great part in	KNOW
causing the (25)......extinction...... of many animals throughout the	EXTINCT
world. This has partly come about due to the (26)....destruction......	DESTROY
of their habitats by cities, towns and villages getting larger. (27)Recently,	RECENT
however, some animals, (28)......including......foxes, have extended	INCLUDE
their habitats by moving into cities. These urban foxes have settled into	
(29)....residential........ areas so well that there has been a noticeable	RESIDENCE
(30)......growth.............. in their numbers. The reason they have adapted	GROW
to urban life is that there are (31)unlimited/limitless.supplies of food.	LIMIT
This has allowed urban foxes to produce (32)......twice..........as	TWO
many cubs as their rural cousins, but there is a (33)...disadvantage.. .	ADVANTAGE
The food lacks vital nutrients such as vitamins A and D, which	
(34).....weakens........the young foxes and makes them more likely to	WEAK
die from mange and other diseases.	

Part 4

For questions **35–42**, complete the second sentence so that it has a similar meaning to the first sentence, using the word given. **Do not change the word given.** You must use between **two** and **five** words including the word given. Here is an example (0).

Example:

0   I didn't expect the weather to be so bad.
THAN
The weather..I expected.

The gap can be filled by the words "was worse than", so you write:

0	WAS WORSE THAN

35   It was very difficult to hear what the lecturer said.
HARDLY
We..................... could hardly hear ....what the lecturer said.

36   What was your reason for running away?
EXPLAIN
Can..................... you explain why you ran .... away?

37   She didn't write her first poem until her fiftieth birthday.
WHEN
She..................... was fifty when she wrote ....her first poem.

38   Brian has finished all his work.
HAVE
Brian..................... doesn't have any more ....work to do.

39   Nobody saw the thief steal the necklace.
WITHOUT
The thief..................... stole the necklace without being ....seen.

40   I can't find my glasses anywhere.
MUST
I..................... must have lost ....my glasses.

41   You'll have to hurry if you want to catch the bus.
UNLESS
You..................... will miss the bus unless ....you hurry.

42   It's about a year since I last ate out.
FOR
I..................... haven't eaten out for ....about a year.

Paper 3: Use of English

Vocabulary Extension

A Vocabulary Building

Complete the unfinished words in the following sentences. All the words are related to health and fitness.

1 You should ex e r c i s e regularly.
2 Henry was over w e i g h t, so he went on a strict d i e t and lost twenty kilos.
3 It is better to build up your sta m i n a than to build up your str e n g t h by lifting weights.
4 Walking up two or three flights of stairs gets your h e a r t pumping and your lu n g s working.
5 We thought he'd broken his ank l e and expected him to return with his leg in pla s t e r, but it was a spr a i n which only required a ban d a g e.
6 The sur g e o n who performed the oper a t i o n was very pleased with his pa t i e n t's progress.
7 I'd get med i c a l adv i c e if I were you.
8 You should avoid eating fish if you've got an all e r g y.
9 If you have got a so r e throat and a co u g h but you haven't got a te m p e r a t u r e, you haven't got flu.
10 I came out in a ra s h all over my body, so my doctor gave me an inj e c t i o n and a pres c r i p t i o n for some antibiotics.

B Word Use

Use the words on the left to complete the sentences on the right. Make sure the word is in the correct form. Use each word once.

1	dense heavy vast massive	a The Sahara, a....vast....area of sand in North Africa, is the largest desert in the world. b A ..heavy.....cold prevented me from going out with my friends. c The airport had to be closed due to ....dense... fog. d Massive...walls surround the film star's property.
2	physical usual natural	a She has a(n) ...natural...talent for drawing. b Being an athlete, I enjoyed .physical..education at school. c I didn't drive to work by my ...usual.....route because of heavy traffic on the motorway.
3	rather except instead other	a Everyone came to the party ....except....Alex. b She watched television ...instead...of studying. c There's nothing you can do ...other.....than wait. d We'd ..rather.....stay at home than go abroad.
4	accuse suspect blame charge	a You can't .....blame....me for what happened. b He won't be .charged...with murder because of new evidence which has come to light. c The detective ..suspected..the gardener of stealing the money. d How dare you ..accuse...me of lying!
5	forged false imitation fake	a It is cheaper because it is made of .imitation...leather. b It is illegal to make a(n) ....false.....statement to the police. c She was arrested for using ...forged...twenty-pound notes. d He tried to make out that the ....fake.....painting he had was genuine.

C   Use of Prepositions

Use the prepositions below to complete the sentences.

at	for	in (x2)	of (x2)	on	with

1 The trees in the forest are......at......least three hundred years old.
2 There's no such product....on........the market as far as I know.
3 What was your reason......for......resigning from the company?
4 They've replaced workers...with......computer-controlled machines in nearly all their factories.
5 There's been an increase......in.......the number of people moving abroad to get a better job.
6 You can't go in unless you're dressed......in........ formal clothes.
7 It was a lack......of.......rain that caused the crop failure.
8 He survived as a result......of........the surgeon's great skill.

D   Word Formation

I Use the word in capitals at the end of each sentence to form a word that fits in the space in the sentence.

1 I was amazed by the rapid ......growth....of the fish at his farm.	GROW
2 The army has been...weakened..by the constant enemy attacks.	WEAK
3 You can't enter this building without...protective... clothing.	PROTECT
4 An economic crisis led to the.....closure.....of the factory.	CLOSE
5 Missiles are highly..destructive.. weapons.	DESTROY

II Choose the odd word out from the following groups of words according to how they form <u>nouns</u>.

1	permit	discuss	admit	<u>embarrass</u>
2	difficult	hard	deliver	modest
3	destroy	attract	civilise	advise
4	respond	intelligent	correspond	patient
5	capable	generous	courageous	secure

Hints on multiple matching (Part 3)

In this part of the Listening Paper, you will hear five short extracts, each from a different speaker. The extracts are always related in some way. For example, in Test 1, the speakers are talking about driving, in Test 2, they are talking about repairs done to electrical equipment and in Test 4, about a present they have received.

During the time given to read through the questions, you should identify and underline any key words which will help you to justify your answer. For example, in Test 1 option A "without a licence" is important, in option B 'nearly had a crash' is important and so on.

Try to make your choices on the first listening so that you can check your answers on the second. Answer all questions, even if this means guessing an answer you are not sure about.

Part 1

You will hear people talking in eight different situations. For questions **1–8**, choose the best answer, **A**, **B** or **C**.

1   Listen to the following conversation. Why was the man's connecting flight from Mumbai delayed?
   A   The weather was bad.
   B   The plane had broken down.
   C   The passengers weren't told.

`C` `1`

2   You hear someone talking about an activity weekend. Why didn't he enjoy it?
   A   The instructor was strict.
   B   He didn't feel comfortable.
   C   He wasn't staying in a very nice place.

`B` `2`

3   You hear someone talking about a film. What was her reaction to it?
   A   She was surprised.
   B   She was disappointed.
   C   She was bored.

`A` `3`

4   You hear a conversation in a shop. How does the customer intend to pay for the items she wants to buy?
   A   in cash
   B   by cheque
   C   by credit card

`A` `4`

5   You hear a radio presenter about to interview a guest. Who is the guest?
   A   a doctor
   B   an inventor
   C   an insurance agent

`B` `5`

6   Listen to a policeman talking to a witness. Where does the conversation take place?
   A   in a library
   B   in a bank
   C   in an office

`C` `6`

7   Listen to someone talking about his family. Who is David?
   A   his uncle
   B   his nephew
   C   his cousin

`C` `7`

8   Listen to someone making a phone call. What is the purpose of the call?
   A   to complain
   B   to apologise
   C   to make an arrangement

`B` `8`

Part 2

You will hear a radio interview about investing money from home. For questions **9–18**, complete the sentences.

INVESTING FROM HOME

People can now invest from home by using | modern technology | 9 |

Now there are twice as many investors as there were | three months | 10 | ago.

The real reason people invest is the feeling of | excitement | 11 | they get.

Quite a few investors make about £ | 5,000 | 12 | a month.

Making money quickly usually requires a lot of | capital | 13 |

To make money quickly, small investors must choose | risky | 14 | shares.

When you buy British shares, there is a commission charge of | 1% / one per cent | 15 |

Many British investors prefer to buy shares in | foreign | 16 | markets.

Some investors have lost so much they have had to | sell their homes | 17 |

You should never invest money that you can't | afford to lose | 18 |

Part 3

You will hear people talking in five different situations. For questions **19–23**, choose the profession of each speaker from the list **A–F**. Use the letters only once. There is one extra letter which you do not need to use.

A shop assistant

B lawyer

C teacher

D sports commentator

E film star

F police officer

Speaker 1	E	19
Speaker 2	C	20
Speaker 3	F	21
Speaker 4	A	22
Speaker 5	D	23

Part 4

You will hear part of a conversation about spending a weekend in the Scottish Highlands. For questions **24–30**, choose the best answer, **A**, **B** or **C**.

24   Who spent the weekend in Scotland?

    A   Carrie and her parents

    B   Carrie and Debbie

    C   Carrie, her cousin and Debbie

    `B  24`

25   Why was the train fare cheaper than normal?

    A   They weren't travelling to a city.

    B   They knew somebody who was working on the train.

    C   They took advantage of special student fares.

    `C  25`

26   Where did they stay?

    A   at a cheap hotel

    B   in a tent

    C   in a kind of hut

    `C  26`

27   How can a climber find out where bothies are located?

    A   by buying a guide book

    B   by getting information at a train station

    C   by asking people who know where they are

    `C  27`

28   All bothies have

    A   a fireplace.

    B   raised sleeping platforms.

    C   wooden floors.

    `A  28`

29   When Carrie says she wished Mike had been in Scotland to protect her, she is

    A   trying to make Mike angry.

    B   joking and making fun.

    C   trying to make Debbie jealous.

    `B  29`

30   When Mike is invited to Scotland, he says

    A   he isn't sure if it would be suitable for him.

    B   he isn't fit enough to walk so far.

    C   he doesn't believe they really want him to go.

    `A  30`

Hints on speaking with a partner using visual prompts (Part 3)

In this part of the Speaking Paper, the interlocutor will ask you to complete a task with the other candidate. The task may involve decision making, problem solving, suggesting, planning etc. You will be given pictures, diagrams and so on to use.

The working towards the completion of the task is important here. You need to be able to express and justify your opinions, agree or disagree with what the other candidate says, take turns and generally exchange ideas with each other. Listen to what your partner says so you can respond logically to his or her comments.

Take every opportunity in class to practise this kind of task. It can be difficult to talk to and understand a person speaking in a foreign language, so you need to get used to it before the examination.

Part 1 (about 3 minutes)

Ask and answer the following questions with a partner.

- Can you tell me something about yourself?
- What do you enjoy most about your studies?
- How much time do you spend studying?
- Which subjects do you find most difficult?
- What qualifications will you need for the job you hope to do?

Part 2 (about 4 minutes)

Practise speaking about the photographs. The photographs for Test Three are on page 157.

Candidate A, here are your two photographs. They show people talking on the phone. Please let Candidate B see them. Candidate A, I'd like you to compare these photographs, saying how important you think the telephone has become today. (approximately 1 minute)

Candidate B, could you please tell us which person the telephone is more useful for? (approximately 20 seconds)

Candidate B, here are your two photographs. They show people involved in exploration. Please let Candidate A see them. Candidate B, I'd like you to compare these photographs, saying what you think about exploring space and the oceans. (approximately 1 minute)

Candidate A, could you please tell us which of these two places you would prefer to explore? (approximately 20 seconds)

Part 3 (about 3 minutes)

Discuss the following with a partner.

Imagine that you have moved into a new house or flat and the plan of your bedroom is the one shown in the diagram on page 158. Talk to each other about which colour or colours would be best for the room and where the furniture and other items should be placed. It is not necessary to agree with each other.

Part 4 (about 4 minutes)

Give each other your opinions about the following questions.

- Who was responsible for decorating your house or flat?
- Is it possible to decorate a room cheaply and well?
- Can the way a room is decorated change your mood?
- How much can you tell about a person from the way his or her home is decorated?
- If you could change one thing in your bedroom, what would it be?

Hints on answering questions

Part 1

Always underline the key words in the question. Then use them to scan the text for similar words to find the answer quickly.

For example, in question 8 on page 83, the most important key word is "ready" because it refers to a specific point in the cheese-making process. Each of the four options is mentioned in the text in the same paragraph, but which one is mentioned after a word that signals the end or the process?

Part 2

Sometimes it is easy to find the correct missing sentence by looking for similar words, phrases or pronouns. However, occasionally these "clue" words can be misleading and can lead to the wrong answer. For example, on page 84, paragraph 3 talks about a disease, SBS, and goes on to refer to its "symptoms". Option B on page 85 mentions both SBS and the word 'symptoms', but is it the correct answer to question 10?

Part 3

In this part it is important to understand the *whole* question and look for similar ideas in the text, rather than just key words from the question. Make sure you refer to the whole article, as sometimes the answer might be somewhere you wouldn't expect it to be. For example, on page 86, question 18 asks which bank mentions a different bank. Instead of looking for matches in the key words to answer the question, try looking for the name of a bank that isn't where it should be!

Part 1

You are going to read a newspaper article about a food expert's visit to Ireland. For questions **1–8,** choose the answer **A, B, C** or **D** which you think fits best according to the text.

Getting smoked

Exquisite cured salmon, aromatic cheese and seaweed pudding are among the delicacies of Cork, the food capital of Ireland.

The airbus had barely lifted its belly off the ground before mine was being filled from a steaming foil tray of black pudding, bacon and sausage. Fortunately, there were no eggs – they always taste like plastic on
5 an aeroplane – to spoil the breakfast.

I had been promising friends for several summers that I would go to Cork, Ireland's food capital, and visit its famous Old English market and some of the region's most notable producers. So when Bord Bia, the Irish
10 Food Board, invited me over, I knew I was in for a superb gastronomic experience.

First, we headed out of the city and on through gently wooded country until we reached Belvelly near Cobh. It was here that we met Frank Hederman, whose
15 smoked salmon is of the very highest quality. He emerged from his factory door to greet us and led the way to the smokehouse. Without hesitation, he opened the door, briefly revealing the hanging bodies of the freshly caught fish inside, and shut it quickly as
20 a puff of smoke threatened to leave. "I think we've seen enough. Let's go and have lunch," he said, satisfied that no smoke had, in fact, escaped.

We set off for Ballymaloe, where we had lunch at Myrtle Allen's country house. The most memorable parts of
25 the meal were an Irish spinach soup and Myrtle's caragheen pudding. Made with caragheen moss, a seaweed gathered on Ireland's Atlantic shores, milk, egg and vanilla, it trembled like white jelly as it was set down before me.

30 Frank was brought up near the sea. "I found myself in this business by good fortune," he said. But it was not so good in the early stages of smoking experimentation. "I built a smoking box like a large wardrobe and used wood from sawn-up whiskey barrels. I'd sit in my
35 grandfather's armchair and read the paper. Every now and then, there would be a large bang due to spontaneous combustion of the alcohol," he added, smiling.

Frank built his factory on the advice of a Dutchman
40 who taught him how to smoke his fish. 'Nothing really changes in how the smoking is done, but the secret of success lies in the detail. You have to learn how to treat the fish, how to pack them and fillet them. My aim is to make Irish smoked salmon a genuine
45 gourmet product. Unfortunately, I have to use farmed salmon as there simply isn't enough wild salmon. So you get the best you can out of them. We dry them for a while and then hang-smoke them. It creates quite a different texture from the fish that's smoked lying flat
50 on mesh where the oil has nowhere to go. We replace the oiliness with smoke,' he explained.

We arrived late at the Ardrahan dairy. I had hoped to meet Eugene and Mary Burns, whose fine cheese has just won two top prizes in the British Cheese Awards,
55 but they were unavailable. Pauline, the third member of the business, showed us round, determined to give us a detailed account of the cheese-making process.

Scrubbed up more thoroughly than a surgeon, the cheese is washed, turned and tended every two days
60 until a crust darkens the creamy part inside. If you put your nose to the cheese, you can smell the grass and hay of the fields in which the cows grazed.

1   What does "mine" in line 2 refer to?
    (A)   the writer's stomach
    B   the writer's tray
    C   the writer's appetite
    D   the writer's eggs

2   How much of the smokehouse did the writer see?
    (A)   He only caught a glimpse of it.
    B   He went inside and looked around.
    C   He got a good look at it from the doorway.
    D   He didn't see it at all.

3   Where did Frank Hederman spend his childhood?
    A   in Holland
    B   near a factory that made whiskey
    (C)   near the coast
    D   in the writer's neighbourhood

4   Why were there bangs in Frank's smoking box?
    A   The fish sometimes exploded.
    B   The pressure from the smoke caused them.
    C   He had used a wardrobe to make the box.
    (D)   The wood he used was not completely dry.

5   If you smoke fish when they are lying down,
    A   the smoke forces out the oil.
    (B)   the fish remain oily.
    C   the process of smoking is much quicker.
    D   the fish sometimes split open.

6   Who are "they" in line 55?
    A   the prizes
    B   the British Cheese Awards
    (C)   Eugene and Mary Burns
    D   the cheeses

7   What does the writer mean by "Scrubbed up more thoroughly than a surgeon" in line 58?
    A   The process is rather like an operation.
    (B)   The cheese is kept very clean.
    C   The dairy looks like a hospital.
    D   The work done at the dairy is dangerous.

8   When is the cheese ready?
    A   when it turns green like grass
    B   in approximately two days
    C   after it has been washed a couple of times
    (D)   when the inside gets darker in colour

Part 2

You are going to read an article about buildings which make people feel sick. Seven sentences have been removed from the article. Choose from the sentences **A–H** the one which fits each gap (**9–15**). There is one extra sentence which you do not need to use.

WHEN THE BLUE MIST ARRIVES, MOVE OFFICES

Despite NASA's efforts to keep the matter secret, reports that the International Space Station could be suffering from 'sick building syndrome' were published in *New Scientist* last month. Last May, after astronauts spent hours inside it installing equipment, they said they had headaches and their eyes were burning. One was sick, blaming bad air.

The problems could not be explained by space sickness caused by weightlessness. It was possible that the Russian module, Zarya, an integral part of the space station, was releasing volatile chemicals. **9 F** In addition, the large amount of Velcro™ might have been releasing other chemicals from its adhesive backing.

SBS was first recognised about 20 years ago. **10 D** One building that caused such symptoms in 1991 was a medical centre in Seattle. Many people who worked there said they developed nasal congestion while they were at work but felt better when they left the building.

That year, 550 SBS complaints were made to councils throughout Britain. The most widely-publicised of these was about a building in Rochdale that was home to a greenish-blue swirling mist. **11 A** There were even stories of people being able to watch it move around the offices.

Experts from the Health and Safety Executive carried out extensive tests but failed to identify it, leaving superstitious staff suspecting a ghost. **12 C**

In an HSE report on sick building syndrome in 1992, ventilation, chemical pollution and high temperatures combined with low humidity and poor lighting were identified as the main contributory factors. In 1995, it was decided to tear down St John's House in Bootle, Merseyside, a 19-storey tax office, at a cost of £36 million. **13 H** Since the early eighties, almost half of the 2000 civil servants who worked there had experienced flu-like symptoms, while their families appeared to be unaffected.

In 1997, another HSE study of the syndrome found that those most at risk were clerical workers who wore contact lenses and worked in front of computer screens in mechanically ventilated buildings. Airborne bacteria became electrically charged and settled either on the screens or on the contact lenses. **14 E**

High-intensity ultraviolet lights have proved effective in wiping out the bacteria and fungi that grow in ducts and ventilation equipment. **15 G** Within three weeks all the bacteria and fungi had disappeared. A survey of all 113 employees, who never knew whether or not the UV lights were on, found that 20 percent fewer work-related symptoms occurred when the lights were on.

A It hovered on one floor, only to vanish and reappear on the floor below a few days later.

B Last month, Reading University researchers claimed that more than a third of SBS symptoms were caused by electromagnetic radiation.

C They were given permission to flee their desks and work elsewhere when the mist appeared.

D The symptoms such as nausea, headaches, dizziness, mental fatigue, neck pain and eye, nose and throat irritation are frustratingly non-specific.

E The same study estimated that between a third and a half of all new or reconditioned buildings had the syndrome.

F A strong smell was reported when its wall panels were opened.

G Earlier this year, some were installed in a Montreal office block which had previously suffered from SBS.

H The Inland Revenue believed that trying to cure it of SBS would be even more expensive.

Part 3

You are going to read an article about a teenager's investigation into opening a young person's bank account. For questions **16–30**, choose from the banks (**A–F**). The banks may be chosen more than once. When more than one answer is required, these may be given in any order.

Which bank or banks

made her listen to terrible music?	**16** E
dealt with her straight away?	**17** C
gave information about another bank?	**18** B
would be best for someone going on holiday abroad?	**19** A
didn't tell her to bring important documents with her?	**20** E
allowed new clients to save money on CDs?	**21** A **22** E
offered no advantages to teenagers?	**23** D
offered her something she couldn't make use of?	**24** C
gave her irrelevant information?	**25** F
had a system which checked a client's bank balance before allowing them to spend?	**26** F
showed little interest in teenagers?	**27** B
said their interest rate was the best for her age group?	**28** D
made a claim that wasn't true?	**29** B
offered a gift that would help customers understand the language used in banks?	**30** E

Banking on it

Which bank is best? Armed with £40, 15–year–old
Claire Pearson found out which bank is best for her.

BANK	THE FIRST PHONE CALL	THE DEAL	THE VERDICT
A Herd's Bank	After being put on hold for over two minutes, I was asked when I would be 16. Since accounts run in age groups, I was offered the Route-15 account, which would cover me until my next birthday. They asked if I wanted to be sent more details.	There was a welcome pack with a personal organiser, a cash card (£50-a-day limit) with Cirrus (for getting money out abroad), a statement every 3 months, 4% interest and 20% off at KZW music stores.	I felt fobbed off by the wait on the phone but when I got through, they showed genuine interest and treated me like an adult – not a kid with a bit of money. The KZW offer was tempting but I'm not sure whether I'd ever need Cirrus.
B Jensen's	After a two-minute wait, they told me that an under-19 savings account would be best for me. They said I should talk to my local branch manager as free gifts vary from branch to branch. They also mentioned that VGB give vouchers!	They offered me a welcome letter with account details, a cash card (£200-a-day limit), 3% interest, a statement every 3 months and mini statements from cash machines.	They didn't seem to be interested. Not knowing what they give clients my age to join was unprofessional (there were, in fact, no free gifts). But I liked the idea of keeping the account until I was 19.
C VGB	The bank dealt with me immediately, suggesting a VGB Plus account. They weren't sure about gifts but said that if I popped into my local branch, they would help.	You got a cash card (£50-a-day limit), interest of 1.5% rising to 3% depending on the amount of money in your account, a paying-in book, statements as requested and an on-line magazine with star interviews and competitions.	I liked the 'no hold' call, but I felt rushed through the conversation. An on-line magazine is not much use if you haven't got a computer (like me). A paying-in book is a good idea because it gives you a useful record of your account.
D Barnsley	After making me wait for a minute or so, they recommended the Express cash account, claiming it had the highest interest rates for my age group. They advised me to go to my local branch.	A cash card (£300-a-day limit) came with mini statements from cash machines and 4% interest if you're under 21.	I was impressed with how helpful they were, but I hated the way they kept on referring to me as "under 21". There was no welcome pack and there were no benefits for teenagers.
E Fast Bank	I had to wait in a phone queue with dreadful music. Finally, I was told the Live Cash account (11-15) with free CD vouchers would suit me best. They also told me about school branches which can be set up by students and teachers.	There was a good welcome pack, including a personal organiser with a wallet, diary, paper, pen and a dictionary of banking terms. They also offered a cash card (£100-a-day limit), 3.75% interest, a music voucher and monthly statements.	They were quite rude, but I'm glad I was patient. The package was impressive, with good interest. My one big criticism was that they didn't offer to send me any information or tell me to bring proof of identity when I went into a branch, which was essential.
F The Big Bank	They asked me which branch I wanted to join and put me on hold. They suggested the Card Plus account, with sports vouchers and good interest but no cheque book until my next birthday.	Their welcome pack contained information on operating an account, a statement folder, card holder and a £10 Sports division voucher. This bank gave monthly statements, 4% interest, a cash card (£250-a-day limit) with SOLO (which checks your balance before allowing you to buy things).	I felt they weren't serious when they dealt with me. Why did they tell me about what I can get at 16 (cheque book) when I can't have one now? Their offer of SOLO was good, though. It would be great for shopping.

Hints on writing an essay

Question 2 in this test is an example of this type of question. Your answer should include opinions and ideas on the subject presented by the teacher.

It is important when writing an essay that you organise your paragraphs in a logical way. Your first paragraph should be a brief but interesting introduction to the subject. The next two or three paragraphs – the main body – should expand your ideas in an organised manner.   Remember to start your paragraphs with a topic sentence and use a different paragraph for each idea.   You should end your essay with a short summary of the points raised and include your own opinion.

Style

The style for this type of essay should be impersonal.   Avoid extensive use of   "I think...".   Use passive structures such as "It is thought ..." or "... is thought to ...".

There are many useful phrases which will help you to structure your essay.

Words and phrases for listing points:

To start with, ..., Firstly, ..., Secondly, ...; Next, ...; Then, ...; Finally, ...

Phrases to add more points in support of an argument:

Furthermore,...; Moreover,...; Another major (dis)advantage (of)...; In addition (to)...; Apart from that,...

Phrases to introduce conflicting arguments:

On the contrary, ...; However,...; On the other hand,...

Phrases to express opinion:

I believe,...; It is believed,...; In my opinion,...; In my view,...

Part 1

You **must** answer this question.

1   You work for a travel agency and you have been asked to arrange a full-day excursion for a group of English tourists who will be visiting your area in the summer. Read the letter from the tour operators and your notes. Then, write a letter to the tour operators, giving suggestions for an itinerary.

> We have decided to include a full-day excursion for this group of tourists. As they are all members of a history society, the excursion should include a visit to a place of historical interest. I have also been informed that the majority are keen nature lovers, so perhaps they would enjoy observing local wildlife. The group will be aged between 50 and 70 so the day should not be too strenuous.
>
> I hope this information will be of assistance to you.
>
> Yours faithfully
>
> *John Gardener*
>
> John Gardener
> (Tours Manager)

10 am	visit to local temple and ruins (with guide, air-conditioned coach) local market (souvenirs)
1 pm	lunch at local hotel (Apollon?) rest in hotel lounge
2:30 pm	visit to sea park (3 hrs) in glass-bottomed boat dolphins, seals, fish and sea birds
6 pm	refreshments at beach cafe
7 pm	board coach to leave

Write a **letter** of between **120** and **150** words in an appropriate style. Do not write any addresses.

This is a model answer for the question in Part 1 on page 89 which may help you to see what a student needs to produce to be successful in the examination.

Dear Mr Gardener,

Thank you for your enquiry about an excursion. I have suggested a possible itinerary below.

The morning will include a visit to a local temple that is over 3000 years old, which would be of great interest to the group. There will be a guide to accompany them and the coach will be air-conditioned. They may buy souvenirs from the local market. Lunch will be served at a local hotel (probably the Apollon), and it will be followed by a rest in the hotel lounge.

At 2:30 there will be a three-hour tour of a sea park in a glass-bottomed boat. There is a wide variety of sea creatures and birds in the park. Refreshments will be served at a beach café and the group will board the coach to return to their hotel at 7 pm.

I look forward to hearing from you.

Yours sincerely,

Evi Papadopoulou

Part 2

Write an answer to **one** of the questions **2–5** in this part. Write your answer in **120–180** words in an appropriate style.

2 Your teacher has asked you to write an essay, giving your opinion on the following statement:

> *Young people do not appreciate the value of money unless they are made to work for it.*

Write your **essay**.

3 You have seen this in an international magazine.

 Your future

Do you have any ideas about what the future holds for you? We want to read them. The best articles will be published in our magazine and the sender of each published article will receive £100.

Write your **article** for the magazine.

4 Your pen friend has been asked to do a project on a foreign country and has chosen to write about your country. This is part of your pen friend's letter.

about your country and I'd like you to help me if you can. We have to write about education, family life and national holidays.

Write a **letter** to your pen friend. Do not write any addresses.

5 Background reading texts

Answer **one** of the following two questions based on your reading of **one** of the set books. Your answer should contain enough detail to make it clear to someone who may not have read the book.

Either·(a) A good book develops the relationship between its characters very well. Write an **essay**, describing the relationship between two of the characters in the book or short story you have read.

or **(b)** Most books have a part which makes them unique. From the book or short story you have read, choose one part which makes the book different from any other. Write an **essay**, describing the part and explaining why it is unique.

Hints on "key" word transformations (Part 4)

In this part of the Use of English Paper, you must complete 8 sentences with between two and five words each. One of the words must be the "key" word given. This "key" word must not be changed in any way. This part of the Use of English Paper tests grammatical structures such as conditionals, direct and indirect speech, modals and so on, as well as lexical phrases and collocations.

You must read the prompt sentence carefully, paying particular attention to tenses. Then, look at the "key" word and decide how it can be used in relation to the prompt sentence. Finally, ensure that the phrase you write makes sense, fits the structure of the sentence and contains a maximum or five words.

Remember that contractions, like *can't, won't, don't*, etc, are counted as two words. Don't forget, however, that *cannot* is one word.

Part 1

For questions **1–12**, read the text below and decide which answer **A**, **B**, **C** or **D** best fits each space. There is an example at the beginning (**0**).

Example:

0 **A** long   **B** early   **C** soon   **D** far

0	A	B	C	D

Submarines

The first craft to be able to travel under water was built as (0).................as the seventeenth century. Over a century (1)................., an American engineer invented a submarine which was used to try and attack a British ship in New York (2)................ . Named *Bushnell's Turtle* (3)..................its inventor, it could only remain submerged for thirty minutes because it had no underwater oxygen supply.

In 1800, the first submarine which was (4)..................in shape to the modern submarine was built. It used compressed air as an underwater oxygen supply but the (5)..................had to rotate a propeller (6)..................hand, so that it could move under water. Towards the end of the nineteenth century, the first submarine with an efficient (7)..................of power was built. Launched in 1898, it used a petrol-driven (8)..................to cruise on the surface and it moved (9)..................an electric motor after it had dived.

In the twentieth century, submarines were used extensively as weapons of war. In the First World War, German submarines, (10)..................as U-boats, sank many British ships. Their effectiveness (11)..................to the development of submarines that could remain submerged for long periods of time without having to surface. By 1950, the record was a distance of just (12)..................5,300 miles.

Nowadays, there are nuclear-powered submarines, many of which can travel about 400,000 miles without having to be refuelled.

1	**A** after	**B** since	**C** later	**D** sooner
2	**A** harbour	**B** bay	**C** gulf	**D** port
3	**A** after	**B** from	**C** through	**D** with
4	**A** alike	**B** same	**C** resembling	**D** similar
5	**A** team	**B** crew	**C** group	**D** gang
6	**A** with	**B** by	**C** in	**D** on
7	**A** origin	**B** state	**C** source	**D** spring
8	**A** generator	**B** machine	**C** engine	**D** device
9	**A** in place of	**B** in accordance with	**C** on account of	**D** by means of
10	**A** named	**B** regarded	**C** recognised	**D** known
11	**A** resulted	**B** led	**C** brought	**D** caused
12	**A** more	**B** above	**C** over	**D** higher

Part 2

For questions **13–24**, read the text below and think of the word which best fits each space. Use only **one** word in each space. There is an example at the beginning (**0**).

Example:

0	OF

Choosing a car

Most people's choice (0)......<u>of</u>.........car is based on looks or performance but, according to the National Back Pain Association, there should be a far more important reason.

In Britain, statistics show that back pain is responsible (13)......<u>for</u>........about 120 million lost working days each year and the Association regards poor car seating and driving position (14).....<u>as</u>......... two of the main causes of back pain. Statistics also show that when you (15).....<u>spend</u>.....several hours a day behind the wheel, you are three (16)....<u>times</u>........ more likely to suffer (17)....<u>from</u>....... back trouble. Consequently, choosing the wrong car can literally (18)....<u>be</u>.......... a pain in the neck.

(19).....<u>The</u>...... best cars in terms of comfort give plenty of adjustment. Ideally, both seats and steering wheel should adjust electrically to give the perfect driving position, but (20)......<u>if</u>......... they don't, the adjusters should be well-placed and easy (21).....<u>to</u>......... use. The driver's seat should provide support at the base and back but should (22).....<u>not</u>........ restrict movement. The doors and boot should be easy to open, even in a crowded car park. Finally, there is visibility. The driver's field of vision should be good (23)...<u>enough</u>.... to allow parking without the driver having to twist so much that unnecessary strain (24).......<u>is</u>........ put on the back.

Part 3

For questions **25–34**, read the text below. Use the word given in capitals at the end of each line to form a word that fits in the space **in the same line**. There is an example at the beginning (**0**).

Example:

0	INVENTIONS

Telephone takeover

The telephone may have been one of the most important (0)..inventions..   INVENT
of the nineteenth century but it can be extremely (25)......annoying.....   ANNOY
at times.

(26)....Personally......, I do not find it amusing when a mobile phone   PERSON
starts ringing in all its (27)....technological.. glory and I am forced to   TECHNOLOGY
listen to one side of a (28)...conversation... . Nor do I think it is funny   CONVERSE
when I am forced to wait (29) ......patiently......when someone keeps   PATIENCE
on (30)..apologising......for having to make a call when they have just   APOLOGY
received a message. It is as if there is a (31)...worldwide........   WORLD
conspiracy to conquer the human race. Perhaps I am too (32)....suspicious   SUSPECT
of these clever little devices, but when I see them (33).....dressed.....   DRESS
up in jackets or made to look like cuddly toys, my (34)......dislike........   LIKE
of them increases even further.

Part 4

For questions **35–42**, complete the second sentence so that it has a similar meaning to the first sentence, using the word given. **Do not change the word given.** You must use between **two** and **five** words including the word given. Here is an example (**0**).

Example:

0   The last time we ate out was six months ago.
FOR
We ....six months.

The gap can be filled by the words "haven't eaten out for", so you write:

0	HAVEN'T EATEN OUT FOR

35   Mark will probably win the darts tournament.
LIKELY
It ....is likely that Mark will..........................win the darts tournament.

36   I'd like to see your essay.
LOOK
I'd like to................(have a / take a) look at.................. what you have written.

37   They weren't doing anything about it when I arrived.
WAS
Nothing..........................was being done..........................about it when I arrived.

38   There wasn't much milk left in the fridge.
ONLY
There............................was only a little............................ milk left in the fridge.

39   Little Ben can get dressed without any help.
CAPABLE
Little Ben..............is capable of getting dressed.............without any help.

40   They tried to rescue the survivors before dark.
ATTEMPT
They...........................made an attempt...........................to rescue the survivors before dark.

41   I wish I could spend my summers on a desert island.
ABLE
I'd love......................to be able to spend.....................my summers on a desert island.

42   The teacher explained the theory to us very clearly.
EXPLANATION
The teacher gave us................a very clear explanation of...............the theory.

Vocabulary Extension

A Vocabulary Building

Complete the unfinished words in the following sentences. The words are all related to shopping and clothes.

1 You'll have a better chance of finding a bar <u>g a i n</u> at the local mar <u>k e t</u>.
2 I had to take the dogs for a walk in the rain so I put on my an <u>o r a k</u> and a pair of Wellington b <u>o o t s</u>.
3 Keep the rec <u>e i p t</u> in case you want to ex <u>c h a n g e</u> the swea <u>t e r</u> for a larger si <u>z e</u>.
4 She was wearing a lot of accessories including ear <u>r i n g s</u>, a neckl <u>a c e</u> and a large br <u>o o c h</u> on her dress.
5 The items sold in that shop may be good val <u>u e</u> for mo <u>n e y</u>, but they won't give you a re <u>f u n d</u> if the goods are fau <u>l t y</u>.
6 He never wears a b <u>e l t</u> to hold up his trousers: he always wears br <u>a c e s</u>.
7 These jeans are too ti <u>g h t</u> around the wai <u>s t</u>; they must have sh <u>r u n k</u> in the wash.
8 They have a cre <u>d i t</u> card which is accepted at almost every department st <u>o r e</u> in town!
9 You can get a dis <u>c o u n t</u> of up to 60% on some goods in the January sa <u>l e s</u>.

B Word Use

Use the words on the left to complete the sentences on the right. Make sure the word is in the correct form. Use each word once.

1 team
   crew
   group
   gang

a Only a few members of the ....<u>crew</u>....had to leave the ship.
b I was forced to join a...<u>gang</u>.....in my neighbourhood to avoid being beaten up.
c Now that he's recovered from injury, he's back in the ...<u>team</u>........ .
d When we find a drummer, we'll be able to form a ...<u>group</u>........ .

2 by hand
   in hand
   on hand

a I don't know whether to type the letter or write it ...<u>by hand</u>.... .
b It was lucky that a lifeguard was ...<u>on hand</u>...to rescue you.
c He told me not to worry because everything was ...<u>in hand</u>.... .

3 origin
   source
   spring

a The ...<u>origin</u>....of this medical term is obviously Greek.
b I'm afraid I can't reveal my <u>source</u>..... of information.
c This water comes from a(n) ...<u>spring</u>.... in the Alps.

4 generator
   machine
   engine
   device

a My car ...<u>engine</u>....is running very smoothly indeed.
b Without our ...<u>generator</u>, we wouldn't have had any electricity.
c His uncle operates a cutting ...<u>machine</u>. in a factory.
d This is a clever little ...<u>device</u>...for finding lost keys.

5 in place of
   on account of
   by means of
   in accordance with

a He got the job ...<u>on account of</u>..his ability to sell.
b The vote must be carried out ......<u>in accordance with</u>..... the rules.
c She reached the top of her profession.<u>by means of</u>..hard work and useful contacts.
d We could use this new method...<u>in place of</u>....the old chemical process.

C Use of Prepositions

Use the prepositions below to complete the sentences.

> at   by   from   in   of (x2)   on (x2)

1 Harold can be a right pain......in........the neck......at........times.
2 She has such an intense dislike.......of.......computers that she doesn't even want to talk about them.
3 You're not capable...of..........running the marathon in under four hours.
4 Sitting in that chair for hours will put a great strain......on........your back.
5 Carla suffers....from.....amnesia.
6 There was something strange floating......on.......the surface.
7 It'll be quicker to write the note.....by........hand.

D Word Formation

I Use the word in capitals at the end of each sentence to form a word that fits in the space in the sentence.

1 It is, as far as I know, electrically powered.	ELECTRICITY
2 When are they going to ...modernise... the sports centre?	MODERN
3 Does ...technogical. progress make us less human?	TECHNOLOGY
4 Jack's such a ...suspicious... character.	SUSPECT
5 Last year the company's ...worldwide.... sales reached almost £10 billion.	WORLD

II Choose the odd word out from the following groups of words according to how they form adjectives.

1   prefer   rely   create   profit

2   atmosphere   addition   critic   education

3   danger   humour   suspect   effect

4   comedy   drama   economy   luxury

5   speed   heat   sun   fog

Paper 4: Listening

Hints on answering multiple-choice questions (Part 4)

In Part 4 of the Listening Paper you will hear a monologue or text involving interactive speakers. There are seven multiple-choice questions with three options.

You will have time before you listen to read the questions. Don't forget to underline key words and make predictions about what you might hear.

Remember that the questions are in the same order as the text, so listen out for key words from the question or stem to signal an answer. You might even hear the exact words from the options on the recording, but that does not necessarily mean it is the correct answer. For example, in Part 4 of Test Four, a speaker will mention that a vet was shot by the police, but is option B the correct answer to question 24?

You will have time at the end of the examination to transfer your answers to the answer sheet. Make sure you transfer your answers accurately and clearly. Check that you have marked the right choice next to the appropriate question number and that you haven't jumped a line.

Part 1

You will hear people talking in eight different situations. For questions **1–8**, choose the best answer, **A**, **B** or **C**.

1 Listen to two people talking. What does the man want the woman to do?
   A to cook a meal
   B to baby-sit
   C to take a phone message

   B 1

2 Listen to two people talking before they go out. Where are they going?
   A to a concert
   B for a meal
   C to a discotheque

   C 2

3 Listen to a conversation in an office. What happened to the woman the previous evening?
   A She got into a fight.
   B She was insulted.
   C She got involved in an argument.

   B 3

4 Listen to a woman telling a friend about a problem at work. Why does she think John caused the photocopier to break down?
   A He was angry about a managerial decision.
   B He wanted to move to another branch.
   C He didn't like his job.

   A 4

5 You hear two people talking. How does the man know Emil Wesker, the famous footballer?
   A They used to play in the same team.
   B They were in the same class at school.
   C They used to live in the same street.

   C 5

6 Listen to two people talking at work. What did the woman do when someone hit her car?
   A She apologised.
   B She got angry.
   C She called the police.

   B 6

7 Listen to two people talking at home. Why won't the remote control work?
   A There's a piece missing.
   B The batteries have run down.
   C It has been dropped.

   A 7

8 Listen to two people discussing an incident which occurred the previous evening. What did the woman do?
   A She ignored the man.
   B She was rude to the man.
   C She lied to the man.

   A 8

Part 2

You will hear part of a radio interview with a film director about making a film. For questions **9–18**, complete the sentences.

Making a Film

Best recent example: *The Blair Witch Project* took 8 days **9** to complete.

10 steps to making a cheap film

1 The Idea. Coming up with a good idea **10** is probably the most difficult part.

2 The Vision. You need to know what kind of film you are going to make and think about

the film's style and soundtrack **11**

3 The Script. You must have believable characters and a well-developed plot **12**

4 The Pitch. An agent might be needed to help sell the film/idea **13**

5 Finance. You can make a film for as little as £300 **14**

6 The Cast and Crew. Finding these people is best done by using email lists **15** to place ads.

7 The Equipment. Cameras are expensive, so it's a good idea to rent one **16**

8 Shooting. Save time by shooting different scenes together.

9 Creating Interest. Good marketing means creating something that will stay in people's minds **17**

10 Festivals. Your film gets shown and hopefully a distributor **18** picks it up.

Part 3

You will hear five different people talking about a present they have been given. For questions **19–23**, choose which of the people **A–F** is speaking. Use the letters only once. There is one extra letter which you do not need to use.

A This person got a present of sentimental value.

B This person saw the present before finding out whose it was.

C This person lost a Christmas present.

D This person was disappointed with the present at first.

E This person got a good present despite financial difficulties.

F This person got a present which couldn't have been bought.

Speaker 1	B	19
Speaker 2	D	20
Speaker 3	F	21
Speaker 4	E	22
Speaker 5	A	23

Part 4

You will hear a converation between two students about an article in a newspaper. For questions, **24–30**, choose the best answer, **A**, **B** or **C**.

24 Dee and Paul mention
   A   a vet who was attacked by a tiger a week ago.
   B   the fact that the police were forced to shoot a vet.
   C   an incident that took place some time ago.

`C` `24`

25 Why doesn't Dee want to become a vet?
   A   It is a potentially dangerous profession.
   B   She doesn't want to get shot by the police.
   C   It involves too much studying.

`A` `25`

26 Why wouldn't Dee run away if she saw a lion?
   A   She thinks it would be better to stand still.
   B   She could not run away fast enough.
   C   She would be too scared to move.

`C` `26`

27 According to the article, the British student
   A   was sleeping outside his tent.
   B   was sleeping when a lion approached him.
   C   had smelly feet, which attracted a lion.

`B` `27`

28 Why didn't anyone help the student?
   A   Nobody heard him calling for help.
   B   The attack happened too fast.
   C   The lions had already run away.

`B` `28`

29 Why wasn't the safari guide blamed for the attack?
   A   He was also attacked.
   B   He didn't know what to do.
   C   He probably prevented other attacks.

`C` `29`

30 How do safari companies avoid paying compensation if a lion attack happens?
   A   They ask clients to sign legal papers.
   B   They hire professional safari guides.
   C   They take their clients to court.

`A` `30`

Hints on speaking with a partner and the interlocutor (Part 4)

In this part of the Speaking Paper, the interlocutor will extend the discussion in Part 3. This part is a three-way conversation between yourself, the other candidate and the interlocutor. Therefore, it is important to talk to and look at both the other candidate and the interlocuter.

Be ready to comment and answer questions, giving reasons for your opinions where necessary. Don't just say: "Science can be dangerous to society." Instead, say: "In my opinion, science can be dangerous to society for many reasons. Genetic engineering, for example, ...".

Part 1 (about 3 minutes)

Ask and answer the following questions with a partner.

- Do you have any hobbies?
- How did you become interested in it/them?
- Which do you prefer, watching TV or going to the cinema?
- What sort of programmes or films do you like to watch?
- What was the last film you saw at the cinema (or on TV)?

Part 2 (about 4 minutes)

Practise speaking about the photographs. The photographs for Test Four are on page 159.

Candidate A, here are your two photographs. They have a connection with crime. Please let Candidate B see them. Candidate A, I'd like you to compare these photographs, saying what kinds of problems these crimes can cause and how we can prevent these crimes. (approximately 1 minute)

Candidate B, could you tell us which of these crimes, in your opinion, is more serious? (approximately 20 seconds)

Candidate B, here are your two photographs. They show places of learning. Please let Candidate A see them. Candidate B, I'd like you to compare these photographs, saying what the differences in attitude of the students are. (approximately 1 minute)

Candidate A, could you tell us which place you would prefer to study at? (approximately 20 seconds)

Part 3 (about 3 minutes)

Discuss the following with a partner.

Imagine that you decide to enter a competition for students while visiting a science museum. The competition rules say that you have to put the inventions illustrated on page 160 in order of importance. Talk to each other about the order in which you would put them. It is not necessary to agree with each other.

Part 4 (about 4 minutes)

Give each other your opinions about the following questions.

- How difficult do/did you find science subjects at school?
- What sort of person do you have to be to become a scientist?
- How important is science today?
- What do you think is the most important recent scientific discovery?
- Can science be dangerous to society?

Hints on improving your reading skills I

The best way to improve your reading skills is through practice. This means reading in English regularly. It is more important to choose something which you would enjoy in your own language than to force yourself to read something you find uninteresting.

Furthermore, recognise and remember that people read different things for different reasons. You would not read a menu in the same way you read a short story! Practise different techniques for the different parts of the examination and work out which parts are easier or more difficult for you.

Try to read *something* in English every week, even if it is just a magazine or a comic. This should be extra to whatever reading your teacher sets you. Do not get "stuck" on difficult words or allow them to get in the way of the general meaning of a sentence or a paragraph. You may even be able to guess the meaning of an unknown word from the context. Remember: practise and you will get better.

Part 1

You are going to read about a traveller's visit to a Nepalese national park. For questions **1–8**, choose the answer **A**, **B**, **C** or **D** which you think fits best according to the text.

Battle to save protected species
In a Nepalese national park, rangers and poachers are in deadly conflict.

In the morning we set off on elephant safari. Rhesus monkeys swung through the trees while deer rushed into the forest before us. Every now and then, we heard a snort, the grass would sway and a rhino would lumber out, take a good 'look' at us and plunge back into the undergrowth. We were hoping to see a tiger, the greatest prize of all, but they are notoriously shy. On our third day out, to our great excitement, we saw some five-toed tiger paw prints (or 'pug prints', as Jitu called them). A tiger had passed by, walking – not running, according to Jitu – first one way, then the other, not more than a few hours earlier. That was the closest we came to a meeting.

Until four decades ago, the Bengal tiger and Indian one-horned rhino ruled the Nepalese jungle. George V came on a hunting expedition in 1911 and shot 39 tigers and 18 rhinos. Then, in the 1950s, malaria was eradicated and people from the mountains migrated to the plains, cutting down the jungle to grow crops.

As their habitat disappeared, so did the tigers and rhinos. By 1962, there were only about 100 rhinos and 20 tigers in Chitwan. That year, Chitwan was declared a rhino sanctuary and protected zone. Today, it is home to about 500 Indian one-horned rhinos, a quarter of the world's population, and 107 Bengal tigers out of a worldwide population of about 3,000.

On the second day, we set off on a gruelling four-and-a-half-hour journey by elephant, boat and jeep to the national park headquarters to meet the warden. He told us that the biggest threat to the animals, apart from other animals, is poachers. In Taiwan, tiger bone sells for nearly £3,000 a pound, while rhino horn can fetch £16,000 a pound in South-East Asia.

Two battalions, of 800 men each, guard the park. One posts sentries around the park and sends out armed patrols daily. The other, the Rhino Patrol, polices the zone between the park and the villages. Occasionally, there are shoot-outs. 'We have run this patrol for the past 25 years,' the cheerful general told us. 'During this period, 25 people have been sacrificed from our side and we have killed as many.'

Poachers can only operate with the support of the locals, who know the animals' habits and habitats and regard the park as a waste of good crop-growing land. So there is great temptation to break the law.

Around the edge of the park, there are ditches filled with water, but they do not keep the animals in. Rhinos and tigers swim across at night to feed on crops and cattle before returning to the safety of the national park. The best villagers can do is bang drums, beat sticks on the ground or make firebrands out of straw to try and scare them away.

'Last week a tiger came and killed some cattle. We lost three,' complained Giri Ram. 'We also get a lot of trouble from rhinos. Three days ago, a mother and baby rhino came at night. The next day, they were still here so we tried to drive them away. One man was hurt very badly; the rhino had gored his side,' he added.

We then had a clandestine meeting with an informat from a different village, who is paid by the national park to watch his neighbours. We talked on the verandah of our small wooden house in the safari camp, away from anyone who might be tempted to listen. 'A rhino was killed by poachers six months ago,' he said. 'A new man had arrived in the village just before it happened. He was talking about killing animals and what price you could get for them.'

Later we went to the viewing platform to look at the endless jungle tinted white in the moonlight. An injured rhino we had spotted earlier had disappeared. Perhaps he had gone to a local rice field for a snack.

1   What did the rhinos do when they saw the writer's safari party?
    A   They made threatening noises.
    B   They attacked the nearest person.
    C   They paused for a moment before leaving.
    D   They started walking around in cirdes.

2   What did Jitu say about the tiger they had missed?
    A   He expected to catch up with it.
    B   It was probably injured.
    C   It kept changing direction.
    D   It had spent a few hours in the same place.

3   Why did the rhinos and tigers begin to disappear in the 1950s?
    A   They died from disease.
    B   The jungle was cut down.
    C   Hunters killed them off very quickly.
    D   They moved into the mountains.

4   The greatest danger to the men who guard the park
    A   comes from wild animals.
    B   comes from poachers.
    C   comes from traps set by hunters.
    D   is a strange, incurable disease.

5   What do the locals think of the park?
    A   It should be used to grow crops.
    B   It is a good idea.
    C   It is important for the economy.
    D   They are proud of it.

6   What do some rhinos and tigers do at night?
    A   They sleep on straw left by the locals.
    B   They make a noise by banging the ground.
    C   They sleep in special cages.
    D   They search for food outside the park.

7   How do the park guards get information about poachers?
    A   Some locals are paid to spy for them.
    B   They go under cover.
    C   They have hidden cameras in the park.
    D   They regularly search for guns in the villages.

8   What is the writer's opinion of the rangers and poachers?
    A   The writer agrees with the rangers.
    B   The writer sympathises with the poachers.
    C   The writer acknowledges both sides of the conflict.
    D   The writer does not give a personal opinion.

Part 2

You are going to read an article about "amenity kits" given to people on long-haul flights. Seven sentences have been removed from the article. Choose from the sentences **A–H** the one which fits each gap **(9–15)**. There is one extra sentence which you do not need to use.

What goes into amenity kits?

Let's see. There are 320,000 Virgin upper class passengers a year, plus 3.5 million in economy class. All of them are given at least one amenity kit, which adds up to 3,820,000 zip-up vinyl pouches, 7,640,000 self-destructing socks, enough miniature toothbrushes for the whole of Lilliput and 7,640,000 tiny marshmallow ear-plugs.

If you multiply those figures by the number of airlines operating, there must be more in-flight amenities lying around in drawers, boxes and attics than any other free gifts. **9** **F**

"That's the whole point," says Dee Cooper. "Our new economy-class kits, on board from this month, are themed around a large, clear rucksack so that people can use them afterwards – for the beach, books, or whatever. **10** **C** They've got a toothbrush, toothpaste, a 2 cm-high plastic duck called Lewis – things people will actually need to use on holiday."

Perhaps it is the airline that is missing the point. Whenever I fly long-haul, I flatly refuse to open the little bag of goodies given to me. **11** **H** I leave that to my children, who take more delight in an amenity kit than they do in any carefully chosen gift I buy them.

"A lot of people like to take their amenity kits home as gifts," agrees Dee Cooper, "so in upper and business class we now give people two kits." **12** **E** The small ones, containing pens, note-pads and key fobs, are intended to be given away as presents.

Still, children's gifts apart, it has to be said there are limits to the usefulness of an amenity kit around the house. Once, as a cost-cutting experiment, I wore a pair of flight-socks for a day to see if they could stand the pace. **13** **G**

For airlines, amenity kits are big business. Virgin spends over 5 million pounds a year on its economy-class rucksacks and half that on its upper-class kits. **14** **A** The product is then perfected by an external design agency.

"It's all to do with knowing what's out there from a fashion point of view. **15** **D** If you're in Japan or New York, say, and you see something early, you're encouraged to bring it back – like those miniature Polo mints, or tissues with 'Achoo!' written on them," says Dee Cooper.

A A team of four industrial designers chooses what goes in them, but aircrews, management and other staff throw in their ideas as well.

B So who decides what goes in the kits?

C They're see-through and they come in five different colours.

D You have to know what's hot, what the future is.

E Launched last year, the large ones – in a camel-coloured fabric that is supposed to look 'traditional with a twist' – are a kind of in-flight washbag.

F Or there may be a much simpler explanation: people really do use them.

G By noon, they had disintegrated into candy floss and I spent the afternoon picking sticky black fibres off the carpet.

H I just can't bring myself to break open the wrapper.

Part 3

You are going to read some information about parks and farms to visit in England. For questions **16–30**, choose from the list of places (**A–F**). The places may be chosen more than once. When more than one answer is required, these may be given in any order.

At which of the places could you

buy clothes? — **16 F**

buy food to give the animals or birds? — **17 C** **18 D**

see animals or birds that were once almost extinct in parts of Britain? — **19 A**

see a famous personality? — **20 C**

see an exhibition? — **21 F**

see animals or birds that are disabled? — **22 B**

see animals or birds that are quiet? — **23 F**

take advantage of facilities for eating outdoors? — **24 E**

see animals or birds that are interested in the people who come to see them? — **25 A**

give animals or birds something to drink? — **26 C**

handle baby animals or birds? — **27 D**

see animals or birds recovering from illnesses? — **28 B**

hear the sound which is being used to protect animals or birds? — **29 E**

be assisted by the animals or birds? — **30 F**

Soft and Cuddly

Parks and farms open to show off their newborn residents to an audience of admirers.

A Otter Trust

A heart-warming success story since it was founded 28 years ago, the *Otter Trust* has reintroduced 117 otters into the wild, reversing a trend that saw them disappearing from large areas of the country. Most have been released into rivers in East Anglia, where they were virtually extinct in the early 1980s. The biggest draw for children, however, are the playful Asian short-clawed otters. They are fed at the same time as their European relatives, but are much tamer and seem genuinely curious about their human visitors, too.

Other attractions

Enclosures with ducks and geese. Café with hot drinks, cakes, etc.

Best buy

Cuddly otter cub, £4.

B Seal Sanctuary

Some of the seals here live in a sheltered community. Their home is a series of pools set among the pastures and woodlands overlooking the Helford estuary. Each one has problems which means they can never be set free. Rocky, for example, was a performer of tricks at a marine centre until he started going blind. The centre also rescues wild seals that are sick, injured or orphaned. They convalesce at the sanctuary (you can visit the hospital where they are treated) until they are fit again.

Other attractions

Underwater observatory, a few retired donkeys, nature trail. Café with ice creams.

Best buy

All sizes of fluffy seals, £2.99–£19.99.

C Sheep Centre

Grazing on the top of chalk cliffs is Terry Wigmore's flock of sheep – 340 adults from 47 British breeds. Down in a couple of old barns in the village of East Dean is the *Seven Sisters* visitor centre, where a team of 15 lambs obligingly lines up to be bottle-fed by waiting children. The Easter holidays are a good time to go, with four or five lambs born every day.

Thirty pence buys you a bag of feed for the ewes and there are plenty of takers, including local celebrity and TV star, Twiggy.

Other attractions

Occasional weaving. Café with light lunches and cream teas.

Best buy

Sheep's milk ice cream, 75p a cone.

D The Wernlas Collection

With 80 breeds, *The Wernlas Collection* claims to be the country's leading conservation centre for rare and traditional breeds of chicken. Each breed has a pen in a large meadow in scenic Shropshire countryside. You get a cupful of wheat · (10p) and wander round the pens, distributing seed to the birds. Highlight of the visit is a glimpse inside the Chick House, where young chicks up to a month old huddle together under warm lamps or run round cheeping wildly. A guide shows children how to hold the tiny bundles of feathers safely.

Other attractions

More animals to visit, including donkeys, goats and lambs.

Best buy

Day-old chicks from £4.

E Abbotsford Swannery

The Swannery is by no means new. It has been managed since at least 1393, when it belonged to a Benedictine monastery. The main problem the management has had since then has been how to protect the cygnets from foxes. A local farmer recently came up with a good solution – Radio 4 should be played through loudspeakers. The present manager, David Wheeler, tried it and it worked!

Highlight of the visit is feeding time, at noon and 4 pm. Hundreds of swans gather to greet a member of staff who pushes a wheelbarrow full of wheat down a path to the lagoon.

Other attractions

Rides in a horse-drawn carriage. Picnic area.

Best buy

Cuddly toy cygnet £3.95.

F Ashdown Llama Farm

The centre is full of displays designed to show why these producers of soft wool are so much nicer than other farm animals. Llamas don't damage trees, they don't make noise and they will happily accompany you on walks and carry your bags for you. Between 60 and 70 llamas and alpacas live here. One of the current stars is two-year-old Tom, a handsome and exceptionally woolly light-brown male. You can see him and the others on a self-guided walk around the farm, where you also meet their relatives, the alpacas and guanacos and learn about these creatures from displays in restored 18th-century barns.

Other attractions

Cashmere and angora goats. Tea shop.

Best buy

Soft alpaca knitwear.

Hints on writing a short story

Questions requiring you to write a short story can be worded in a variety of ways. Often, as in Test Two, Question 3, you may be required to write your story for a short story competition. In Test Three, question 2, you are required to write your short story for an English-language magazine. Whatever the case, you will probably be given a sentence to include in your story. It is very important to make sure that this sentence ties in with your story.

The easiest way to ensure this is to "question the question". Let's look at question 3 in Test Two and do this. Your story must begin with *As I was passing a newspaper stand, I saw a picture of my best friend next to the headlines.* Questions raised by this sentence are:

a Were you surprised to see your best friend's photograph in the newspaper, or were you expecting to see it there?

b What were the headlines? What was the story in the newspaper? How was your best friend involved?

c If you were expecting to see his or her photograph, how did you have knowledge of what had happened?

d Is the story about something good or bad?

As long as your story includes these points, the opening sentence should "fit in" well.

Remember that you do not want to give the story away in the first paragraph. It is important to hold the readers' attention and make them curious about what is to come. In this way, they will want to continue reading.

Do not introduce too many different characters or events. 120-180 words is not a very long story, so keep it simple.

Part 1

You **must** answer this question.

1   You are a member of the sports committee at your college. A number of students have expressed interest in a tennis course coached by a professional tennis player. An agreement has been made, but the coach has written to you asking for more information about the course.

Read his/her letter and your notes and write a reply to him/her.

Fine!
no change

24 maximum

You stated that the course would last from the 12th-19th July, but these dates were not confirmed. Have there been any changes made to the original dates? I would also like to know how many students will be attending the course, their ages and what level they are at. There is also the question of courts and how long each session will last. Please send me more information about these points. Finally, have you planned a tournament or anything for the last couple of days?

16–20

Grass (4)

Beginners, intermediate, advanced

Up to the coach, 1 hour or 1 and 1/2 hours, which prefer?

Yes, great idea!
+buffet dinner afterwards to present awards, prizes, etc.

Write a **letter** of between **120** and **150** words in an appropriate style. Do not write any addresses.

This is a model of what would be expected at the FCE level.

Dear Ms Connor,

Thank you for your letter. I would be glad to give you the information you requested.

The dates for the course have not been changed,   so they are still 12th-19th July as you stated.   There will be a maximum of 24 students,   aged between 16 and 20 and they will be divided into three groups: beginners, intermediate and advanced.   As far as the courts and length of sessions are concerned,   there are four grass courts at the college and the sessions can either last for one hour or ninety minutes.   It all depends on which you prefer.

I had not planned anything for the last two days but I found your idea marvellous. There will now be a tournament, the prizes for which will be presented at a buffet dinner.

I hope these arrangements are satisfactory.

Yours sincerely,

Dimitris Papantonis

Part 2

Write an answer to **one** of the questions **2–5** in this part. Write your answer in **120–180** words in an appropriate style.

2 You have seen this announcement in an international magazine.

 Dog World

Enter our exciting short story competition and win a year's supply of pet food! Write a short story beginning with these words:

If it hadn't been for my dog, that day would have ended in disaster.

Write your **story** for the magazine.

3 You have had a class discussion about the following statement:

Both parents and young people complain that communication between the two generations is very difficult.

Now your teacher has asked you to write an essay about the statement, giving reasons for the situation and possible solutions to the problem.

Write your **essay**.

4 You have just returned from a five-day holiday organised for the first time by your college. You have been asked to write a report about the holiday to help with the planning of future holidays. You have been asked to include the following in your report: transport, accommodation, facilities and entertainment.

Write your **report.**

5 Background reading texts

Answer **one** of the following two questions based on your reading of **one** of the set books. Your answer should contain enough detail to make it clear to someone who may not have read the book.

Either (a) If you could have one of the experiences that one of the characters has in the book or one of the short stories you have read, which one would it be? Write an **essay**, describing both the character and experience you have chosen.

or (b) A good book or story must be able to hold a reader's attention. Write an **essay**, explaining how the book or short story you have read managed to hold your attention.

Hints on answering questions

Part 1

Question 6: Which of the four options means "the physical location of a library building"?

Question 9: Which verb describes the giving of a present?

Question 12: Which pronoun refers to the "readers"?

Part 2

Question 19: Look at the word after the gap. It tells you that the missing word is part of the verb "to be". Which tense is needed in this sentence?

Question 20: Which preposition collates with "discovery"?

Question 21: Which pronoun is needed here?

Part 3

Question 25: What kind of word can we put immediately before a noun to define it?

Question 29: In this question the missing word is a noun. Look at the verb after the gap. Is the noun needed singular or plural?

Question 34: The word after the gap is a verb, so that tells us that we need to form an adverb from "hope" to answer the question.

Part 4

Question 36: Along with the "key" word "best", a verb is also needed to make this sentence complete. What verb phrase fits in this gap?

Question 39: Notice now the sentence has changed from active to passive voice. Change the verb in the given sentence to passive to complete the gap, using the "key" word.

Question 42: A verb is needed in this gap. How can you form a verb with the word "used"?

Part 1

For questions **1–12**, read the text below and decide which answer **A, B, C** or **D** best fits each space. There is an example at the beginning (**0**).

Example:

0   **A** possible   **B** likely   **C** reasonable   **D** sure

0	A	B	C	D
	▬	—	—	—

THE BRITISH LIBRARY

Nowadays, it is (0)..............to find libraries throughout Britain, (1)..............in some relatively small villages. Many of these were built in the 1960s and (2)..............1970s as part of a national literacy campaign. The largest library established at this time was the British Library, which was (3)..............up as a national centre for reference, study and information. This library is regarded as (4)..............since it attempts to represent every (5)............. of civilisation, every language and every topic.

The British Library moved to its new (6)............. in St Pancreas in north London in 1997. The current building has about 340 km of shelf (7)............. Perhaps the most impressive part of the building is the King's Library, with a (8)............. of 65,000 volumes, which was (9)............. to the nation by George IV in 1823. This particular collection is housed in the Tower of Books, an imposing glass structure of six (10)............. .

The British Library's collection consists of more than 18 million volumes, built up over the last 250 years. In addition to this material, there are 33 million patent specifications, about 2 million maps, 8 million stamps and millions of manuscripts. Among the collection is the earliest known copy of the Anglo-Saxon poem "Beowulf". Every year its reading (11)............. are used by over 500,000 readers, twenty per cent of (12)............. are from overseas.

1	**A** still	**B** also	**C** even	**D** yet
2	**A** early	**B** beginning	**C** start	**D** low
3	**A** taken	**B** made	**C** set	**D** brought
4	**A** only	**B** unique	**C** single	**D** particular
5	**A** age	**B** time	**C** term	**D** interval
6	**A** place	**B** area	**C** setting	**D** site
7	**A** area	**B** range	**C** room	**D** space
8	**A** number	**B** calculation	**C** total	**D** sum
9	**A** presented	**B** granted	**C** provided	**D** pleased
10	**A** levels	**B** layers	**C** decks	**D** storeys
11	**A** offices	**B** rooms	**C** wards	**D** studios
12	**A** which	**B** those	**C** them	**D** whom

Part 2

For questions **13–24**, read the text below and think of the word which best fits each space. Use only **one** word in each space. There is an example at the beginning (**0**).

Example:

0	FAR

Rulers of the Sky

The history of dinosaurs, as (0)....far...... as we know, is quite complete, but the history of pterosaurs, flying reptiles, is still (13).....in...... some doubt. What is generally accepted, however, is that the first pterosaurs were about the size of a blackbird and that the early forms were poor fliers that (14)...could... only stay in the air by constantly flapping (15)....their... wings.

Palaeontologists also know that they grew to huge sizes, but (16)...until.... recently, nobody could have suspected just (17).....how.. big. In 1975, the remains of a Quetzalcoatius, (18)...with..... a wingspan of 33 feet, were found in Texas. This creature (19).....had....... been considered the largest one capable of getting into the air before the recent discovery (20).....of....... the Solana Dragon.

The Solana Dragon, named after the area in (21)...which... it was found, had a bigger wingspan than that of a small executive jet and cruised the skies of what is now called Spain (22).between.... 144 million and 66 million years ago. Although its wingspan of 39 feet allowed it to attack large reptiles, there must have been some disadvantages. A fairly strong wind, for instance, would (23)...have... put the Dragon's wings under great pressure, making flight very difficult, if (24)...not...... impossible.

Part 3

For questions **25–34**, read the text below. Use the word given in capitals at the end of each line to form a word that fits in the space **in the same line.** There is an example at the beginning (**0**).

Example:

0	KNOWLEDGE

Satellites

It is common (0)....knowledge...... that satellites play a very important | KNOW
role in (25).......global......... communications, but contrary to what | GLOBE
most people believe, they will not orbit our planet for ever. Satellites
are (26).....dependent..... on energy to keep working, so when their | DEPEND
batteries run down they (27)....effectively...... 'die'. Since satellites are | EFFECT
extremely expensive to build and launch, the (28)........loss........ of | LOSE
one due to energy failure is costly. As a result, (29)......scientists... | SCIENCE
are trying to find a way of keeping them in orbit. One (30).suggestion.. | SUGGEST
that has been put forward is the (31)......addition........ of solar panels, | ADD
which would allow the satellite to keep on (32)......circling........above | CIRCLE
us as there would always be (33)........available... energy from the | AVAIL
sun.   Indeed, any excess energy could be sent back to earth using
lasers, (34)....hopefully....... solving any energy crisis that may occur | HOPE
in the future.

Part 4

For questions **35–42**, complete the second sentence so that it has a similar meaning to the first sentence, using the word given. **Do not change the word given.** You must use between **two** and **five** words including the word given. Here is an example (**0**).

Example:

0 Crowd trouble led to the match being abandoned.
RESULT
The match had to ....of crowd trouble.

The gap can be filled by the words "be abandoned as a result", so you write:

0	BE ABANDONED AS A RESULT

35 Mark doesn't drive as carefully as Wendy does.
DRIVER
Wendy is ....a more careful driver than............Mark is.

36 I'll help you in any way I can.
BEST
I'll ....do/try my best to...............help you.

37 Take a packed lunch because there might not be a shop in the area.
CASE
Take a packed lunch...............in case there isn't............ a shop in the area.

38 You can't leave the exam room before eleven o'clock.
EARLIEST
Eleven o'clock ....is the earliest you can...............leave the exam room.

39 You can't send this letter unless there is a stamp on it.
ONLY
This letter ....can only be sent if............ there is a stamp on it.

40 'May I use the laboratory after school, please?' the boy asked.
PERMISSION
The boy asked...............(for) permission to use............... the laboratory after school.

41 We finally managed to find a solution to the problem.
ABLE
We...............were finally able to solve............... the problem.

42 I would visit the funfair with my father every weekend.
USED
My father ....used to take me to............... the funfair every weekend.

Vocabulary Extension

A Vocabulary Building

Complete the unfinished words in the following sentences which are related to science and technology.

1 Make sure your mo b i l e phone is switched off during the performance.

2 Doing chemistry exp e r i m e n t s in the lab o r a t o r y was one thing I enjoyed at school.

3 The house we've rented has air con d i t i o n i n g and central h e a t i n g.

4 Astronauts fl o a t around in space because there is no gra v i t y inside their space station.

5 Leave a message on my answ e r p h o n e if I'm out when you call.

6 The price they quoted for the computer includes spea k e r s, a pri n t e r, a mou s e and some soft w a r e.

7 It won' work because there's either a short cir c u i t or a f u s e has blown.

8 Put the pl u g in the soc k e t in the corner and switch on the vac u u m cleaner.

9 A water mole c u l e consists of two hydrogen at o m s and one ox y g e n at o m.

10 Metals like copper are good cond u c t o r s, while rubber and plastic are good ins u l a t o r s.

B Word Use

Use the words on the left to complete the sentences on the right. Make sure the word is in the correct form. Use each word once.

1	take up make up set up bring up	a This committee was .....set up.......to investigate the air crash. b Charlie was .....brought up... in a big city. c When did you .....take up......golf? d If I hadn't .....made up..... that story, they wouldn't be angry with me now.
2	only unique single particular	a I am not a(n) .....only........ child; I have a younger brother. b She was .....single...... when I last saw her. c Each ring is .....unique.....because it is specially made for the customer. d He shouted at me for no .....particular..... reason.
3	present grant provide please	a The company will .....provide..... you with all the material. b Do well in the exams and you'll .....please...... your father. c He was .....presented..... with a gold watch when he retired. d I'll .....grant....... you your wish and take you to Disneyland.
4	level layer deck storey	a I prefer sitting on the top .....deck...... of a sightseeing bus. b The top .....layer........of the cake contained strawberries and cream. c He lives in a ten .....storey...... building. d He's not good enough to compete at international.....level......... .
5	room ward studio office	a There were five other patients in the .....ward.........I was taken to. b I had to spend an hour in the waiting .....room...... before I saw the dentist. c Jack does most of his paintings in his .....studio......... . d I share a(n) .....office..... with two other secretaries.

C Use of Prepositions

Use the prepositions below to complete the sentences.

in (x4)	of	to (x2)	under

1 The detective was ....in......... no doubt as to who the murderer was.
2 People do best in the subjects they are interested ....in.......... .
3 Contrary ....to.........what most people believe, koalas are not bears.
4 Journalists very often work ......under.......great pressure.
5 My uncle has a collection ....of.........over 5000 stamps.
6 I don't know how many satellites there are ....in........ orbit around our planet.
7 Sequoias can grow ....to......... a height of over 300 feet.
8 The magician's assistant appeared to be floating ....in........ the air.

D Word Formation

I   Use the word in capitals at the end of each sentence to form a word that fits in the space in the sentence.

1 Being away at a conference, the manager was ...unavailable... for comment.   AVAIL
2 The team suffered from a ......loss........ of form just before the final.   LOSE
3 Who gave you ..permission... to fish in this river?   PERMIT
4 Their ...suggestions...were not practical.   SUGGEST
5 It is such a huge organisation that it operates ...globally...... .   GLOBE

II   Choose the odd word out from the following groups of words according to how they form adjectives.

1	arrogance	attract	include	produce
2	misery	fashion	suit	influence
3	muscle	triangle	circle	cube
4	courage	person	infect	poison
5	doubt	forget	excite	peace

Hints on improving your listening skills I

The Listening Paper often makes students feel anxious because they cannot control the speed at which they work. They also spend time worrying about questions which they have missed rather than concentrating on listening for the next answer.   It is important to make good use of listening practice in class so that you familiarise yourself with the style of tasks you will face in the examination.   In this way,   you will feel as confident as possible on the exam day.

You can improve your listening skills outside the classroom too.   If you enjoy watching English-language films,   try covering up the subtitles with a sheet of paper and see how much of the film you can follow.   Don't be too concerned about understanding every word.   Instead,   concentrate on understanding and following the main storyline. You could also spend time listening to songs in English and trying to understand the words or even write them down.

The more practice you get at listening for a reason, the better you will become. Remember: practice makes perfect!

Part 1

You will hear people talking in eight different situations. For questions **1–8**, choose the best answer, **A**, **B** or **C**.

1 Listen to this conversation between a woman and a man. What does the woman do?
   A   She makes an appointment.
   B   She makes a suggestion.
   C   She offers sympathy.

B **1**

2 Listen to a man talking about his job. Where does he work?
   A   in an office
   B   at a port
   C   in a school

C **2**

3 Listen to a woman speaking on the phone. Why is she making the call?
   A   to make some extra changes
   B   to check that some changes have been made
   C   to check that the spelling is correct

B **3**

4 You hear two people talking about a book. What does the man say about it?
   A   Very few people have read it.
   B   Very few people can understand it.
   C   Very few people have bought it.

A **4**

5 You hear two people talking about an exhibition they went to. What was their opinion of it?
   A   It was boring.
   B   It was interesting.
   C   It was disappointing.

B **5**

6 Listen to a man talking to a friend about a trip he went on. Why didn't he stay in the town he was visiting?
   A   All the hotels were fully booked.
   B   The hotels were too expensive.
   C   The hotels were terrible.

A **6**

7 Listen to a woman talking on the phone. What is the relationship between her and the person she is talking to?
   A   They are colleagues.
   B   They are friends.
   C   They are relatives.

C **7**

8 Listen to two people talking about a man who has been arrested. What crime did he commit?
   A   robbery
   B   burglary
   C   murder

B **8**

Part 2

You will hear two people making enquiries about cars for sale. For questions **9–18**, complete the sentences.

CAR 1

The price of this car is   £17,970   **9**

It has done a little more than   2,000   **10** miles.

The caller would like to know if the car is manual or   automatic   **11**

The car is   silver   **12** in colour.

As well as an alarm system and car stereo, the car also comes with   air conditioning   **13**

A viewing appointment was made for Wednesday 13th, between   six and eight   **14**

CAR 2

The second car is   (Africa) grey   **15** in colour.

It is   two years   **16** old.

The seller will accept £13,000 in   cash   **17**

CAR 3

This car has been   sold   **18**

Part 3

You will hear five different people talking about why they were punished while they were at school. For question **19–23**, choose which of the people **(A–F)** is speaking. Use the letter only once. There is one extra letter which you do not need to use.

A He cheated in an examination.

B He got involved in a fight.

C He wrote on a wall.

D He had the wrong attitude.

E He played a practical joke on a teacher.

F He let someone copy his answers in an examination.

Speaker 1	F	19
Speaker 2	E	20
Speaker 3	D	21
Speaker 4	A	22
Speaker 5	B	23

Part 4

You will hear a conversation about predicting the future. For questions **24–30**, choose the best answer, **A**, **B** or **C**.

24 Dave mentions a supposed prediction in the beginning
  A to show how easy it is to trick people.
  B to make fun of Linda.
  C to tell a funny story.

  A 24

25 The woman who predicted the attack on Ronald Reagan
  A made a film about the event.
  B had special powers.
  C tried to trick people with a recording.

  C 25

26 The American who predicted a plane crash
  A had never travelled by plane.
  B had the same dream more than once.
  C didn't really believe there would be one.

  B 26

27 The strangest thing about the plane crash was that
  A a jet plane had never crashed in this way before.
  B it happened just after the plane had taken off.
  C it happened in Chicago.

  A 27

28 The woman who spoke about the explosion before it happened
  A had a dream about the accident.
  B knew exactly when it would happen.
  C had a strange experience while watching TV.

  C 28

29 How did the woman feel after watching the newsflash with her friend?
  A She felt ashamed for having lied.
  B She was frightened.
  C She thought it was funny.

  B 29

30 In the end, Dave
  A believes in predictions completely.
  B thinks people might be able to predict the future.
  C gets very angry with Linda and Carol.

  B 30

Hints on improving your speaking skills I

You will be assessed on a variety of points in the Speaking Paper. You will be given good marks for sounding natural in English. Pronunciation and intonation are important here.

To improve your pronunciation, you could practise reading out loud and even record your voice so you can hear for yourself what you sound like. Make sure you speak clearly rather than swallowing your words or speaking from behind your hand.

Intonation is also important. When you ask a question, make sure it sounds like one. Your voice must rise at the end of the question. If you have finished commenting on something, your voice should fall. Avoid leaving unfinished sentences hanging in the air. Don't mention two or three points and then say "and ..." without having anything to add.

Take advantage inside and outside the classroom of any opportunities to use and practise your English.

Part 1 (about 3 minutes)

Ask and answer the following questions with a partner.

- What kind of sports are you and your friends interested in?
- What kind of music do you enjoy most?
- How do you usually spend your holidays?
- Is there anywhere you would particularly like to visit?
- What is your favourite time of the year? Why?

Part 2 (about 4 minutes)

Practise speaking about the photographs. The photographs for Test Five are on page 161.

Candidate A, here are your two photographs. They show different conditions for growing vegetables. Please let Candidate B see them. Candidate A, I'd like you to compare these photographs, saying what you think are the advantages and disadvantages of growing vegetables in these ways. (approximately 1 minute)

Candidate B, could you please tell us which of these methods produces tastier and healthier food? (approximately 20 seconds)

Candidate B, here are your two photographs. They show people communicating in different ways. Please let Candidate A see them. Candidate B, I'd like you to compare these photographs, saying what you think are the advantages and disadvantages of communicating in these ways. (approximately 1 minute)

Candidate A, could you please tell us which of these ways of communicating you prefer? (approximately 20 seconds)

Part 3 (about 3 minutes)

Discuss the following with a partner.

Imagine that you have been asked to help organise an end-of-term show for the older pupils aged nine to eleven at your younger brother's primary school. Talk to each other about which of the acts on page 162 should be included in the show and how long each one should last. The show should last about one hour. It is not necessary to agree with each other.

Part 4 (about 4 minutes)

Give each other your opinions about the following questions.

- How important is entertainment today?
- What kind of entertainment is the most popular in your country?
- Do entertainers deserve to be paid so much?
- What would you like to be famous as? Why?
- What are the advantages and disadvantages of being famous?

Hints on improving your reading skills II

Apart from managing your time efficiently in the examination, it is also important to read in an effective way. It can be easy to make the mistake of reading so quickly that you do not always take in what you have read.

You should try to increase the speed you read at gradually. The more you read, the faster you will get. You could try reading a short passage fairly quickly and make notes on the main points. Then, go back and check your points against the text.

Another way to improve your scanning skills is to get a friend to read a short passage to themselves and ask you a question about a specific piece of information. Then, see how quickly you can find the answer to their question.

Part 1

You are going to read an article by the author of a best-selling novel. For questions **1–8**, choose the answer **A**, **B**, **C** or **D** which you think fits best according to the text.

Great White Lies

"Jaws" cast the great white shark as public enemy number one, but more than 25 years later its author, Pefer Benchley, admits it was safe to go into the water after all.

"Shark on the bait!" shouted André Harman, pointing to a spot a few yards behind the outboard motors. His voice gave no indication of panic, but the crew suddenly became tense and fixed their eyes on the
5 water. And there it was. Its steel-grey dorsal fin was slicing the glass-calm sea as we stood and stared. Slowly, smoothly, André drew in the bait. The big shark followed. No one asked what kind of shark it was. Everything about it, from its colour to its shape,
10 broadcast its identity: a great white shark.

André lifted the bait aboard and quickly knelt. Placing himself between the two motors, he plunged his right hand into the water just as the great conical head reached the first motor. "For goodness sake, André!" I
15 said. His hand grabbed the snout, moving it away from the shaft of the motor, guiding the shark's head up as it rose out of the water. There, in an instant was its mouth, the jaw dropping to reveal rows of serrated triangular daggers. André's hand held the snout,
20 almost stroking it. No one spoke. No one breathed. The moment seemed endless. In fact, it lasted a couple of seconds, certainly less than five, before André pulled his hand back. For one more heartbeat, the shark remained suspended and then half-slid,
25 half-fell backward, slipping beneath the surface down into the gloom.

Still nobody spoke. Then André smiled and said: "The first time was an accident. I was just trying to move a shark away from the motor. Sharks are attracted to
30 motors by their electrical signals and have a habit of biting them to see if they are edible." A former commercial fisherman, André has worked with great white sharks for years. "My hand landed on its nose,

and it sort of paused, so I kept it there, and when I did let go, the shark snapped and snapped as if it was 35 searching for whatever it was that had hypnotised it."

By now the photographer David Doubilet and I were becoming used to the unusual. Nearly every encounter we had had with the great whites had been totally illogical. The more we learned, the more we realised 40 how little was really known about them. Despite vast leaps of knowledge since *Jaws* was published more than a quarter of a century ago, no one yet knows what causes one great white shark to attack, kill and eat a human being and another to bite and spit out its victim. 45

Still, considering the knowledge which has been accumulated about great whites in the past 25 years, I have become convinced that I couldn't possibly write *Jaws* today – at least, not in good conscience. Back then, it was generally accepted that great whites ate 50 people by choice. Now we know that almost every attack on a human is an accident in which the shark mistakes a human for its normal prey.

Back then, we thought that once a great white scented blood, it would launch a feeding frenzy that would lead 55 to death. Now we know that nearly three-quarters of bite victims survive, perhaps because the shark recognises that it has made a mistake and doesn't return for a second bite. Back then we believed that great whites attacked boats. Now we know that their 60 sensory systems detect movement, sound and electrical fields and they are just coming to investigate. Finally, back then it was fine to demonise a creature that appeared to be infinite in number.

1   Why didn't anyone ask what kind of shark was on the bait?
    Ⓐ   The answer was obvious.
    B   Everyone was too frightened to speak.
    C   No one could see the whole shark.
    D   None of the crew was an expert.

2   Why did the writer say, "For goodness sake, André!"?
    A   He thought André would fall in.
    B   It wasn't the right time for Anaré to repair the engine.
    C   He felt annoyed by Anaré 's behaviour.
    Ⓓ   André was about to touch the shark.

3   Why did André touch the shark?
    A   He wanted to look inside its mouth.
    Ⓑ   He was trying to protect it from the motor.
    C   He was feeding it.
    D   He didn't mean to touch it.

4   Why did everyone remain silent and stop breathing?
    A   They thought they were all going to die.
    Ⓑ   They were both amazed and frightened.
    C   The air was very thin.
    D   They were getting ready to give into the sea.

5   What does "they" in line 31 refer to?
    A   electrical signals
    B   sharks
    C   boats
    Ⓓ   motors

6   How does the writer describe his encounters with great whites?
    A   frightening
    B   pointless
    Ⓒ   educational
    D   ridiculous

7   Why does the writer feel he couldn't write *Jaws* today?
    A   It wouldn't be a success.
    B   He is too busy with research.
    C   He wouldn't be paid enough.
    Ⓓ   We now know a lot more about sharks.

8   Why do most bite victims of shark attacks survive?
    A   Sharks need at least two bites to kill a human.
    B   Most people manage to swim to safety.
    Ⓒ   The shark stops attacking.
    D   Swimmers are taught how to fight off sharks.

Part 2

You are going to read a book review. Seven sentences have been removed from the review. Choose from the sentences **A–H** the one which fits each gap (**9–15**). There is one extra sentence which you do not need to use.

Pea–Brained Geneticist

Anthony Daniels praises a life of the monk who laid the foundations of modern genetics.

*A Monk and Two Peas: The Story of Gregor
Mendel and the Discovery of Genetics*
by Robin Marantz Heinig
Weidenfeld & Nicolson, £14.99 278 pp

Every school pupil learns in a few science lessons what it took many great scientists years of deep thought and hard work to discover. So, unless the history of science is taught, it is all too easy to assume that what is now common knowledge and appears to be obvious has always been known. It is just as important, therefore, to learn from the errors of the past as it is to appreciate the achievements.

The name of Gregor Mendel is familiar to every child who learns biology. **9   B** He was, in effect, the first person to give genetics a scientific basis.

It was Mendel who also discovered that inheritable characteristics may skip a generation and reappear. **10   D** Then, Dutch geneticists suddenly appreciated its importance.

That, unfortunately, is the extent of most biology students' knowledge of Mendel. **11   H** To some, he was a lone and heroic genius but to others, he was a semi-educated amateur who hardly knew what he was doing.

12   A His archives were burnt by his successor in the monastery as being of no importance and Robin Marantz Heinig's biographical study of Mendel and the acceptance of his ideas is, therefore, padded out to make it longer. Nevertheless, it is a useful and even inspiring book which rejects the notion that Mendel was merely a bumbling amateur who stumbled quite by chance upon an important discovery, but was otherwise undistinguished.

The sheer amount of work and the care with which he did it, crossing and recrossing thousands of pea plants over many years, should convince anyone that Mendel knew exactly what he was doing. This is not the way lucky strikes are made. Genius was required to appreciate the significance of the skipped generation and the fixed ratios of inherited characteristics that appeared in later generations of crossed plants. **13   C**

There is deep sadness in the story of a great scientist who was given no recognition during his lifetime. **14   E** Because of exam nerves, he did not even pass his teacher's certificate but, as we now know, he contributed far more to human knowledge than the examiners who judged and failed him.

Mendel sent reprints of his revolutionary papers to Darwin, whose work he greatly admired. Darwin, as is well known, had no understanding of the mechanism of heredity, and Mendel's papers might have enlightened him. **15   G**

A   Very little is known about the man.

B   He was a Catholic monk who lived in a monastery in Moravia in the middle of the 19th century and who discovered the laws of inherited characteristics by crossing peas of various shapes and colours.

C   Most people would not even have noticed them; and if they had, they wouldn't have understood their meaning.

D   His work, published in an obscure local journal, was neglected for 35 years until 1900.

E   Mendel's fame was only achieved after his death.

F   They disapproved of genetics for political reasons and removed Mendel's statue from the square.

G   But he never even read them: they were found uncut in his library after his death.

H   Even among historians of science, his reputation has varied considerably.

Part 3

You are going to read some book reviews. For questions **16–30**, choose from the list of reviews (**A–G**). The reviews may be chosen more than once. When more than one answer is required, these may be given in any order.

Which review(s)

mentions people's lives being made difficult by others?	16 G
mentions a change of opinion?	17 B
are about books set in two different times?	18 B 19 C
is about a book that was not originally written in English?	20 G
suggests you might read the book in one go?	21 D
refers to the supernatural?	22 C
mention a journey abroad?	23 A 24 F
mentions a change of neighbourhood?	25 E
mentions a character who is being watched?	26 D
is about a book that is very surprising?	27 A
mention people who are physically challenged?	28 F 29 G
mentions a character who is good at drawing?	30 E

Who is your most readable author?

Our younger readers choose their favourites.

A Postcards from No Man's Land

By Aidan Chambers
Age: 14+ (Bodley Head, £10.99)

SIAN BATES

Jack goes on a journey to Holland to meet the people who cared for his grandfather before he died during the Second World War. When he gets there, he finds more than he expected. I really enjoyed this book. It's very moving and shows how emotions can change and how people can hide secrets for years. By the end, you are left in a state of shock by all that has happened.

B King of Shadows

By Susan Cooper
Age: 10+ (Bodley Head, £10.99)

SARAH MAILE

Nat Field, a young actor, has lost both his parents. While rehearsing a play by Shakespeare, Nat falls ill and finds himself transported back in time to 1599, when he works with Shakespeare himself and performs in front of Elizabeth I. I love this book. The characters are great and the plot is impressive. It has completely changed my outlook and attitude towards Shakespeare.

C The Rinaldi Ring

By Jenny Nimmo
Age: 11+ (Mammoth, £4.99)

SERENA FULLER

Eliot's mother has been murdered and his father, unable to cope, sends him to live with his aunt. There, he is haunted by the ghost or a woman named Mary Ellen, who tells him about her lost fiancé, Orlando Rinaldi. Set both in the present day and in 1914, when the First World War broke out, the book is both emotional and exciting.

D Tightrope

By Gillian Cross
Age: 12+ (Puffin, £4.99)

EMMA GRIFFITHS

Gillian Cross creates an atmosphere of tension and fear in this story. Ashley is happy to be part of the excitement surrounding Eddie Beale and his gang until she realises she is being followed. The most amazing part of the book is the way the suspense builds as Ashley tries to find out who is following her. Once you start reading, you can't put it down.

E Kit's Wilderness

By David Almond
Age: 11+ (Hodder, £4.99)

SEAN KERRIGAN

Kit is an excellent story-teller who starts at a new school after his parents move to look after his elderly grandparents. He meets John Askew, a dark-souled boy, who illustrates some of the scenes of Kit's stories and invites Kit to join his gang of friends, who play very strange games. *Kit's Wilderness* looks on the dark side of life but it's also quite sentimental.

F Gift of the Gab

By Morris Gleitzman
Age: 10+ (Puffin, £4.99)

LOUISE FURLONG

This book is sad in some places and funny in others. It's all about an Australian girl, Rowena Balts, who was born with bits missing from her throat and has to use sign language. Rowena is trying to track down her mum's killer and her mission takes her and her dad on a journey to France. *Gift of the Gab* is a very exciting and adventurous read.

G Dreaming in Black & White

By Reinhard Jung
Translated by Anthea Bell
Age: 14+ (Mammoth, £3.99)

SIMON DAVIES

Dreaming in Black & White is the sort of book that whispers about horror instead of screaming at it and is all the more powerful for it. A disabled student called Hannes and a friend experience prejudice because of their differences from those around them. Eventually the prejudice extends beyond the classroom and invades their homes.

Hints on writing a report

A report is usually written for a particular person. It could be for your boss at work or for a teacher at school. This would require a formal style. However, it is possible that you will be asked to write one for club members or class-mates, which would require a more relaxed style.

The best approach to this type of question is as follows:

a Read the question very carefully to identify who you are writing the report for and exactly what kind of information is needed. For example, are you asked just to relate facts or to include suggestions and recommendations, too?

b Make a plan and paragraph your ideas well. You need an introduction to state the topic of your report and who it has been written for. Then, the main body of your report should present the main information under headings. Finally, your conclusion should contain a summary of your findings, a recommendation or suggestions.

Style
Try to keep your writing formal or semiformal in style. Avoid using contractions, phrasal verbs, expressions or idioms.

Hints on answering the task for the set books

Question 5 of the Writing Paper always consists of a choice of two tasks based on the set reading texts. You will not be able to answer this question unless you have read the book more than once and had guidance from your teacher as to what is expected.

Questions are usually concerned with the characters, the plot or the settings of the book. The tasks set are general enough to apply to any of the books set.

Part 1

You **must** answer this question.

1   You have decided to take part in a summer student exchange programme with student from Britain.   You are going to spend a month with a British family and have received the following email from your host.

Read the email and the notes you have made.   Then,   using the information write an email to your host, giving him all the details asked for.

email

From: Kevin Caddick
Sent: 21st June
Subject: Student exchange programme

Dear Mark,

changed yesterday, now Fri. 2nd July   *Thank them!*

leaves 9:30, gets in 3 pm local time

We have been informed of the day of your arrival,   but not the time.   Could you please let us know what time your flight gets in so that we can pick you up from the airport? By the way, can you send us a photo of yourself so that we will be able to recognise you?   We would also like to know if you cannot eat any kind of food or if you have any dietary needs.   We have also been told by the organisers that there will be some free days and we would like to organise some activities for you. Could you let us know what sort of things you like doing during your free time?

OK!

allergic to tomatoes, not used to big English breakfasts

playing tennis, swimming, visiting historical sites

If there is anything else you would like us to arrange for you, do not hesitate to tell us. We all look forward to meeting you.

if possible, go on a picnic in the wonderful countryside

Best wishes,
Kevin Caddick

Write an **email** of between **120** and **150** words in an appropriate style. Do not write any addresses.

This is a model of what would be expected at the FCE level.
Dear Mr Caddick,
Thank you for your email.
The date of my flight was changed yesterday to Friday 2nd July. The flight leaves at 9:30 am and arrives at 3 pm local time.   I would like to thank you in advance for coming to the airport to pick me up.   I have attached a recent photograph of myself to help you recognise me.   I can eat any kind of food except tomatoes, but I must say that I am not used to large English breakfasts!
I am quite active and I enjoy playing tennis and swimming. My ambition is to become an archaeologist, so I find historical sites extremely interesting. I would also find a picnic most enjoyable.
Thank you once again for your kindness and I look forward to meeting you and your family on 2nd July.
Yours sincerely,
Konstanainos Sourlas

Part 2

Write an answer to **one** of the questions **2–5** in this part. Write your answer in **120–180** words in an appropriate style.

2 Your brother has recently celebrated his eighteenth birthday by having a party. Your cousin, who lives abroad, was due to attend the party but was unable to do so. Write a letter to your cousin, describing the party. Describe the preparations, what you did during the party and include some details about the guests who came to the party. Do not write any addresses.

Write your **letter.**

3 You have decided to enter a short story competition. The competition rules say that the story must begin with the following words:

It wasn't worth any money after all.

Write your **story** for the competition.

4 An international magazine has invited its younger readers to suggest useful ways of making their neighbourhood a better place to live in. Write an article for the magazine, giving your suggestions.

Write your **article.**

5 Background reading texts

Answer **one** of the following two questions based on your reading of **one** of the set books. Your answer should contain enough detail to make it clear to someone who may not have read the book.

Either (a) Good books are set in interesting places. Write an **essay** describing one of the places mentioned in the book and refer to an unusual incident that took place there.

or (b) You believe that the book you have read can help solve a penfriend's problem. Write a **letter** to your penfriend, explaining what you have learnt from the book and how this can help solve the problem.

Hints on improving your Use of English skills

The best way to improve your skills for this paper is by keeping thorough, organised notes including vocabulary, useful expressions and collocations. You need to read these notes regularly without spending time learning them off by heart.

Practice makes perfect – so it is important to familiarise yourself fully with all four different tasks so that when you are in the examination, you know exactly what you are doing.

In addition to improving your reading skills, reading anything in English will also help your Use of English skills. This is because you will improve your instincts about what "sounds" right in English and what doesn't.

Part 1

For questions **1–12,** read the text below and decide which answer **A, B, C** or **D** best fits each space. There is an example at the beginning (**0**).

Example:

0   **A**   section   **B**   part   **C**   piece   **D**   time

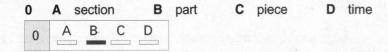

A house with a history

One of the oldest houses in England, with a history that can be traced back the best (0)............. of a thousand years, is Abbot's Hall in Essex. In 1066 it was worth £12. In those days, for that (1)............. of money you not only got a manor house but also 1,400 acres of land, three town houses, 20 oxen, 2 horses, 14 pigs, 230 sheep and 8 workers. It was obviously a(n) (2).............at a time when £1 was (3)............. to just over £100 in today's money. (4)............. with many other great houses, it was taken over by the medieval monasteries.   Renamed Abbess Hall,   the estate was owned by Barking Abbey until the (5)............. 1530s.

As Abbess Hall, it (6)............. very unlucky for two of its owners, Lord Cromwell and the Duke of Norfolk, both of (7)............. were executed. In 1647 Sir Mark Guyen bought Abbess Hall. It was then handed down from generation to generation, so it (8)............. the property of his ancestors until 1810, when it was sold for £23,500. The property was sold again in 1950. Amazingly, it (9)............. only £21,000, which represented 140 years without a (10)............. increase!

Between 1950 and 1966, however, the value of the house, now (11)............. as Abbot's Hall, reached £159,000. Now the asking price is around £2.3 million. If prices (12)............. up this millennium at the same rate, Abbot's Hall will be worth £52.9 billion in 3000!

1	**A**	total	**B**	quantity	**C**	much	**D**	sum
2	**A**	chance	**B**	offer	**C**	bargain	**D**	discount
3	**A**	identical	**B**	similar	**C**	equal	**D**	valued
4	**A**	In common	**B**	Resembling	**C**	Like	**D**	Sharing
5	**A**	last	**B**	final	**C**	end	**D**	late
6	**A**	turned	**B**	proved	**C**	showed	**D**	came
7	**A**	whom	**B**	them	**C**	those	**D**	which
8	**A**	kept	**B**	remained	**C**	stopped	**D**	stayed
9	**A**	bought	**B**	got	**C**	fetched	**D**	took
10	**A**	value	**B**	price	**C**	cost	**D**	sale
11	**A**	known	**B**	named	**C**	called	**D**	regarded
12	**A**	take	**B**	go	**C**	stay	**D**	carry

Part 2

For question **13–24**, read the text below and think of the word which best fits each space. Use only **one** word in each space. There is an example at the beginning (**0**).

Example:

0	IT

ICE CLIMBING

For most people who have tried (0).....it........ , rock climbing is probably the most dangerous sport they would ever wish to take (13).....up..... . Mark Twight, a Canadian in his mid-thirties, however, is not (14)...one..... of them. As soon as he found out about ice climbing, he was determined to accept the challenge. He and many others like him are among a growing (15).number.. of climbers who regard the sport as the best way of testing (16)..their..... physical and mental abilities.

One of the most challenging climbs in the world is Curtain Call, a waterfall which is frozen solid during the winter months. The face of this frozen waterfall is vertical, so climbers cannot afford to lose concentration for a moment. In addition to the shape of the climb, there are other dangers. Hidden pockets of air in the ice can cause huge pieces of the waterfall, as (17)...much... as 15 kilos in weight, to crash to the ground (18)..if/when.. a climber's axe hits the ice around one. The cold can also make things difficult for climbers since typical climbs take place in (19).temperatures... of about -15℃.

Now that the sport (20)....has..... gained popularity, there are organised contests. Every winter, climbers meet in Courcheval, France, (21)..where.. a huge man-made ice cube has (22).been.... built around a vertical steel structure. Climbers race up the 'Ice Cube', which is about 30 metres (23)....high.., in a contest of speed and style. Such contests, however, are rare and the majority (24)....of...... climbers, including Mark, see the sport as a way of testing themselves.

Part 3

For questions **25–34**, read the text below. Use the word given in capitals at the end of each line to form a word that fits in the space **in the same line**. There is an example at the beginning (**0**).

Example:

0	EMPLOYEE

Stress at work

Although it is well known that stress affects almost every (0)..emp̱ḻo̱y̱e̱e̱.,   EMPLOY

only a few people act (25).....e̱f̱f̱e̱c̱ṯi̱v̱e̱ḻy̱.... enough to prevent it from reaching   EFFECT

(26)..u̱ṉa̱c̱c̱e̱p̱ṯa̱ḇḻe̱... levels. By this time, it is likely that medical help will   ACCEPT

be required to treat both the (27)..p̱s̱y̱c̱ẖo̱ḻo̱g̱i̱c̱a̱ḻ.. and physical problems   PSYCHOLOGY

that stress causes. So it is absolutely necessary to (28).....e̱ṉs̱u̱ṟe̱....... that   SURE

there is a positive response to the early (29)...........w̱a̱ṟṉi̱ṉg̱.......... signs such   WARN

as (30).....a̱ṉx̱i̱e̱ṯy̱......... , a loss of sense of humour, poor decision-making   ANXIOUS

and (31)......ṯi̱ṟe̱ḏṉe̱s̱s̱...... . First of all, a diary should be kept so that   TIRE

all the (32)........s̱ṯṟe̱s̱s̱f̱u̱ḻ...... activities can be identified. Once this has   STRESS

been done, a (33).ḏe̱ṯe̱ṟm̱i̱ṉe̱ḏ... effort should be made to remove the   DETERMINE

source of stress. If this is impossible, the job is probably (34)......u̱ṉs̱u̱i̱ṯa̱ḇḻe̱....

and it may be best to look for a new one.   SUIT

Part 4

For questions **35–42**, complete the second sentence so that it has a similar meaning to the first sentence, using the word given. **Do not change the word given**. You must use between **two** and **five** words including the word given. Here is an example (**0**).

Example:

0   It's unfair that he should be given a second chance.
     DESERVE
     He ....given a second chance.

The gap can be filled by the words 'doesn't deserve to be' so you write:

0	DOESN'T DESERVE TO BE

35   Our friendship began twenty years ago.
     FRIENDS
     We .... have been friends for .... twenty years.

36   Why didn't you use your dictionary to find the meaning of this word?
     LOOK
     Why didn't you .... look up this word in/look this word up in .....your dictionary?

37   Nobody had scored so many points in one game before.
     HIGHEST
     It .... was the highest number of ....points anyone had scored in one game.

38   She is quite a good singer, isn't she?
     WELL
     She .... sings quite well, doesn't ....she?

39   How about spending ten days in the Caribbean this summer?
     HOLIDAY
     How about having a .... ten-day summer holiday ....in the Caribbean?

40   I'm not sorry I wrote that letter to her.
     REGRET
     I .... don't regret writing .... that letter to her.

41   Use a separate piece of paper for each answer.
     TWO
     Do not .... write/put two answers on .... one piece of paper.

42   There aren't many parcels left for us to deliver.
     FINISHED
     We............... have nearly/almost finished delivering ...the parcels.

Vocabulary Extension

A Vocabulary Building

Complete the unfinished words in the following sentences, which are all related to the theme of travel and tourism.

1 When you stay in a holiday re s o r t, you don't get much of a chance to learn about other cul t u r e s and tra d i t i o n s.

2 While we were waiting in the dep a r t u r e lounge for our flight to be ann o u n c e d, we decided which d u t y-free goods we would buy.

3 If you've got an EU pass p o r t, you won't need a v i s a.

4 According to the holiday bro c h u r e, the hotel is so popular that you have to make a res e r v a t i o n six months in advance.

5 As the train was almost empty, there was only one other pass e n g e r in the com p a r t m e n t.

6 On retiring, she decided to book a world cr u i s e on a luxury li n e r. She also decided to book an expensive cab i n.

7 We passed through cus t o m s with only our hand lu g g a g e because our suit c a s e s had been lost!

8 The coach fa r e was surprisingly cheap.

9 The price includes sight s e e i n g tours and first class acc o m m o d a t i o n.

10 My travel ag e n t arranged for us to have our own gu 5 d e for the whole holiday.

B Word Use

Use the words on the left to complete the sentences on the right. Make sure the word is in the correct form. Use each word once.

1	chance offer bargain discount	a	He told me he'd accept any reasonable.....offer.... for his car.
		b	There's a(n) .discount.. of up to 25% on all clocks.
		c	At just £5, the jacket was a(n) .bargain..... .
		d	A holiday in Bali for so little is the...chance... of a lifetime.

2	turn prove show come	a	A sting from a box jellyfish can...prove..... fatal.
		b	She...turned.... out to be a world-class tennis player.
		c	The news that he was a thief...came..... as a shock.
		d	Can you...show..... me how to use the dishwasher?

3	whom them those which	a	There were several tables, a few of ...which....were antiques.
		b	The students, some of ...whom...were foreign, were given a guided tour of the college.
		c	I bought a dozen eggs, but some of ...them....were broken.
		d	I'll tell you about...those.... photos some other time.

4	value price cost	a	This watch isn't worth much but it has great sentimental ...value...... .
		b	The ...cost...... of living has risen considerably in the past year.
		c	Can you read the ...price..... tag on that ring?

5	similarity likeness comparison	a	That's not John in the photo, but there is a ..likeness... .
		b	We have to make a comparison between these two short stories for homework.
		c	I'll admit that there are similarities. but they are not the same.

C Use of Prepositions

Use the prepositions below to complete the sentences.

> as   by   from (x2)   of   on   to   with

1 The man in the photo is not the same .....as....... the one involved in the robbery.
2 My new job is very different ....from..... what I expected.
3 I'm sure her sense ......of...... humour was a factor in her getting promoted.
4 That photograph was taken.....by....... the bride's father.
5 We're never bored .....with..... her lectures.
6 How can I prevent the children ....from..... climbing over the wall?
7 He can never relax, even when he's .....on........ holiday.
8 I knocked the vase off the table and it crashed ......to....... the floor.

D Word Formation

I   Use the word in capitals at the end of each sentence to form a word that fits in the space in the sentence.

1 Please ..ensure.... that all the windows are closed when you leave.   SURE
2 Don't fire him this time; just give him a .warning... .   WARN
3 It was ..amazingly. difficult to answer all the questions in the time allowed. AMAZE
4 My new neighbours aren't as ....noisy...... as the previous ones.   NOISE
5 A lack of vitamins may be the reason for your constant ..tiredness... .   TIRE

II Choose the odd word out from the following groups of words according to how they form <u>opposites</u>.

1	honest	advantage	appear	(emotional)
2	legal	(lawful)	logical	legible
3	possible	(paid)	mortal	mature
4	(reliable)	regular	responsible	relevant
5	fair	safe	(correct)	certain
6	accurate	(organised)	complete	sensitive

Hints on improving your listening skills II

One aspect of effective listening is concentration. You must be patient and ignore outside distractions such as traffic noise.

Practise making notes in English while you continue to listen to what is said. You could do this with a friend. Ask your friend to read something aloud while you make some notes. Then, give your friend a summary of the passage. In this way, your ability to think and write while listening will improve.

Part 1

You will hear people talking in eight different situations. For questions **1–8**, choose the best answer, **A**, **B** or **C**.

1   Listen to two people talking about an injury. How did the man burn his hand?
   A   There was a fire in his kitchen.
   B   He got hot liquid on it.
   C   He touched a very hot pan.

`B 1`

2   Listen to a man talking about a football match. How did he feel immediately afterwards?
   A   shocked
   B   embarrassed
   C   frustrated

`A 2`

3   Listen to a man talking to two friends. What is he doing?
   A   giving a warning
   B   making fun of his friends
   C   telling a joke

`C 3`

4   You hear this conversation in a restaurant. Why is the man complaining?
   A   His food is undercooked.
   B   His food is cold.
   C   He was given the wrong order.

`B 4`

5   Listen to a man telling a woman about a famous person. Who was the famous person?
   A   a business executive
   B   a sporting figure
   C   an actress

`C 5`

6   Listen to a woman who has moved house talking on the phone. Where has she moved to?
   A   another country
   B   another city
   C   a village

`C 6`

7   Listen to a woman talking about a recent holiday. What was the weather like?
   A   wet
   B   sunny
   C   cold

`A 7`

8   Listen to a radio announcer giving some motoring information. What has blocked the A30?
   A   a vehicle
   B   a tree
   C   floods

`A 8`

Part 2

You will hear a radio interview with two experts on keeping unusual pets. For questions **9–18**, complete the sentences.

Geckos

All six species of Rhacodactylus come from islands 1,500 km from | Australia | **9**

Adult gargoyle geckos have long dark stripes and their body is either | orange or red | **10**

In their natural habitat, they eat flowers, pollen, small lizards, | spiders and insects | **11**

In their tanks, they need a carpet, branches to climb up and | water | **12**

They eat live crickets covered in | powder | **13** containing minerals and vitamins

Sometimes they have a huge | appetite | **14**, but at other times they don't want to eat anything.

Monitors

As they need lots of care, they shouldn't be kept by | beginners | **15**

In each tank (120 cm × 50 cm × 75 cm), there should be no more than | three animals | **16**

Their tanks should be kept at 30-33°C and the humidity should be | at least 65%/near(ly) 100% | **17**

They eat crickets with powdered calcium daily and baby mice every | two weeks | **18**

Part 3

You will hear five different people talking about the way they look. For questions **19–23**, choose which of the people **A–F** is speaking. Use the letters only once. There is one extra letter which you do not need to use.

A Her biggest fear is that she won't be able to buy fashionable clothes.

B Her friends sometimes make her feel very unhappy.

C She is dissatisfied with one of her features in particular.

D She is completely satisfied with her appearance.

E She feels very sad when she gains weight.

F She has mixed feelings about the way she looks.

Speaker 1	E	19
Speaker 2	B	20
Speaker 3	C	21
Speaker 4	F	22
Speaker 5	D	23

Part 4

You will hear part of a conversation in which three people talk about where and how they were brought up. For questions **24–30**, choose the best answer, **A**, **B**, or **C**.

24 Where did Terry grow up?
  A on a boat
  B on an estate
  C in an expensive suburb

  `B` `24`

25 What impression of people did Marion have when she was a child?
  A She thought some people were poorer than her.
  B She thought everyone read books.
  C She thought everyone had at least one car.

  `C` `25`

26 Which person had the poorest upbringing?
  A Charles
  B Marion
  C Terry

  `C` `26`

27 What does Terry think of the upper classes?
  A He is jealous of them.
  B He thinks they look down on the poorer classes.
  C He dislikes them.

  `B` `27`

28 Why was Terry lucky?
  A He received financial help to go to university.
  B He could afford to go to university.
  C He went to university in the 1950s, when everyone could afford it.

  `A` `28`

29 Why does Marion disagree with Charles's attitude?
  A He thinks only talented people should go to university.
  B He thinks poor people want to go to university.
  C His opinion is old fashioned.

  `C` `29`

30 Why does Terry suggest the group goes for a cup of coffee?
  A He wants a hot drink.
  B He is angry with Charles and Marion.
  C He thinks the conversation might get out of hand.

  `C` `30`

Hints on improving your speaking skills II

Vocabulary and structure are important aspects of speech. You will get a good mark if you show the examiners that you have a wide vocabulary and vary your use of structures according to the task in hand.

Practise new vocabulary or expressions as often as possible in class so that you begin to use them correctly and naturally. Do not be afraid of using things wrongly. Your teacher will be able to help you identify mistakes so you can correct them.

Remember, no matter how shy or nervous you feel in the examination, you must show the examiners that you can communicate clearly and effectively in English.

The examiners can only mark what they hear, so try to provide a good sample of your spoken English.

Part 1 (about 3 minutes)

Ask and answer the following questions with a partner.

- What do you hope to do in the next few years?
- How important is English in your future plans?
- What do you hope to be doing in five years' time?
- Where would you like to live in the future? Why?
- What is your main ambition?

Part 2 (about 4 minutes)

Practise speaking about the photographs. The photographs for Test Six are on page 163.

Candidate A, here are your two photographs. They have a connection with appearance. Please let Candidate B see them. Candidate A, I'd like you to compare these photographs, saying how important it is to be slim in today's society. (approximately 1 minute)

Candidate B, could you please tell us how often you eat the wrong kind of food? (approximately 20 seconds)

Candidate B, here are your two photographs. They show ways that people can get information. Please let Candidate A see them. Candidate B, I'd like you to compare these photographs, saying what the advantages are of these ways of getting information. (approximately 1 minute)

Candidate A, could you please tell us which of these ways you prefer to use to get information? (approximately 20 seconds)

Part 3 (about 3 minutes)

Discuss the following with a partner.

I'd like you to imagine that you are going to organise a tour for a group of tourists from your country who are going to visit Britain. Talk to each other about which places on the map on page 164 you would include in the tour. Your group ranges in age from 25–60. It is not necessary to agree with each other.

Part 4 (about 4 minutes)

Give each other your opinions about the following questions.

- What facilities are there for tourists in your area?
- How do people in your country get on with tourists?
- In what ways do you think tourists have an effect on your country?
- How important is it to have a holiday every year?
- What are the attractions of a holiday abroad?

Candidate A

What do you think about the kinds of relationships shown?

Candidate B

Where would you like to live and why?

Which two of the following would be most useful to the school and its pupils?

Candidate A

What are the advantages of shopping at each of these places?

Candidate B

What do you think of these ways of making money?

· Which of these professions would you like to enter after your studies?
· Which would offer the most job astisfaction and money?

architect

dentist

doctor

lawyer

stockbroker

teacher

mechanical engineer

Candidate A

How important do you think the telephone has become today?

Candidate B

What do you think about exploring space and the oceans?

- What colour or colours would be best for the bedroom?
- Where should the furniture and other items be placed?

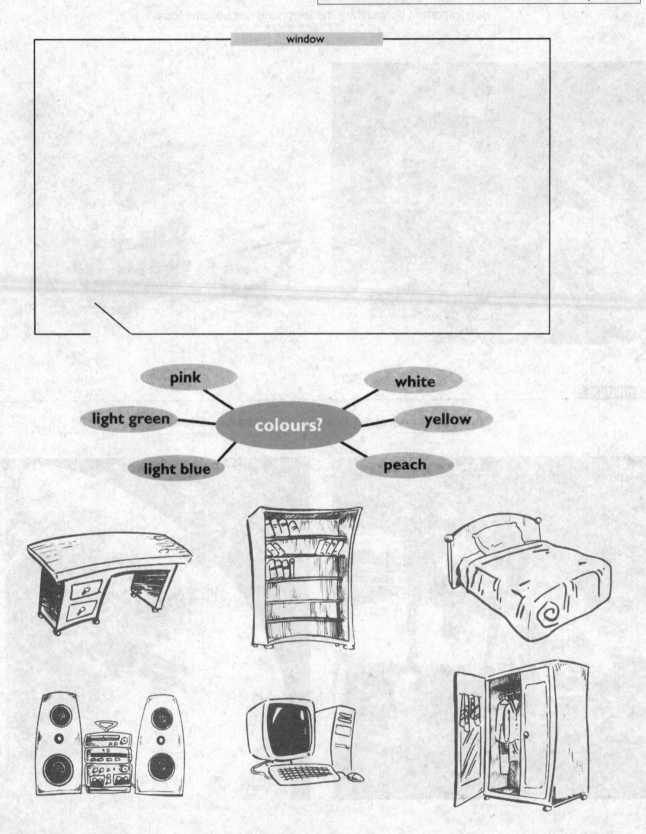

window

pink

white

light green

colours?

yellow

light blue

peach

Candidate A

What kinds of problems can these crimes cause and how can we prevent them?

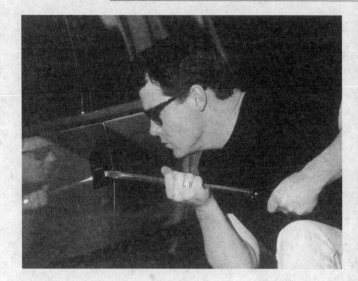 

Candidate B

What are the differences in attitude between these students?

Put these inventions in order of importance.

Candidate A

What are the davantages and disadvantages of growing vegetables in these ways?

Candidate B

What are the advantages and disadvantages of communicating in these ways?

- Which acts should be included in a show for pupils aged nine to eleven?
- How long should each one last? (The show should last about an hour.)

Candidate A

How inportant is it to be slim in today's society?

Candidate B

What are the advantages of these ways of getting information?

Which places would you include in a tour of Britain for a group of tourists form your country aged 25-60?

Edinburgh

Birmingham

Stratford

Newmarket

Windsor

London

Test One

READING, PART 1

mains plug (n) the place on a wall where you can connect an electrical device to a supply of electricity

valve (n) a part of a tube or pipe that opens and shuts like a door to control the flow of liquid, gas, air, etc passing through it

synthetic (adj) not of natural origin; man-made

indicator (n) a pointer on a machine that shows temperature, pressure, speed, etc

moderate (adj) not excessive or extreme

conventional (adj) ordinary rather than different

stain (n) a mark on material that does not disappear when the material is washed

recommence (v) to begin again

READING, PART 2

enthusiast (n) a person who has a strong liking for something

assign (v) to give someone something

blend (n) a combination of two or more things

obscure (adj) not famous or well-known

disregard (n) when someone does not care about or show any interest in someone or something

READING, PART 3

straightforward (adj) saying clearly and honestly what you think

business executive (n) a person who has authority in a business

budget (n) the total sum of money needed or available for a purpose

furiously (adv) with lots of energy and speed

underestimate (v) to think that something is smaller, less expensive or less important than it really is

nightmare (n) an experience that is frightening or distressing

faceless (adj) impersonal

seal a deal (phr) to make a deal or agreement official

Test Two

READING, PART 1

harmony (n) good feelings

authoritative work (n) a book that is trusted because it was written by someone who knows a lot about a subject

virtually (adv) almost

tempt (v) to make someone want to have or do something

poach (v) to cook something by putting it in gently boiling water or other liquid

nutritionist (n) an expert on the subject of food and the way it influences your health

promotional trip (n) a trip that is made with the purpose of persuading people to buy or use a new product or service

toddler (n) a young child who has just learnt to walk

urge (v) to strongly advise

stereotype (v) to have a fixed idea about what a particular type of person is like, especially an idea that is wrong

crunchy (adj) crunchy food is pleasantly hard and makes a noise when you eat it

seaweed (n) a plant that grows in the sea

appealing (adj) attracting interest

difficult eater (n) a person who does not like a lot of foods or is fussy about what they eat

speciality (n) a dish or food that someone makes very well

crush (v) to break into tiny pieces

fragmented family life (phr) life in a family whose members spend little time together

household (n) all the people who live together in a home

plantation (n) a large farm where crops are grown on a large scale

processed food (n) food that is prepared in a factory

license (v) to give official permission for someone to do something

foolproof (adj) not likely to fail

convenience food (n) packaged food or a meal that can be prepared quickly and easily

bother (v) to take the time or trouble to do something

READING, PART 2

tee up (phr v) to hit the ball towards a hole in a game of golf

rawhide (n) leather that is in its natural state

hammer (v) to hit something with a hammer (= a tool used for hitting nails into wood)

shilling (n) an old British coin

substantial (adj) large

conservative (adj) traditional; unwilling to change

apprentice (n) a person who works for a skilled person in order to learn a trade

craftsman (n) a person who is highly skilled in their work

hickory (n) a type of tree or the wood from that tree

shaft (n) a long handle on a tool or piece of equipment

club (n) a stick that is used by a golfer to hit a golf ball

mould (n) a container that you pour liquid into so that the liquid will take its shape when it becomes solid

swirl (n) a curving, twisting pattern

READING, PART 3

content (adj) satisfied or happy with something

alongside (prep) next to

construct (v) to build something such as a house, bridge, etc

latter (n) the second of two people or things mentioned

descent (n) the process of going down

commentary (n) a spoken description of an event which is given while the event is happening

flock (v) if people flock to a place, they go there in large numbers

playwright (n) a person who writes plays

latter years (n) the years towards the end of someone's life

be associated (with someone/something) (phr) to be related to a particular subject, activity, etc

insight (n) a clear understanding of a problem, situation, etc

transplant (v) to move something from one place to another

well-stocked bookshop (n) a bookshop with a wide range of books for sale lavish (adj) luxurious

estate (n) a large area of land in the country which is owned by a family or organisation

heir (n) a person who will receive money, property or a title from another person when that other person dies

distillery (n) a factory where alcoholic drinks are produced

acquire (v) to buy; to obtain

Edwardian (adj) relating to the reign of Edward VII of England (about 1900—1910)

Test Three

READING, PART 1

immobiliser (n) a device fitted to a car which stops it from moving so that it cannot be stolen

be insured (v) to protect yourself against risk by paying a sum of money at regular intervals to a special company that will pay you money if your possessions are damaged, destroyed or stolen

transmitter (n) a device for sending a message

device (n) an object or machine which has been invented for a particular purpose

via (prep) through; using

critical (adj) very important because what happens in the future depends on it

READING, PART 2

vital (adj) very important

determined (adj) having a strong desire to do something so that you will not let anyone stop you

mansion (n) a very large house

service charge (n) an amount of money paid to the owner of a block of flats for services such as cleaning the stairs

studio flat (n) a large one-room apartment

commute (v) to travel back and forth regularly between work and home

council flat (n) a flat that is provided by the local council for a very low rent

READING, PART 3

job-sharing scheme (n) an arrangement in which a single full-time job is shared between two or more people

lie-in (n) an occasion when you stay in bed longer than usual in the morning

accountant (n) a person whose job is to keep and check financial accounts, calculate taxes, etc

multinational (n) a large company that has offices or factories in several countries

worn out (adj) very tired because you have been working hard

assembly worker (n) a person who works in a factory in which the products move past a line of workers who each make or check one part

shift (n) if workers work shifts, they work for a particular period of time during the day or night and are then replaced by others so that there are always people working

deadline (n) a date or time by which you have to do or complete something

restricted (adj) limited

unearthly hour (n) a very early or very late hour and therefore extremely inconvenient

Test Four

READING, PART 1

exquisite (adj) excellent; wonderful

cured salmon (n) salmon that has been prepared by salting, drying, smoking, etc

delicacy (n) a special food that is usually expensive or rare

foil (n) thin metal paper for wrapping food

black pudding (n) a dark sausage, one of whose ingredients is blood

notable (adj) widely known and deserving attention

superb (adj) excellent

smoked salmon (n) salmon that has been dried and cured by hanging in wood smoke

emerge (v) to appear

hesitation (n) the act of pausing

reveal (v) to display; to show

spinach (n) a type of green leafy vegetable

moss (n) any tiny, leafy-stemmed, flowerless plant that reproduces by spores and grows on moist ground, tree trunks, rocks, etc

sawn-up (adj) cut with a saw (=a tool that consists of a thin blade of metal with a series of sharp teeth)

spontaneous combustion (n) burning caused by chemical changes inside something rather than by heat from outside

fillet (v) to remove the bones from a piece of meat or fish

gourmet (adj) relating to very good food and drink

mesh (n) material made from threads or wires that have been woven together like a net

scrub up (phr v) to wash your hands and arms, usually before doing a medical operation

tend (v) to take care of; to look after

crust (n) the hard outer layer on bread or other kinds of food

hay (n) grass that has been cut and dried for use as food for animals

graze (v) if an animal grazes, it eats grass that is growing

READING, PART 2

syndrome (n) a pattern of symptoms indicative of some disease

integral (adj) belonging as a part of the whole

volatile (adj) a volatile liquid or substance changes easily into a gas

adhesive backing (n) a sticky material at the back of an object

nasal congestion (n) a blocked nose

swirling (adj) moving in a twisting or circular motion

superstitious (adj) believing in supernatural forces

ventilation (n) the process of replacing stale air with fresh air

humidity (n) the level of water in the air

clerical worker (n) a person who does office work

effective (adj) successful; working in the way that was intended

wipe out (phr v) to kill or destroy completely

fungus (n) (plural: fungi) a simple type of plant that has no leaves or flowers

duct (n) a tube or pipe, usually inside a building

READING, PART 3

account (n) an arrangement between a bank and a customer that allows the customer to pay in and take out money

interest (n) money paid to you by a bank when you keep money in an account there

fob off (phr v) to put someone off; to ignore someone

branch (n) a local bank or business that is part of a larger bank or business

voucher (n) a document or coupon which can be exchanged for goods or services equivalent to the value shown on the document or coupon

statement (n) a document that shows the recent activity in your bank account

paying-in book (n) a receipt book for paying money into your bank account

benefit (n) something that is advantageous or good

suit (v) to be acceptable or convenient for a particular person or in a particular situation

term (n) a word or expression with a particular meaning, especially one that is used for a specific subject

proof of identity (n) a document that proves who you are, eg a passport

Test Five

READING, PART 1

ranger (n) someone whose job is to look after a nature reserve and the animals in it

poacher (n) someone who hunts or fishes illegally

deadly (adv) causing or capable of causing death

conflict (n) a fight or struggle between two opposing groups or individuals

sway (v) to move back and forth or sideways

lumber (v) to move in a slow, awkward way

plunge (v) to move suddenly forwards or downwards

notoriously (adv) well-known or famous for something bad

eradicate (v) to destroy completely

migrate (v) to go from one country, region or place to another

gruelling (adj) exhausting

post a sentry (phr) to make a guard be in a particular place in order to protect a building, check who enters or leaves a place, watch something, etc

patrol (v) to go around an area at regular times to check that there is no trouble

ditch (n) a long narrow hole in the ground

gore (v) if an animal gores a person or another animal, it wounds that person or animal with its horn(s) or tusk(s)

clandestine (adj) secret

tint (v) to slightly change the colour of something

READING, PART 2

amenity kit (n) a bag containing useful items provided by an airline company on long flights for its customers

pouch (n) a container for holding or carrying things

ear-plug (n) a small piece of soft material which you put into your ear to keep out noise or water

economy class (n) the cheapest available seating area on a flight

flatly refuse (phr) to refuse in a direct and definite way

key fob (n) a ring for carrying keys

upper-class (adj) the most expensive seating area on a flight

READING, PART 3

cuddly (adj) soft to touch and nice to hug

otter (n) a small mammal that lives in rivers or the sea and eats fish

trend (n) a general development or change in a situation

draw (n) an attraction

tame (adj) not wild and not frightened or people

community (n) a group of people or animals living in the same area and interacting with each other

pasture (n) an area where grass grows and where animals graze

estuary (n) the wide part of a river where it approaches the sea and the fresh water of the river mixes with the salt water of the sea

convalesce (v) to get better after an illness or injury

flock (n) a group of sheep

obligingly (adv) in a way that shows you are willing or eager to help

ewe (n) a female sheep

weave (v) to make cloth on a machine by crossing threads under and over each other

pen (n) a small piece of land surrounded by a fence to keep farm animals in

scenic (adj) surrounded by views of beautiful countryside

huddle (v) to gather or crowd together

cheep (v) to make a noise like young chicks

monastery (n) a building where men live as a religious community

cygnet (n) a young swan

wheelbarrow (n) a cart with handles and one or more wheels, used for carrying small loads, usually on a farm or in a garden

lagoon (n) a body of water separated from the sea by a reef of sand or coral

horse-drawn carriage (n) a vehicle pulled by horses, used for carrying people

restore (v) to repair something old

barn (n) a farm building for storing grain or animal feed and housing farm animals

Test Six

READING, PART 1

cast (v) to regard or describe a person or animal as a particular type of person or animal

bait (n) food used to attract fish or animals so that you can catch them

dorsal fin (n) the fin on the back of a fish

broadcast (v) to indicate clearly

snout (n) the long nose of some kinds of animals

shaft (n) a revolving rod that transmits power to drive an engine

instant (n) a very short period of time

serrated (adj) having an edge made of a row of small points like teeth

dagger (n) a knife like a sword, used for stabbing

gloom (n) darkness

edible (adj) suitable for use as food

snap (v) if an animal snaps, it closes its jaws suddenly

encounter (n) an unexpected meeting

vast (adj) enormous

spit (v) to force something out of your mouth

accumulate (v) to collect

in good conscience (phr) if you do something in good conscience, you do it because you think it is right

scent (v) to smell

feeding frenzy (n) an occasion when animals like sharks eat something in a very excited way

detect (v) to discover; to notice

READING, PART 2

monk (n) a member of a religious group of men who live in a monastery and who do not marry or have personal possessions

foundation (n) an idea or a fact that something is based on

genetics (n) the scientific study of the ways in which different characteristics are passed from each generation of living beings to the next

achievement (n) something important that you succeed in doing

inheritable characteristic (n) a characteristic that can be passed from one member of a family to another

generation (n) all the people living at the same time or of approximately the same age

successor (n) someone who takes a position previously held by someone else

pad out (phr v) to make a speech or piece of writing longer by adding unnecessary words or details

inspiring (adj) exciting and encouraging you to do or feel something

notion (n) an idea; a belief

bumbling (adj) behaving in a careless way and making mistakes

stumble upon (phr v) to find or discover by chance

undistinguished (adj) not interesting, successful or attractive

cross (v) to mix two types of plant to form a new one

lucky strike (n) a lucky discovery

ratio (n) the relationship between two amounts

mechanism (n) the way that something works

heredity (n) the biological process whereby characteristics are passed from one generation to the next

enlighten (v) to make someone understand something

READING, PART 3

rehearse (v) to practise a play, music, etc before performing it in front of an audience

outlook (n) an attitude

cope (v) to deal with a situation, problem, etc

haunt (v) if a ghost haunts a person or place, it appears to that person or in that place often

tension (n) a nervous and anxious feeling

gang (n) a group of friends

suspense (n) the feeling you have when you are waiting for something terrible, frightening, exciting, etc to happen

sentimental (adj) showing feelings like love or sadness too strongly

sign language (n) a language that uses hand movements, used by deaf people

mission (n) an important job that a person is given to do

prejudice (n) when people do not like or trust someone who is different, for example because they belong to a different race, country or religion

extend (v) to stretch out over a distance, space or time

invade (v) to enter a place without permission

TEST 1
First Certificate Practice Test One. Paper Four. Listening.

Hello. I'm going to give you the instructions for this test. I'll introduce each part of the test and give you time to look at the questions. At the start of each piece you'll hear this sound:

tone

You'll hear each piece twice. Remember, while you're listening, write your answers on the question paper. You'll have time at the end of the test to copy your answers onto the separate answer sheet.

The tape will now be stopped. Please ask any questions now, because you must not speak during the test.

PAUSE 5 seconds

PART 1
Now open your question paper and look at Part One. You will hear people talking in eight different situations. For questions 1–8, choose the best answer, A, B, or C.

One
Listen to a commentator describing a race on the radio. What kind of race is being described?

A   a motorbike race
B   a horse race
C   a cycling race

PAUSE 5 seconds – tone

Question 1
Commentator: ... and as they race towards the final furlong, it's James Isaac on the far side and Nicholas Mistress on the near side. They're two lengths ahead of Mr Majica back in third, with King of Peru fading in fourth. Inside the final furlong and James Isaac goes on with Tom Barker finishing fast on the wide outside coming to challenge. And as they race towards the line. it's James Isaac just holding on from Tom Barker with Mr Bergerac in third. A good win then for James Isaac by a head at 6-1. Of course, we'll have to wait for the official result, but I think Ray Cochrane kept him up to his work without using the whip too much in the final furlong ...(fade)

PAUSE 2 seconds – tone

Repeat Question 1

PAUSE 2 seconds

Two
You hear two people talking. How does the man feel about his cousin's haircut?

A   He is shocked by it.
B   He disapproves of it.
C   He thinks it suits her.

PAUSE 5 seconds – tone

Question 2
Jason: What have you done to your hair? (pleasantly surprised)
Mary: Don't you like it them?
Jason: No, ... I mean let me have a look at you. I've never seen you with short hair before.
Mary: You don't like it, do you?
Jason: It's not that. I just feel as if I'm talking to a different person. I didn't know a person's hairstyle could have such an effect on the way they look.
Mary: Of course it can! You still haven't answered my question.

Jason: Well ... if you weren't my cousin, I'd ask you to go to the dance with me!

PAUSE 2 seconds – tone

Repeat Question 2

PAUSE 2 seconds

Three
You hear a person telling a story. Where did the story take place?

A   in a jeweller's
B   in a bank
C   in a bus station

PAUSE 5 seconds – tone

Question 3
Woman: There was a man in front of me and he seemed to have a problem. Apparently, he had forgotten to empty his pockets before he put his trousers into the wash. He had left everything in them including a watch and a bus pass. I don't know why he insisted on telling the whole story in detail. Anyway, he pulled out the contents of his wallet and put them on the counter. The notes were all stuck together and he wanted to know if they could be replaced. I don't know what he'd put in the wash-bleach, perhaps, but I could hardly make out what he had in front of him. They looked like ordinary bits of paper.

PAUSE 2 seconds – tone

Repeat Question 3

PAUSE 2 seconds

Four
Listen to this radio advertisement. What is being advertised?

A   a car breakdown service
B   a car insurance company
C   a car manufacturer

PAUSE 5 seconds – tone

Question 4
[sound of a car breaking down]
Jack: I knew you shouldn't have borrowed Mark's car. What are we going to do now?
Nicki: Don't worry. I've got AA cover.
[sound of a number being dialled on a mobile phone]
Voice: Yes, if you join the AA now you can get a year's cover for you and your partner for just £15. And You don't even have to be related or married to include cover for a partner. You just have to share the same home address.
AA man: Yes, what seems to be the problem?
Voice: We have the world's largest patrol force so we're more likely to get you back on the road without delay!
[sound of a car starting]
Nicki: You see. We're not going to be late after all thanks to the AA!
AA man: To our members we're the fourth emergency service. Call free on 0800 444999 ... now!

PAUSE 2 seconds – tone

Repeat Question 4

PAUSE 2 seconds

Five
Listen to a woman talking about her home town. What is her profession?

A She is an artist.
B She is a sociologist.
C She is an architect.

PAUSE 5 seconds – tone

Question 5
Woman: Of course when the town changed, the people in it changed, too. There were also outsiders who came to live here when large companies moved in. Health centres, shopping centres, sports centres and new schools have sprung up all over the place. It has also been a time of growth for service industries. The town is booming and I just hope it continues because I'm involved in everything. We're easily the biggest ones in town and almost everyone who wants to build comes to us to have designs made. They're looking for something modern and that's exactly what we specialise in.

PAUSE 2 seconds – tone

Repeat Question 5

PAUSE 2 seconds

Six
You hear a conversation about a shopping trip. What does the woman say about it?

A The shopping trip didn't cost as much as expected.
B The shopping trip was unusual.
C It was an awful shopping trip.

PAUSE 5 seconds – tone

Question 6
Paul: [surprised] I hear you went on a shopping trip with Barbara.
Carol: Yes, I did. Who told you?
Paul: Never mind. You were brave, weren't you? You know what Barbara's like. It's not unusual for her to spend five or six hundred pounds without blinking.
Carol: Well, that's not what happened this time. Barbara was awfully nice. I think she realised that I don't have as much money as she does so she didn't make me feel bad by spending it like water. I actually came back from the trip with change! Barbara's not nearly as bad as people make out you know.
Paul: So how much did you spend then?
Carol: Mind your own business!

PAUSE 2 seconds – tone

Repeat Question 6

PAUSE 2 seconds

Seven
You hear two university students talking about some reading they have to do. What subject are they talking about?

A history
B psychology
C chemistry

PAUSE 5 seconds – tone

Question 7
William: Have you done any reading for Professor White yet?
Stuart: Yes, a little. I read a couple of pages last night.
William: What did you think of it?
Stuart: Honestly? After the first paragraph, I couldn't understand a word. I'll have to read it again this evening.
William: You're not the only one. I've asked April and Charles and they said the same thing. There are so many references to theories about human behaviour in early civilisations that I haven't even heard of! I mean what has it got to do with the way we think today?
Stuart: Perhaps we have to do some background reading before we even look at this book.
William: That's a good idea. Why don't we get together with April and Charles on this?

PAUSE 2 seconds – tone

Repeat Question 7

PAUSE 2 seconds

Eight
You hear two people talking in a hotel. What are they talking about?

A a mobile phone
B a DVD player
C a camera

PAUSE 5 seconds-tone

Question 8
Janet: You can't do that!
Wayne: [cheekily] Why not?
Janet: It's not yours!
Wayne: Yes, but I found it here. I'm not going to take it. I'll put it back when I've finished.
Janet: Yes, but you're wasting film and when the person gets it developed, they'll wonder what on earth has happened.
Wayne: Oh, I don't know. I think they'll appreciate my artistic talent, actually.
Janet: Put it down before the owner gets back!

PAUSE 2 seconds – tone

Repeat Question 8

PAUSE 2 seconds

That's the end of Part One. Now turn to Part Two.

PART 2
You will hear part of a radio interview about banking. For questions 9–18, complete the sentences.

You now have forty-five seconds in which to look at Part Two.

PAUSE 45 seconds-tone

[fade in]
Presenter: ... so we've seen that nearly all banks offer students incentives like money to open an account. Now, what else do they offer, Naomi?
Naomi: Well, basically from the moment they open an account, they are treated almost the same as other customers and they have to be aware of charges for using cashpoint cards, for example.
Presenter: I thought that using cash machines was free for the customer.
Naomi: Generally speaking, it is if you use a cash machine belonging to a bank where your account is or a subsidiary of that bank, but it's not that simple. Kaspa's, for example, charge £1 for each withdrawal at its machines in stores or petrol stations whether you are a customer or not.
Presenter: What will you be charged if you use another bank's cash machine?
Naomi: There is a fee of between 60p and £1.50. For example, someone who has a bank account with VGB will be charged £1.50 if they use a The Big Bank machine. There is one notable exception, though. Herd's Bank is free for cash withdrawals, whichever bank the customer uses and they have 25,000 machines throughout Britain. On the other hand, you may even be charged twice if you use the wrong machine. If

an Allanbee customer withdrew money from a VGB machine, Allanbee would slap on a £1.50 charge for disloyalty and VGB would also charge £1. In fact, you could end up paying a fee of 12.5% to take out £20!

Presenter: How do you know how much you will be charged if you can't get to the right cash machine?

Naomi: Well, it's almost impossible. Details of charges are given when you open an account and if there are changes, you are given 30 days' notice. There are also some machines programmed to warn users of the charges, but these are in the minority.

Presenter: What about using your card abroad?

Naomi: There is usually an initial charge of at least 1.5% and a second foreign usage charge of 2.5-2.75%. So, in general, you shouldn't. But it may sometimes be cheaper than buying foreign currency before you leave. If, for example, you want to change £500 before you go to France, you will get 4,700 francs. But if you get 4,700 French francs with a Gold VGB card in Paris, it will cost you £492.93.

Presenter: It sounds like a minefield!

Naomi: It is. You should always check carefully before you use your card, otherwise it could turn out to be expensive... [fade out]

PAUSE 10 seconds – tone

Now you'll hear Part Two again.

Repeat Part Two

PAUSE 5 seconds

That's the end of Part Two. Now turn to Part Three.

PART 3

You will hear five different people talking about experiences they have had while driving. For questions 19–23, choose from the list A–F what happened in each case. Use the letters only once. There is one extra letter which you do not need to use.

You now have thirty seconds in which to look at Part Three.

PAUSE 30 seconds – tone

Speaker 1

We decided to take a short cut to my sister's wedding which was held in a small church in the country. For a while we thought it was a good idea because there was hardly any traffic. Then, suddenly, a tractor pulled out in front of us. The narrow, winding road made it impossible to overtake without taking a risk. Soon, the traffic built up behind us and John kept on telling me to overtake. Fortunately, I took no notice even though I was getting rather frustrated and wanted to get past. The person behind me did try and ended up in a ditch because there was a lorry coming the other way. I don't think anyone was hurt, but it can't have done the car any good. A couple of minutes later the tractor turned into another field and we got to the wedding on time.

PAUSE 2 seconds

Speaker 2

I was driving in a part of town that I don't normally visit. As usual, I was thinking about the meeting I was going to more than my driving. I kept looking at the car clock and finally I was satisfied that I would be there on time so I didn't have to rush. Then, suddenly, a police car pulled out behind me with the lights flashing. I glanced at my speedometer but I wasn't going fast. Anyway, I pulled over and wound down my window. The policeman asked me whether it was my car, took a look at my licence and insurance, which were in order, and then told me I was travelling the wrong way down a one-way street. I was shocked because it didn't use to be one, but he simply pointed to prove his point. I'd missed it completely and apologised. Luckily, I got off with a warning.

PAUSE 2 seconds

Speaker 3

I was driving home late one evening when I was stopped for a spot check. I hadn't been drinking but I was exhausted. I'd been at a conference in Birmingham all day. They asked me for my licence and insurance and asked whether I'd been drinking. I must have been the worse for wear because they asked me to blow into the bag which, of course, came out negative. Then one officer looked at me and said: "I suppose you think this is some kind of joke!" I was flabbergasted. Then he showed me the driving licence I'd given him. It had my girlfriend's photo on it and then I remembered I'd put it in my wallet for safekeeping. I explained the situation and went to the station with her the next day to show them mine and to prove I hadn't stolen the other one. Even though it was a genuine mistake, I got the feeling they didn't quite believe me that evening.

PAUSE 2 seconds

Speaker 4

It happened just after I'd passed my test. I'd got my full driving licence that morning and I went out for a drive. On my way back, I decided to take a short cut. This involved going down a steep hill which I didn't like at all. I don't know why, but my driving instructor took me down it on one of my first lessons and it terrified me. While I was going down and picking up speed, I tried to brake but hardly anything happened. I kept going faster and for some reason the car wouldn't stop. I kept a cool head and changed down into second. This slowed me down a little, but the engine was roaring. Then I remembered a road which forked to the left and went slightly uphill for a short while. I got on to this road and managed to stop the car. I think I did quite well in the circumstances.

PAUSE 2 seconds

Speaker 5

We had an away game not far away so we didn't hire a mini-bus. We went by car and Chris and I drove. He's got one of those seven-seaters. A few of the team went by motorbike. I was driving in front of Chris and there wasn't anything in front of me. As I was approaching one set of traffic lights, I saw the lights turn green so I drove on. Suddenly, I heard a horn blaring and I saw a car coming towards me from the left. He just missed me and shook his fist at me. He looked really angry. Well, we got angry too and stopped. Chris, who was behind us, also stopped and started shouting at the other driver. We weren't the only ones. At the lights other people were shouting at each other. Then we realised that all the lights were green so we called the police. It could have been much worse!

PAUSE 10 seconds – tone

Now you'll hear Part Three again.

Repeat Part Three

PAUSE 5 seconds

That's the end of Part Three. Now turn to Part Four.

PART 4

You will hear a radio interview with a policeman who was successful in tracking some burglars. For questions 24–30, choose the best answer, A, B or C.

You now have one minute in which to look at Part Four.

PAUSE 1 minute-tone

Presenter: And now it's time for our personality of the week. Well, in fact there are two this week, Police Constable George Walters from Alnwick, North-East England, and his five-year-old Alsation dog, Carl. Welcome to the programme PC Walters. I believe you were involved in a thrilling chase last week.

PC Walters: Well, I'm not sure you could call it thrilling. It was pretty hard work. I can tell you!

Presenter: Yes, I can imagine. You've been praised for your doggedness (forgive the pun) in the situation. You've even been compared to a Canadian Mountie who always gets his man. Tell us what happened.

PC Walters:	Well, at 2:30 am on 9th February the alarm went off at a WH Smith shop in Alnwick High Street. By the time we got there, the burglars had disappeared, so we went after them.
Presenter:	How did you know which way to go?
PC Walters:	It had been snowing that morning so we were able to follow their tracks through the fresh snow. When the tracks ran out, Carl picked up the scent.
Presenter:	How far did you follow the burglars?
PC Walters:	About 8 miles. First we went through the Duke of Northumberland's private park and then through the local high school. We found the stolen goods – £1,300 worth of cigarettes and cigars – hidden in the bushes in the Duke's park. There was still no sign of the burglars, but we continued.
Presenter:	Were you tempted to give up at any time?
PC Walters:	No, because Carl still had the scent. We then went out over open countryside and farmland until we got to a main road, the Al. Then we climbed a steep slope, went over a wall, went through the woods and crossed the River Aln twice.
Presenter:	Weren't you cold?
PC Walters:	The cold didn't bother us. With all the physical effort I was quite warm. I didn't even think about it. I just concentrated on the job in hand. Eventually, at about 6 am we spotted the burglars at Alnmouth railway station. They were huddled together, trying to keep warm in a waiting room. They obviously thought they'd got away with it.
Presenter:	Didn't they try and make a run for it?
PC Walters:	No, they just looked at us in astonishment. I don't think they could quite believe what was happening. They'd had enough. I'll never forget the looks on their faces when we arrived.
Presenter:	How many burglars were there?
PC Walters:	Three. They were all from Morpeth and they confessed to the crime. They will be sentenced on 30th June.
Presenter:	How did you feel when you caught them?
PC Walters:	Pleased and exhausted. I think Carl and I make a pretty good double act.
Presenter:	You certainly do! Well, congratulations PC Walters...[fade out

PAUSE 10 seconds – tone

Now you'll hear Part Four again.

Repeat Part Four

PAUSE 5 seconds

That's the end of Part Four.

There'll now be a PAUSE of five minutes for you to copy your answers onto the separate answer sheet. I'll remind you when there is one minute left so that you're sure to finish in time.

PAUSE 4 minutes

You have one more minute left.

PAUSE 1 minute

That's the end of the test. Please stop now. Your supervisor will collect all the question papers and answer sheets. Goodbye.

TEST 2

First Certificate Practice Test Two. Paper Four. Listening.

Hello. I'm going to give you the instructions for this test. I'll introduce each part of the test and give you time to look at the questions. At the start of each piece you'll hear this sound:

tone

You'll hear each piece twice. Remember, while you're listening, write your answers on the question paper. You'll have time at the end of the test to copy your answers onto the separate answer sheet.

The tape will now be stopped. Please ask any questions now, because you must not speak during the test.

PAUSE 5 seconds

PART 1
Now open your question papers and look at Part One. You will hear people talking in eight different situations. For questions 1–8, choose the best answer, A, B or C.

One
You hear two people talking. What was the cause of the problem?

A The woman's answerphone wasn't working.
B The woman didn't receive the message.
C The woman forgot about the message.

PAUSE 5 seconds – tone

Question 1
Woman:	(angrily) Where have you been? I've been waiting here for over half an hour. You said you'd be here at seven and it's now nearly twenty to eight!
Man:	Didn't you get my message, then?
Woman:	What message?
Man:	I left a message on your answerphone to say that I had to work late and that I'd meet you just after half past seven.
Woman:	Well, I haven't been home. Don't you remember me telling you I'd meet you straight after work?
Man:	Yes, but you don't have to go home to get your messages on the answerphone.
Woman:	(more angrily) Look, I didn't get your message, OK! So let's just forget about it, shall we? We haven't got time for a drink now, so let's go straight to the theatre.
Man:	That's fine by me.

PAUSE 2 seconds – tone

Repeat Question 1

PAUSE 2 seconds

Two
You hear two people talking about an electricity bill. Why does the woman think the man's bill is smaller than usual?

A It is a mistake.
B The man's family has been away.
C The electricity company doesn't charge as much now.

PAUSE 5 seconds – tone

Question 2
Man:	Have you had an electricity bill, recently?
Woman:	No, it hasn't arrived yet but I'm expecting it any day now. Why do you ask?
Man:	I got mine this morning and it seems to be wrong. I always pay about £80, but this bill is for just over £60.
Woman:	Perhaps you've used less this time.
Man:	No, I'm sure that's not it. We've been using the same amount for ages. I think I'd better go and check because I don't want a huge bill when the electricity board find out they've made a mistake.
Woman:	Wait a minute! I remember reading about reductions in bills. They were going to cut distribution charges because the companies wanted to be "consumer friendly".
Man:	Oh, that's nice! I'll just pay the bill and hope you're right.

PAUSE 2 seconds – tone

Repeat Question 2

PAUSE 2 seconds

Three
Listen to the following conversation. Who is Bob Turner?

A   a private investigator
B   a research scientist
C   a police detective

PAUSE 5 seconds – tone

Question 3

Mr Johnson: Good morning. My name's George Johnson and I'm managing director at Watkins.
Mr Turner: Good morning. I'm Bob Turner. How may I help you?
Mr Johnson: Well, I believe we have a problem with security at the factory.
Mr Turner: But you have your own guards who check staff at the gate, don't you?
Mr Johnson: Yes, but the problem is not with stolen goods from the factory. It's industrial espionage. We believe that one of our competitors has obtained important research results and is now using them to develop a new product.
Mr Turner: Have you informed the police yet?
Mr Johnson: Not officially. I spoke to a detective friend of mine who suggested I should see you first to get evidence so that they can build a case.
Mr Turner: Fine. Well now, I'll require more details. (fade out)

PAUSE 2 seconds – tone

Repeat Question 3

PAUSE 2 seconds

Four
You hear two people having a discussion. What are they talking about?

A   a film
B   a play
C   a concert

PAUSE 5 seconds – tone

Question 4

Martin: I thought that was rather good.
Wendy: It was fine for you, but I must have had a basketball team sitting in front of me. I could hardly see what was happening on stage. It was the same as when we went to see that film that won all those Oscars-remember?
Martin: Yes, but surely you could tell how good the acting was.
Wendy: I could hear the whole thing and I could see the scenery, but the only indication I really had of how good it had been was the applause at the end. I was really disappointed.
Martin: Right! Why don't we go again at the weekend. I'd love to see it again and the concert I was going to see has been cancelled.
Wendy: You're on.

PAUSE 2 seconds – tone

Repeat Question 4

PAUSE 2 seconds

Five
Listen to two people talking about a friend's wedding preparations. In what way will the wedding be different?

A   It will take place on another planet.
B   It will take place under the sea.
C   It will take place in the air.

PAUSE 5 seconds – tone

Question 5

Paul: Guess who I ran into the other day.
Marion: Who?
Paul: Bill ... Billy Carr.
Marion: What's he doing now? I haven't seen him for ages.
Paul: He's working for a computer company and guess what. He's getting married next month and we've both been invited to the reception.
Marion: Where's the wedding?
Paul: That's the strange part. We won't be able to attend the actual ceremony.
Marion: Why not?
Paul: Apparently, he's joined an extreme sports club and taken up sky diving and parachuting and that sort of thing and they're going to get married on the way down. He met his fiancée at the club.
Marion: I don't believe you. You're pulling my leg.
Paul: No, no, it's true. I swear.
Marion: Look, I've heard of people getting married in scuba diving gear but ...
Paul: It's true. Honest! By the way, how about putting off our wedding until we can have it on Mars?
Marion: Be serious for once, will you?

PAUSE 2 seconds – tone

Repeat Question 5

PAUSE 2 seconds

Six
Listen to a conversation between two people at home. Why can't they go shopping?

A   The man has lost his credit card.
B   The man has left his wallet at work.
C   The man has no money in his bank account.

PAUSE 5 seconds – tone

Question 6

Sylvia: I thought we could go to the supermarket first. I've got the shopping list here somewhere. Yes, here it is. You see there's hardly anything that needs to go in the fridge.
Tom: Yes, that's true, but do we really need all this cleaning stuff? If we keep on buying so much from the supermarket, we'll be broke.
Sylvia: Stop complaining. Anyway, you've always got your credit card. Then, I thought we'd go window shopping and perhaps get some new slippers. Your old ones are full of holes.
Tom: Fine. I'll just get my jacket. (pause) Have you seen my wallet anywhere?
Sylvia: think you had it in your blue jacket.
Tom: Oh, no! I left my jacket in the office yesterday. You see, we had a meeting and I didn't go back for it and it's got my credit card in it. Haven't you got any money?
Sylvia: No, I'm afraid not.

PAUSE 2 seconds – tone

Repeat Question 6

PAUSE 2 seconds

Seven
You hear two people talking about a friend who has moved to a village called Caldy. Where is Caldy?

A   in England
B   in Scotland

C   in Wales

PAUSE 5 seconds – tone

Question 7
Tamsin: Talking of old friends, I got a letter from Justin the other day.
William: Oh, really. Do you write to each other often then?
Tamsin: Not really – Christmas cards and a few letters a year. That's all.
William: Where did he move to? I haven't heard from him since he left the area. We weren't very close friends, as you know.
Tamsin: He now lives in a small village called Caldy.
William: Caldy? That's in Scotland, isn't it?
Tamsin: No, you're thinking of Kircaldy. He lives in Caldy. It's in the north-west of England, between Liverpool and Wales.
William: So, he hasn't moved abroad then.
Tamsin: No, he'...

PAUSE 2 seconds – tone

Repeat Question 7

PAUSE 2 seconds

Eight
You hear two people talking. Who is the man?

A   a doctor
B   the woman's boss
C   a friend

PAUSE 5 seconds – tone

Question 8
Woman: Ouch.
Man: What's the matter?
Woman: Nothing really – it's just that when I lift my right arm up, I get a sharp pain here in my ribs.
Man: Well, It's certainly got nothing to do with your heart.
Woman: (sarcastically – jokingly) That's a comfort, doc.
Man: How long have you had the pain?
Woman: A couple of days. I thought it would pass but it seems to be getting worse.
Man: You haven't taken a knock there, have you?
Woman: I don't know. I don't think so.
Man: So what are you going to do about it?
Woman: I won't be going to work in the morning. I asked my boss for a couple of hours off and he agreed that I should get some medical advice.
Man: Let me know how it goes. Give me a ring at work when you get back.

PAUSE 2 seconds – tone

Repeat Question 8

PAUSE 2 seconds

That's the end of Part One. Now turn to Part Two.

PART 2
You will hear a man ordering goods from a supermarket over the telephone. For questions 9–18, complete the sentences.

You now have forty-five seconds in which to look at Part Two.

PAUSE 45 seconds – tone

[telephone ringing]
Woman 1:   Good morning, Star Supermarket.
Man: Good morning, I'd like to place an order, please.
Woman 1:   Hold the line, please.
[pause]
Woman 2:   Good morning, Star Supermarket orders. How may I help

you?
Man: I'd like to place an order, please.
Woman 2:   May I have your name and address, please?
Man: Yes, it's Coleman. That's C-O-L-E-M-A-N and my address is 16 Neston Drive, Neston.
Woman 2:   Mr Coleman, 16 Neston Drive, Neston. And what time would you like it to be delivered?
Man: Between 5 and 5:30, if that's possible.
Woman 2:   Well, our drivers finish at five o' clock so it'll have to be between half past four and five o'clock if that's all right with you.
Man: Yes, that'll be fine.
Woman 2:   Now, may I have your order?
Man: Yes, I'll start with the fruit and veg. I'd like half a dozen bananas, 3 kilos of oranges, 2 kilos of apples, 10 kilos of potatoes and 2 kilos of tomatoes. Have you got that?
Woman 2:   ··· and 2 kilos of tomatoes. Yes. Is that all the fruit and veg?
Man: Yes, now, I'd like 2 frozen chickens – large ones, if possible – and a dozen eggs.
Woman 2:   What size eggs would you like?
Man: Medium, please.
Woman 2:   Fine.
Man: I would also like a large packet of cornflakes and 2 litres of milk – you know, that long-life milk.
Woman 2:   Is that all, sir?
Man: No, I need 2 bags of flour, a kilo of sugar and 250 grams of butter.
Woman 2:   Does it matter what brand of butter it is?
Man: No, just as long as it's unsalted. Now, where was I?Yes, I'd like 2 loaves of brown bread, ten slices of ham with the lowest fat content you have and 5 lamb chops – again, could you make sure the fat is trimmed off, please. Er ... that's all for the moment, I think.
Woman 2:   Could you give me your telephone number in case we need to contact you?
Man: Certainly, it's 982 4791. You can leave a message if I'm out.
Woman 2:   Thank you, Mr Coleman. Goodbye.
Man: Goodbye.

PAUSE 10 seconds – tone

Now you'll hear Part Two again.

Repeat Part Two.

PAUSE 5 seconds

That's the end of Part Two. Now turn to Part Three.

PART 3
You will hear five different people talking about electrical items that they have had repaired. For questions 19-23, choose from the list A-F which item is being described. Use the letters only once. There is one extra letter which you do not need to use.

You now have thirty seconds in which to look at Part Three.

PAUSE 30 seconds – tone

Speaker 1
Well, it started giving signs that something was going wrong with it, but I hoped that any problem would sort itself out. Of course it didn't and it got gradually worse until last week when the clothes came out with powder on them. Apparently, the rinse cycle had stopped working properly, so I had no choice but to get it repaired. It won't be cheap either because they said that there was also a problem with the heating element and that the water wasn't getting hot enough on some programs. I can't really complain because it's the first time it has gone wrong since I bought it almost ten years ago.

PAUSE 2 seconds

Speaker 2

I was told it wouldn't be worth getting one unless it was one of the best. I had to pay more but I followed the advice I was given. Unfortunately, about six weeks after I'd bought it, it started leaking. Water would drip continuously when it was switched on so there would be hardly any steam coming out of it while I was trying to use it. Obviously, I couldn't get the creases out of my shirts because it wasn't hot enough for materials like cotton. Luckily, it was covered by the guarantee so I didn't have to pay a penny to get it fixed. It needed a new plate and now it works perfectly. I just hope it stays that way because someone at the repair shop said the spray button on the model I bought wasn't very good.

PAUSE 2 seconds

Speaker 3

It wasn't very easy to choose one. There are so many on the market. I chose this one because it can also wash carpets and not just clean them like other models. It doesn't do the job as well as the ones professionals use but it's quite good. It's probably the best I could afford but it does have one big disadvantage. The bag which collects all the dirt is very small so it needs to be changed regularly. If you forget, the motor overheats, which is exactly what happened to mine. There wasn't too much damage done, though. Oh, you can also use it to clean curtains and sofa covers when you put it on a lower setting and use the range of attachments provided.

PAUSE 2 seconds

Speaker 4

I got it because the whole family was sick of doing them by hand. Now I really can't understand how I did without one for so long. Some of the smaller ones aren't very good because the water doesn't come out of the jets fast enough. This one does the job very well, I'm pleased to say. There's plenty of space inside and apart from the odd bit of crockery or cutlery that still has a stubborn bit of egg on it at the end, this model gets everything sparkling clean. You've got to check the filter regularly, though, otherwise you can have problems. This one had to be serviced early because some food had blocked up the filter. Okay, so the special powder and salt you have to buy cost quite a lot, but it beats getting your hands wet when you'd rather be relaxing.

PAUSE 2 seconds

Speaker 5

I'd always wanted one of these but I felt that if I bought one, people would laugh. I mean if you have one, it seems that you are lazy. Anyway, I was in the chemist's one day and there were several different kinds in boxes right next to the counter. I just couldn't resist buying one. It cost me almost £50. It has two brushes so my wife can use it too. It may seem to be a bit of a luxury but it does a good job. The brush rotates quickly and gets all the bits of food out and after using it a few times, you realise just how fresh your breath can be. You have to recharge the battery every few days or so. This was a problem at first as the charger didn't work properly but it didn't take much to get it fixed. Now, I believe it's more of a necessity than a luxury.

PAUSE 10 seconds – tone

Now you'll hear Part Three again.

Repeat Part Three

PAUSE 5 seconds

That's the end of Part Three. Now turn to Part Four.

PART 4

You will hear part of a radio programme about teenagers who have left home. For questions 24-30, choose the best answer, A, B or C.

You now have one minute in which to look at Part Four.

PAUSE 1 minute – tone

[intro music]

Presenter:	Welcome to the sixth of our "Adolescence to Adulthood" programmes. This week's programme is called 'Moving Out' and, in the studio today, we have two teenagers who have taken the giant leap of going to live on their own and two parents whose children have left home. [slight pause] I'll begin with you, Brian. How long has it been since you moved out?
Brian:	I moved out four months ago, but it wasn't what you might call a clean break. I didn't move out all in one go. I did it gradually and spent most of the week with my parents at first. I started by spending the weekends at my new flat so that I could get used to living alone slowly.
Presenter:	So it wasn't a case of having to get out at all costs.
Brian:	No, not at all. My parents have given me a great deal of financial support recently. They were really understanding when I told them where I wanted to move to. You see, I wanted to go somewhere quiet – a place where I could paint without any distractions.
Presenter:	Does living such a long way from your parents, and presumably your friends, cause problems?
Brian:	I suppose it would if I didn't have a car. The local bus service is pretty infrequent and it stops relatively early in the evening.
Presenter:	Now, on to you, Carolyn. You moved out under quite different circumstances from Brian, didn't you?
Carolyn:	That's right. I wish I had moved in the same way as Brian did, but that just wasn't possible.
Presenter:	Why not?
Carolyn:	I finally left home about six months ago. I really had no other choice. My parents and I just didn't see eye to eye on many issues, but the worst thing of all was that they wouldn't really give me any degree of freedom. They wouldn't let me stay out later than ten, even at weekends.
Presenter:	Do you think you made the right decision?
Carolyn:	Yes, I do. It was very hard at first. I severed all direct contact with my parents and we communicated through my younger brother. Things have improved somewhat since then with the occasional telephone call, but our relationship is still a bit frosty. I hope it will get better but we'll have to take it one step at a time.
Presenter:	So, apart from freedom, what else have you gained?
Carolyn:	Maturity. I've become quite a different person over the past six months. I'd say that I'm far more reliable and self-confident than I was.
Presenter:	What about you, Brian?
Brian:	I don't think the move has affected me as much as Carolyn. Perhaps I'm a little more appreciative of what my parents have done for me – not just now but before the move as well.
Presenter:	Finally, I'd like to ask you for some advice you would give to a teenager who was thinking of leaving home.
Brian:	Before you move, you'd better make sure you can cope financially, otherwise you'll be miserable.
Carolyn:	I think that's important, too, but I believe that the main point is to have a good reason for leaving home and not just move for the sake of moving. I mean you shouldn't do it just because it sounds like fun.
Presenter:	Thank you both. After the break, we'll be meeting some parents whose children have left home ... (fade out)

PAUSE 10 seconds – tone

Now you'll hear Part Four again.

Repeat Part Four

PAUSE 5 seconds

That's the end of Part Four.

There'll now be a pause of five minutes for you to copy your answers onto the separate answer sheet. I'll remind you when there is one minute left so that you're sure to finish in time.

PAUSE 4 minutes

You have one more minute left

PAUSE 1 minute

That's the end of the test. Please stop now. Your supervisor will collect all the question papers and answer sheets. Goodbye.

TEST 3

First Certificate Practice Test Three. Paper Four. Listening.

Hello, I'm going to give you the instructions for this test. I'll introduce each part of the test and give you time to look at the questions. At the start of each piece you'll hear this sound:

tone

You'll hear each piece twice. Remember, while your listening, while your answers on the question paper. You'll have time at the end of the test to copy your answers onto the separate answer sheet.

The tape will now be stopped. Please ask any questions now, because you must not speak during the test.

PAUSE 5 seconds

PART 1

Now open your question paper and look at Part One. You will hear people talking in eight different situations. For questions 1—8, choose the best answer, A, B or C.

One

Listen to the following conversation. Why was the man's connecting flight from Mumbai delayed?

A The weather was bad.
B The plane had broken down.
C The passengers weren't told.

PAUSE 5 seconds – tone

Question 1

Mary: Hello, John. How was India?
John: Tiring. Our connecting flight from Mumbal was delayed several times.
Mary: What caused the delay?
John: Well, you see we had to go to a port miles from a big city and there wasn't a major airport nearby. The closest airport was a military base which is sometimes used by a local airline.
Mary: So what time was your flight due to leave?
John: At 10:30 in the morning, but they told us it would leave at 12:30, then at two o'clock and then at three o'clock.
Mary: Perhaps there was a technical problem or a storm.
John: Perhaps, but the military do not allow civil flights to land after five o'clock so we had to fly to another airport further away from our destination.
Mary: That must have been frustrating.
John: Yes, it was.

PAUSE 2 seconds – tone

Repeat Question 1

PAUSE 2 seconds

Two

You hear someone talking about an activity weekend. Why didn't he enjoy it?

A The instructor was strict.
B He didn't feel comfortable.
C He wasn't staying in a very nice place.

PAUSE 5 seconds – tone

Question 2

Man: And I thought I'd try one of those weekend courses. You know, the ones where you stay at a college during the holidays. Well, I decided to spend a weekend – no, don't laugh – learning how to knit. I thought it might come in useful in the future. The course was supposed to be for beginners, but all the others seemed to be determined to show off their skills. Oh, the college facilities were better than expected and the instructor did her best to help me. I think she knew how I felt, but I didn't really fit in.

PAUSE 2 seconds – tone

Repeat Question 2

PAUSE 2 seconds

Three

You hear someone talking about a film. What was her reaction to it?

A She was surprised.
B She was disappointed.
C She was bored.

PAUSE 5 seconds – tone

Question 3

Woman: In my opinion, the film is unique. Normally, when you have so many things going against you, the chances of success are slim. I mean, you've got a film based on a book and, as you well know, that's often a recipe for boredom and failure, Then you've got a marvelous director, Rob Reining, who was known as a director of comedies and romances before this one – and that doesn't always work out well. So, as you can see, I didn't expect much of it. Thankfully, I was completely wrong. The performances by James Cannon and Kathy Brace and the direction were superb.

PAUSE 2 seconds – tone

Repeat Question 3

PAUSE 2 seconds

Four

You hear a conversation in a shop. How does the customer intend to pay for the items she wants to buy?

A in cash
B by cheque
C by credit card

PAUSE 5 seconds – tone

Question 4

Assistant: The TV and video together cost £1,285.
Woman: Fine. I'll take them. When will you be able to deliver them?
Assistant: This afternoon between two and four. How would you like to pay?
Woman: Do I have to pay extra if I pay by instalment?
Assistant: Yes, but it's only ... let me see ...
Woman: Never mind. I think I have enough on me. I'll get it over and done with now.
Assistant: You can pay half by cheque if you like.
Woman: No, that's all right. Here you are.

PAUSE 2 seconds-tone

Repeat Question 4

PAUSE 2 seconds

Five
You hear a radio presenter about to interview a guest. Who is the guest?

A   a doctor
B   an inventor
C   an insurance agent

PAUSE 5 seconds – tone

Question 5
Presenter: Welcome to the third in our series about the elderly. In this programme, we'll be looking at ways in which old people can become more mobile and independent. We'll be discussing medical and insurance aspects of all the latest developments in the second half of the programme. But first I'd like to welcome to the studio, Martin Gray, whose new device, "a seeing and talking" Zimmer frame, will help frail and poor-sighted elderly people to move around with confidence ...

PAUSE 2 seconds – tone

Repeat Question 5

PAUSE 2 seconds

Six
Listen to a policeman talking to a witness. Where does the conversation take place?

A   in a library
B   in a bank
C   in an office

PAUSE 5 seconds – tone

Question 6
Witness: ... and then I heard a loud bang. I turned round and looked out of the window – that one over there. I was doing some photocopying at the time.
Officer: What exactly did you see?
Witness: Two men leaving the bank. One of them was holding a bag. I assume it was full of money.
Officer: Can you describe them?
Witness: Not really, except for the fact that they were both quite tall and slim. Then they jumped into a waiting car parked outside the library opposite. Perhaps you'll find an eye witness who was in there at the time.
Officer: What kind of car was it?
Witness: A blue Ford, I think.

PAUSE 2 seconds – tone

Repeat Question 6

PAUSE 2 seconds

Seven
Listen to someone talking about his family. Who is David?

A   his uncle
B   his nephew
C   his cousin

PAUSE 5 seconds – tone

Question 7
Speaker: I have one brother. He's younger than me. We don't look at all alike. He takes after my father and I take after my grandfather on my father's side. I think he acts more like my mother at times, though. The only person I really resemble is David. He takes after my grandfather, too, and that's strange because neither of our fathers, who are brothers, takes after him. They both take after their mother, my grandmother.

PAUSE 2 seconds – tone

Repeat Question 7

PAUSE 2 seconds

Eight
Listen to someone making a phone call. What is the purpose of the call?

A   to complain
B   to apologise
C   to make an arrangement

PAUSE 5 seconds – tone

Question 8
Speaker: Hi, it's me, Janet. I've been trying to get hold of you all evening. Don't say anything, just let me explain what happened. I got a phone call from my boss this afternoon and he wanted me to meet a client at the airport. I told him about our arrangements for this evening, but he said I was the only one available. I suppose Vicki complained about me not being there. Well, I just wanted to say sorry for not making it and for any problems I caused ...

PAUSE 2 seconds – tone

Repeat Question 8

PAUSE 2 seconds

That's the end of Part One. Now turn to Part Two.

PART 2
You will hear a radio interview about investing money from home.

For questions 9-18, complete the sentences.

You now have forty-five seconds in which to look at Part Two.

PAUSE 45 seconds – tone

Presenter: Good evening and welcome to the last in the series of "Money Matters". We'll be back with a new series in September so don't worry because you'll get plenty of advice about how to make your money work for you after the summer holidays. Today, we have with us in the studio Justin MacDonald of Barclays Stockbrokers. Welcome, Justin.
Justin: Thank you, Miriam, and congratulations on the series. I've really enjoyed it.
Presenter: Thank you, Justin. Justin is here this evening to talk about a new type of investor – the amateur investor who uses modem technology at home to buy and sell shares.
Justin: Yes, first of all, I must give listeners an idea of the number of people trading from their own homes. There are now about 400,000 active individual investors and the number is growing. In fact, it has actually doubled in the last three months.
Presenter: That's an incredible increase. Is there a simple explanation for it?
Jason: Well, many reasons have been given, but I believe that the real reason is excitement. There is a chance of making some real money on the stock market so people are willing to take risks.
Presenter: How much chance is there of making some real money?
Jason: I'll give you a typical example. Last Wednesday, one investor bought $83,600 worth of shares in a mobile phone company – that's about £50,000 worth. Just one minute later, he sold them at a profit of £175 and half an hour later he repeated the deal, making another £45. And this is repeated day after day. So, he ends up with, monthly profit of about £5.000!
Presenter: It sounds like using a mackerel to catch a sprat if you ask me! I mean you need quite a lot of capital, don't you?
Jason: Yes, indeed. If you want to make money like this, you have to

be willing to use a large sum of money in order to make a relatively small amount quickly. But £5,000 a month is definitely worth having and I don't think it's worth turning your nose up at.

Presenter: If it's as easy as all that, why doesn't everyone do it?

Justin: Firstly, not everyone has that much capital and secondly, not all shares can go up all the time.

Presenter: There are dangers, then?

Justin: Definitely the small investor has to choose risky shares to make money - that is, shares that climb quickly in price. Personally, I believe this type of share will become less attractive and people will prefer long-term winners.

Presenter: The example you mentioned earlier occurred in the US. What about Britain?

Justin: There has been a great deal of interest here, but because the structure of the London Stock Exchange is archaic, you have to deal through a stockbroker. You can't deal directly on the market and you have to pay to do so.

Presenter: What sort of charges are we talking about?

Justin: If you buy one share for £2, you may be able to sell it for £1.96 immediately. Then, on top of that, there is a charge of 1% in commission and 0.5% in tax. This means that the share has to rise by about 4% before you make a profit. Few shares increase this sharply so it's not a very attractive proposition.

Presenter: Does that mean that investors look elsewhere?

Justin: Yes. Many prefer foreign markets to our own because they can trade directly without these charges. Therefore, the smallest change in share price can lead to instant profit.

Presenter: What effect has this had?

Justin: Britain's first day-trading centre opened last week. The fee paid by investors to join allows direct dealing in American stocks. Already more than 2000 British investors are trading in American shares and the worst practices in the States have already been seen here. They are not illegal but things can go wrong.

Presenter: In what way?

Justin: Only a few people make a fortune. Many more lose large amounts of money. In America, hundreds of investors have been forced to sell their homes to cover their losses. But it can be much worse. Mark Burton from Atlanta, Georgia, lost $100,000 before killing his wife and children earlier this year. Then he shot dead nine people at two firms of stockbrokers.

Presenter: How terrible! Is anything being done to prevent a repetition?

Justin: Yes, the first steps to limit the amount of money private investors can borrow to make deals.

Presenter: Finally, Justin, can you give the listeners a word of advice?

Justin: Certainly! Only invest money you can afford to lose.

Presenter: Thank you, Justin. And now I'd like to welcome to the studio someone who is no stranger to the programme···

PAUSE 10 seconds – tone

Now you'll hear Part Two again.

Repeat Part Two.

PAUSE 5 seconds

That's the end of Part Two. Now turn to Part Three.

PART 3

You will hear people talking in five different situations. For questions **19–23**, choose the profession of each speaker from the list **A–F**. Use the letters only once. There is one extra letter which you do not need to use. You now have 30 seconds in which to look at Part Three.

PAUSE 30 seconds – tone

Speaker 1

Yes, it was a role I really wanted. When I was a teenager, I wanted to be a lawyer, so I had no hesitation in accepting when I was approached by Jack. I used to watch all those courtroom dramas and imagine myself defending an innocent person charged with murder, so it kind of felt like I was achieving this aim in a way. Of course, working with Bruce and Nicole was just great. Nicole's husband gave us great support, and when we were off set, we'd play basketball together. And Bruce is just a great guy, too. I really enjoyed it. what's next? Well, I may be involved in a project to do with a famous sports star, but I don't want to say any more right now. You'll have to wait and see!

PAUSE 2 seconds

Speaker 2

Please sit down. I'm sorry I had to ask you to come in this evening, but we do feel that it's a rather serious matter. Some sports equipment was stolen from the changing rooms last Wednesday evening after basketball practice and Peter was one of those who had access to it. Now, I know he has assured you he had nothing to do with it. However, he did witness what happened, and since nobody is prepared to come forward to tell the truth, we have no option but to expel all those who were present. We were hoping you might have a word with him so that he realises the seriousness of the situation.

PAUSE 2 seconds

Speaker 3

Look, Mrs Hawkins, the bottom line is that your daughter is only ten years old, therefore, she is not legally responsible for her actions. This means you will have to face charges yourself. Do you have a lawyer, Mrs Hawkins? I realise that all this sounds a bit unfair, seeing as neither of you have been in trouble before, but unfortunately, there was a witness, the goods were found on your daughter by the security guard, and the store has said that it intends to press charges. Now, is there anything you would like to say before we...

PAUSE 2 seconds

Speaker 4

I understand your frustration, Madam, but I'm afraid if you haven't got one, I can't do anything about it, regardless of whether it was a gift. This is store policy. I can plainly see that the garment is one of ours, but as you have no proof that it was bought in this particular store, I cannot help you. You see, articles are frequently stolen and then returned to us for a refund. Now, I'm not suggesting for one minute that you stole the item, but I simply cannot do anything without proof of purchase. Would you like to see the manager perhaps?

PAUSE 2 seconds

Speaker 5

Well, what can I say? There was a great deal of relief when the verdict was announced this afternoon. If the judge had awarded damages to Paul Jones, it would have been a real blow to the game. And I think the biggest effect would have been on the players. There would be no player on a pitch without insurance and a good lawyer. That's OK for professionals, but what about the amateur game or school matches? I believe the judge got it right in court today. Mind you, let me say how sorry I am that Paul's playing days are over, and that I wouldn't wish the horrific injuries that he sustained on anyone. But it's all part and parcel of the game, isn't it?

PAUSE 10 seconds – tone

Now you'll hear Part Three again.

Repeat Part Three

PAUSE 5 seconds.

That's the end of Part Three. Now turn to Part Four.

PART 4

You'll hear part of a conversation about spending a weekend in the Scottish Highlands. For questions 24–30, choose the best answer, A, B or C.

You now have one minute in which to look at Part Four.

PAUSE 1 minute – tone

Mike:	Hi, Carrie. Where were you at the weekend? I called you several times but there was no answer. Did you stay with your parents?
Carrie:	No, I went away for the weekend. I did some walking up in Scotland.
Mike:	Did you go by yourself?
Carrie:	No, I was going to go with my cousin, but I went with Debbie instead. Here she comes now.
Debbie:	Hi, Mike. How are you?
Mike:	Fine. I hear that you went up to Scotland for the weekend.
Debbie:	Yes, we did. It was great to get away from the dirt and noise of the city.
Mike:	It must have cost quite a bit. How can you afford to spend so much on a weekend break? I'm almost broke.
Carrie:	It wasn't too expensive. We got the train up to Corrour Halt.
Mike:	Where?
Carrie:	Corrour Halt. It's up near Fort William. We got a cheap ticket – you know, one of those student reductions on off-peak trains.
Mike:	What about the hotel? They're never cheap and even a hostel costs something.
Debbie:	We didn't stay in either.
Mike:	Don't tell me you took a tent with you.
Debbie:	No, we stayed in bothies.
Mike:	Bothies? What are bothies?
Debbie:	They're huts high in the mountains. I believe the word comes from the Gaelic word "bothan", which means hut. Apparently they started in Scotland in the Thirties, when people wanted to get away from the towns at weekends.
Mike:	That's the first I've heard of them.
Carrie:	That's because they're a pretty well-kept secret. They're not marked on maps or anything.
Mike:	So, how did you find them, then?
Carrie:	A friend of ours, Angus, told us about them. He drew a little map for us. After we'd found the first one, we were told by other walkers where we could find others. That's how it works.
Debbie:	They're pretty basic but they're free so you can't complain. The bothies we stayed in had no furniture to speak of, just some raised sleeping platforms where you can lay your sleeping bag. We were lucky because we were told that in some bothies you have to sleep on the floor.
Mike:	Weren't you cold? It must have been freezing up there in the Highlands.
Debbie:	No, not really. We made a fire and had a hot drink and my sleeping bag is warm. It was a bit cold in the morning but you soon get warm when you start moving around.
Carrie:	The only rule they have is that you must leave the bothy as you found it so you have to replace the wood that you burnt the night before. All bothies have a fireplace so they are quite cosy, really.
Mike:	Were you alone in the bothies? It must have been frightening in there in the middle of nowhere at night.
Debbie:	No, we were fine. Because it was a weekend, there were quite a few other walkers and climbers around. Perhaps there are fewer people during the week.
Carrie:	Actually, I said to Debbie that I wished you had been with us to protect us in case anything bad happened.
Mike:	Well, ... er ... if you'd asked ...
Debbie:	Take no notice of her. She's pulling your leg.
Carrie:	Sorry, I couldn't resist it. Seriously, though, why don't you come with us next time? You'd enjoy it.
Mike:	Wasn't it tiring?
Carrie:	It was a bit, but it was worth it. The scenery was marvellous and there's quite a bit of wildlife up there. We saw our first deer almost as soon as we got off the train at Corrour Halt.
Mike:	To tell the truth, I don't really know if it's my cup of tea.
Debbie:	Come on Mike. Where's your sense of adventure?
Mike:	I don't know. Tell me some more about when you ... [fade out]

PAUSE 10 seconds – tone

Now you'll hear Part Four again

Repeat Part Four

PAUSE 5 seconds

That's the end of Part Four.

There'll now be a pause of five minutes for you to copy your answers onto the separate answer sheet. I'll remind you when there is one minute left, so that you're sure to finish in time.

PAUSE 4 minutes

You have one more minute left.

PAUSE I minute

That's the end of the test. Please stop now. Your supervisor will now collect all the question papers and answer sheets. Goodbye.

TEST 4

First Certificate Practice Test Four. Paper Four. Listening.

Hello. I'm going to give you the instructions for this test. I'll introduce each part of the test and give you time to look at the questions. At the start of each piece you'll hear this sound:

tone

You'll hear each piece twice. Remember, while you're listening, write your answers on the question paper. You'll have time at the end of the test to copy your answers onto the separate answer sheet.

The tape will now be stopped. Please ask any questions now, because you must not speak during the test.

PAUSE 5 seconds

PART 1
Now open your question papers and look at Part One. You will hear people talking in eight different situations. For questions 1–8, choose the best answer, A, B or C.

One
Listen to two people talking. What does the man want the woman to do?

A to cook a meal
B to baby-sit
C to take a phone message

PAUSE 5 seconds – tone

Question 1

Woman:	I really don't know. I don't want the responsibility. What if something goes wrong?
Man:	Look, it's only until seven o'clock. I'll be back by then, I promise you.
Woman:	But I've never done it before.
Man:	Don't worry. He won't be any trouble. He'll play by himself for hours. You won't even know he's there.
Woman:	Can you give me your mobile phone number just in case?
Man:	Yes, here you are. It's on my card there, but I'm sure you won't need it.
Woman:	All right, but don't be late. I'm having some friends round this evening and I've got to prepare dinner.
Man:	I won't and thanks, Barbara.

PAUSE 2 seconds – tone

Repeat Question 1

PAUSE 2 seconds

Two

Listen to two people talking before they go out. Where are they going?

A   to a concert
B   for a meal
C   to a discotheque

PAUSE 5 seconds-tone

Question 2

Bill: Aren't you ready yet?
Alan: No, come in for a second, will you? [door closes]
Bill: What's taken you so long? When I phoned you an hour ago, you told me you were getting ready.
Alan: I know, sorry. But I don't know what to wear. I wasn't sure if I have to wear a jacket and tie to get in.
Bill: I think you've just got to be smart – no jeans – that sort of thing. I don't think you'll need a tie. After all, it's not a restaurant.
Alan: OK. Just give me a minute.
Bill: Oh, and don't wear anything too tight. You'll be moving around most of the night, especially if Tamsin gets her way. You know her – she's always on the dance floor.
Alan: Thanks for the advice. I'll be right with you. Take a seat and put on a CD if you want.

PAUSE 2 seconds   tone

Repeat Question 2

PAUSE 2 seconds

Three

Listen to a conversation in an office. What happened to the woman the previous evening?

A   She got into a fight.
B   She was insulted.
C   She got involved in an argument.

PAUSE 5 seconds – tone

Question 3

Man: You look dreadful. You must have had a great night out.
Woman: No, actually I stayed up to watch the late night film.
Man: I thought you were going out for a meal and then on to a club.
Woman: Well, things didn't quite work out that way.
Man: Oh, why not?
Woman: We all met outside the restaurant at about nine and everything seemed fine. There was Gary, Vicky, Mick, Jennie, Dave and Gary's cousin, Sheila, from Australia. She was really weird. She didn't like me at all.
Man: Are you sure? I remember Gary saying she was on the quiet side.
Woman: She wasn't last night. She started saying nasty things about the dress I was wearing. OK, so it was a bit short, but there was no need to say what she said.
Man: Did you shout at her?
Woman: No. I felt like hitting her but I just bit my lip instead. She didn't stop, so I got up and left. I couldn't get to sleep, so I watched TV until the early hours.
Man: Have you spoken to Gary yet?
Woman: No, and I'm not sure I want to.

PAUSE 2 seconds – tone

Repeat Question 3

PAUSE 2 seconds

Four

Listen to a woman telling a friend about a problem at work. Why does she think John caused the photocopier to break down?

A   He was angry about a managerial decision.
B   He wanted to move to another branch.
C   He didn't like his job.

PAUSE 5 seconds – tone

Question 4

Kate: How's work these days?
Penny: The job's fine, thanks, but there's one thing I can't stand in the office.
Kate: What?
Penny: The way the staff hate everything the managers do. They always complain or worse and make everyone else's life a misery. Take what happened just this morning. Someone tried to force paper into the photocopier for some reason and it broke down.
Kate: Do you know who did it?
Penny: I'm not absolutely sure but I think it was John from accounts.
Kate: What makes you say that?
Penny: Everyone thought he was going to be promoted, but the company brought someone in from outside – another branch actually. Since then, he's been quite upset. I've seen him break a few pens and pencils deliberately while he was on his own.
Kate: Didn't you say anything?
Penny: No, of course not.
Kate: Haven't you ever felt like doing something like that?
Penny: Yes, but I've never broken anything on purpose. It's pretty childish if you ask me.
Kate: You're right. It is.

PAUSE 2 seconds – tone

Repeat Question 4

PAUSE 2 seconds

Five

You hear two people talking. How does the man know Emil Wesker, the famous footballer?

A   They used to play in the same team.
B   They were in the same class at school.
C   They used to live in the same street.

PAUSE 5 seconds – tone

Question 5

Woman: Who was that you were talking to over there? It wasn't Emil Wesker, was it?
Man: Yes, as a matter of fact, it was.
Woman: How come you know him? You were never good at football, were you?
Man: I wasn't good enough to become a professional but I wasn't that bad.
Woman: So how do you know him? Did you go to school together?
Man: Yes, we did.
Woman: Did you know him well?
Man: Quite well, but we weren't what you would call good friends. We were practically next door neighbours but we didn't really hang round together because I'm three years older than him.
Woman: Was he a good player back then?
Man: Yes. Everyone knew he was going places. He was by far the best player at school. Now that he's famous, he's still OK. He's not a snob or anything.

PAUSE 2 seconds – tone

Repeat Question 5

PAUSE 2 seconds

Six
Listen to two people talking at work. What did the woman do when someone hit her car?

A She apologised.
B She got angry.
C She called the police.

PAUSE 5 seconds – tone

Question 6

Man:	What's up? You seem worried.
Woman:	Worried? I'm not worried.
Man:	What's wrong then?
Woman:	Some idiot scraped my car in the car park and then had the nerve to say it was my fault because I'd parked too near the white line.
Man:	Had you?
Woman:	Don't you start! My car was between the white lines, in the proper place!
Man:	What happened then?
Woman:	He accused me of being a typical woman driver and I'm sure he expected me to apologise for what he'd done. I can't describe the look on his face. I just lost my temper. For one moment I thought and Shelley – she saw it, too – thought I was going to hit him.
Man:	You had a witness then.
Woman:	Yes, there was Shelley and Mr Banks – he saw it, too. The man who scraped my car threatened to call the police but he backed down. He knew he was in the wrong.
Man:	That's OK, then.
Woman:	I hope so.

PAUSE 2 seconds – tone

Repeat Question 6

PAUSE 2 seconds

Seven
Listen to two people talking at home. Why won't the remote control work?

A There's a piece missing.
B The batteries have run down.
C It has been dropped.

PAUSE 5 seconds – tone

Question 7

Woman:	[shouts] Can you come in here for a moment?
Man:	Hold on. I'll be right with you. What's up?
Woman:	The TV control isn't working.
Man:	But the TV is on.
Woman:	I know. I switched it on manually but I can't change channel.
Man:	When was the last time you used it?
Woman:	Last night. But Mark changed the batteries this morning because they were running down.
Man:	Did he check the control afterwards?
Woman:	I don't know.
Man:	Has it been dropped? You know these things are pretty sensitive.
Woman:	Well, all I did was pick it up off the table.
Man:	OK. Let's have a look inside. Oh dear! Look!
Woman:	What is it?
Man:	A piece of metal has broken off, so the batteries aren't connecting properly, No wonder it's not working.
Woman:	Now that you mention it, Mark did say he'd had to force the batteries into position.
Man:	I think we'll have to use a piece of aluminium foil for the time

being. That should do the trick.

Woman:	Right. I'll get some from the kitchen.

PAUSE 2 seconds – tone

Repeat Question 7

PAUSE 2 seconds

Eight
Listen to two people discussing an incident which occurred the previous evening. What did the woman do?

A She ignored the man.
B She was rude to the man.
C She lied to the man.

PAUSE 5 seconds – tone

Question 8

Michael:	Look! It's about time we had a talk, Tina.
Tina:	What about?
Michael:	About our relationship.
Tina:	Can't it wait?
Michael:	No, it can't. I won't beat about the bush. I don't think you take me seriously any more. You just take me for granted.
Tina:	Now, you know that's not true. What's got into you?
Michael:	Me? Don't you remember what you did last night?
Tina:	What are you getting at? Are you getting jealous? Can't I talk to anyone when I'm with you?
Michael:	Of course you can, but who was that guy you were talking to? You didn't even know him.
Tina:	Yes, but I can make friends if I want, can't I? Anyway, he bought me a drink so he must have been nice.
Michael:	And what was I supposed to do? You didn't take any notice of me at all. And as for being nice, he said: "What are you looking at, mate?" when I wanted to attract your attention.
Tina:	I don't want to talk about this now. Let's discuss it when you've calmed down. Oh, is that the time? I've got to dash. Bye.

PAUSE 2 seconds – tone

Repeat Question 8

PAUSE 2 seconds

That's the end of Part One. Now turn to Part Two.

PART 2
You will hear part of a radio interview with a film director about making a film. For questions 9–18, complete the sentences.

You now have forty-five seconds in which to look at Part Two.

PAUSE 45 seconds – tone

[fade in]

Interviewer:	Is that really possible when we read about films with sets costing hundreds of thousands of dollars?
Guest:	Yes, it has been done. I'm not suggesting it is easy but if we take *The Blair Witch Project* as an example, you'll see that it's not impossible.
Interviewer:	But surely that film is the exception that proves the rule. I mean, it's never happened before.
Guest:	Not in terms of success, it hasn't, but that doesn't mean it can't happen again. Dan Myrich and Eduardo Sanchez used a 16mm hand-held camera and took just eight days to shoot the film with a budget of only a few thousand dollars.
Interviewer:	And I believe that it has grossed about $150 million.
Guest:	That's right. It also made Myrich and Sanchez millionaires overnight.
Interviewer:	What do you think is the key to making a successful film on a

	limited budget?
Guest:	You have to get a number of things right. There are ten steps in the process. First and foremost, you need a good idea, which may be the hardest part of making a film.
Interviewer:	I'm sure there are many listeners out there with good ideas, so what's the next step?
Guest:	You've got to decide what sort of film you want it to be. You've got to decide on the soundtrack, the style and whether it's going to be a comedy or a thriller, for example. I call this step 'The Vision'. Once you've made your decision, you can go on to the third phase, which is the script. It sounds obvious but the story has to have a beginning, a middle and an end. The characters have to be introduced in the opening section, the plot needs to be developed in the middle and the consequences of the plot come at the end. One important thing to bear in mind here is to make the characters believable.
Interviewer:	All this sounds fairly straightforward. Are there any difficult steps?
Guest:	Well, I did say that getting the idea was hard and the next step, which is the pitch, is crucial, too.
Interviewer:	The pitch? What exactly do you mean?
Guest:	Even if you've got a great script, it won't sell itself. You have to convince other people how good it is and you have to do it quickly. You really should be able to sell either the idea or the finished film in 30 seconds. You might need the help of a sales agent at this stage.
Interviewer:	Is this expensive?
Guest:	You get what you pay for, just like anything else. And that brings me to the fifth step, which is finance. Although experts reckon you can make a good short film for £300, you generally need quite a bit more. Robert Rodriguez, for example, made a $7,000 movie called *El Mariachi* for the Mexican video market, which was picked up by Columbia Pictures and re-made as *Desperado* starring Antonio Banderas. It all depends on why you want to make the film. Normally, the first film is used as a stepping stone.
Interviewer:	Can you get any help with funding?
Guest:	Yes, the British Film Institute's booklet lists all the media organisations that give grants to film makers.
Interviewer:	What about the cast?
Guest:	The cast and crew is the next step. Even if you've got very little money, you can get your cast and crew by placing ads on email lists. Many young actors are keen to impress and get their first break. Then there are steps seven and eight, which deal with the equipment needed and shooting the movie. A Canon XMI digital video camera costs around £1800 so it's best if you contact camera hire companies in order to rent one. And if you're shooting the film yourself, work out which scenes you can shoot at the same time. This will save you time as you will only have to set up the equipment once.
Interviewer:	How should you go about publicising the film?
Guest:	I was coming to that. It's the second to last step and unfortunately you have to have a marketing idea. You've got to create something that will stick in people's minds. Advertising on the net is always a good idea.
Interviewer:	I believe *The Blair Witch Project* was very successfully marketed, wasn't it? Didn't they put fake police reports and a history of the Blair witch dating back to 1700 on the net?
Guest:	That's absolutely right. It's probably what made the film. And that brings me to the final step, which is festivals. This is the all important place where your film gets shown and hopefully picked up by distributors from all over the world.
Interviewer:	Well, thank you, Tim. I think you've given young film makers some real encouragement today. That's all we've got time for today. Next week ... [fade out]

PAUSE 10 seconds – tone

Now you'll hear Part Two again.

Repeat Part Two.

PAUSE 5 seconds

That's the end of Part Two. Now turn to Part Three.

PART 3

You will hear five different people talking about a present they have been given. For questions 19–23, choose which of the people A–F is speaking. Use the letters only once. There is one extra letter which you do not need to use.

You now have thirty seconds in which to look at Part Three.

PAUSE 30 seconds – tone

Speaker 1

When I was in my third year at university, I decided to go home for the Easter holidays because I'd spent my Christmas holidays skiing with some friends in Austria. When I got home, I saw my mother's car and my father's four-wheel drive parked in the driveway together with a new sports car. I opened the front door, but nobody greeted me. They just said. 'Hello' as if I'd just got back from doing the shopping. I felt as if they were giving me the cold shoulder because I hadn't gone home at Christmas. It was really depressing and I thought it would be best if I went straight up to my room. When I opened the door, I saw a huge "Welcome Home" banner on the wall with some car keys hanging underneath it. I was so overcome that I burst into tears and hugged every member of my family, who had sneaked up the stairs behind me.

PAUSE 2 seconds

Speaker 2

About four or five years ago, I asked my family for one large Christmas present rather than several smaller ones. My brothers, my sister and my parents said they would all contribute to one big present, so I was happy. I also hinted that I would like something made of gold or silver. I really wanted a necklace but I didn't say so because I thought that would be going too far. Anyway, Christmas day arrived and we all exchanged presents. I opened my present eagerly, hoping to see a gold necklace. Unfortunately, it was a small silver ornament inlaid with gold. As soon as I saw it, I thought it was a joke but I realised it wasn't when my mother said: "It'll look lovely on your bedside table, dear." I forced myself to smile and thank them, but I felt like bursting into tears. Actually, things weren't that bad because I got a jeweller to make a necklace with the metal from the ornament soon after Christmas and, what's more, I chose the design.

PAUSE 2 seconds

Speaker 3

After I'd finished university, I tried to get a job near home. I applied to a local company but I was offered a good position in their overseas branch. I didn't really want to live abroad but my parents encouraged me to go. The salary was excellent, but I soon got homesick. Fortunately, I managed to get a week's holiday and I decided to take it during the week when it was my birthday. I arrived the day before my birthday and my father and sister met me at the airport. They both seemed very excited, so I thought they had bought me a really expensive present. Suddenly, my sister let the cat out of the bag and said that I had a big surprise waiting for me but she wouldn't tell me what it was. When we got home, they told me to close my eyes. I did so and I opened them when I got into the living room. There, in front of me, was my cousin Janet. I was so moved that I burst into tears when I hugged her. You see, she'd gone missing in Africa a few months earlier and we'd all thought ... but we never lost hope. The embassy said her chances were slim. Luckily, they were wrong. It was the best birthday present I could have wished for.

PAUSE 2 seconds

Speaker 4

I think the best presents you get are those you get at Christmas when you are a child, and this is certainly true in my case. All my friends had racing bikes that could go much faster than my rusty, old second-hand bike and I kept on asking my parents whether they could buy me one for Christmas. They told me that it would be very difficult because things were very tight.

We were quite poor so we didn't have much money to spare to buy presents. Anyway, to cut a long story short, I got my new bike on Christmas day. I really didn't expect to get it and I don't think I would have minded if I hadn't. I did appreciate it, though, and realised that my parents must have made sacrifices in order to please me. I remember feeling proud as I went out for a ride with my friends on my new ten-speed bike.

PAUSE 2 seconds

Speaker 5
It's not always the biggest or most expensive presents that are the best. The best present I have ever been given was neither big nor expensive. I was about fourteen at the time I got it and I remember how much it meant to me. When I was young, I lived with my grandmother because my father was in the army and my parents thought it would be best if I didn't travel round with them so that I wouldn't have to change schools all the time. I got used to living with my grandmother and enjoyed her company, but there came a day when she could no longer take care of me because of illness. My parents came back to England to pick me up and on the day we were about to leave, my grandmother gave me a book she used to read as a child. It was the same book she'd read to me when I first went to live with her. I never saw my grandmother again but I still have the book in my bookcase at home.

PAUSE 10 seconds – tone

Now you'll hear Part Three again.

Repeat Part Three

PAUSE 5 seconds

That's the end of Part Three. Now turn to Part Four.

PART 4
You will hear a conversation between two students about an article in a newspaper. For questions 24–30, choose the best answer, A, B or C.

You now have one minute in which to look at Part Four.

PAUSE I minute – tone

Dee: Have you read this article about the British student who was attacked by lions?
Paul: Not another big cat story! There was that case of a vet being shot by police as he was trying to escape from a tiger just recently. All these stories with big cats seem to occur together.
Dee: That was ages ago.
Paul: Are you sure? It seems like just last week.
Dee: Yes, I'm positive. It was when I was studying for my biology test and I remember thinking that if being a vet involved running away from tigers, I'd rather not become one.
Paul: Yes, you're right. I remember now. Anyway, what does it say about the British student?
Dee: He was on safari in ...er ... Mat ... su ... adona national park which is in Zimbabwe. It says here that he may have provoked the attack by running away from his tent.
Paul: Yes, they can't resist running after a moving target. But I don't suppose it'd be easy to stand still if a lion was walking towards you. What would you do?
Dee: I'd be petrified, I don't think I'd be able to move a muscle, let alone run away. But, according to the paper, he was surprised by a lion trying to smell his feet while he was asleep. They think his feet were sticking out of the tent. He woke up, ran and was chased.
Paul: Wasn't there anyone there to help him?
Dee: There was an investigation and they found out that by the time anyone could do anything, it was too late – he'd already been attacked by ten or twelve lions.
Paul: Who was in charge of the safari?
Dee: A guide – just a normal guide. He's been accused of not checking the student's tent.

Paul: What are they going to do about it?
Dee: Nothing. Apparently, a British family on the safari came to his defence, saying he'd shown [as if reading from the article] tremendous personal bravery and clear thinking during the incident. They also said that if he hadn't been so alert, others might have been attacked as well. It also says here that this kind of encounter is extremely rare.
Paul: It just goes to show that safaris can be dangerous.
Dee: That's exactly what it says here. The companies that run safaris warn their clients about the dangers and ask them to sign forms which don't allow them to claim against the company in court if anything goes wrong.
Paul: Are you doing anything this afternoon, Dee?
Dee: No. Why?
Paul: I thought we could spend a few hours at the zoo!

PAUSE 10 seconds – tone

Now you'll hear Part Four again.

Repeat Part Four

PAUSE 5 seconds

That's the end of Part Four.

There'll now be a pause of five minutes for you to copy your answers onto the separate answer sheet. I'll remind you when there is one minute left so that you're sure to finish in time.

PAUSE 4 minutes

You have one more minute left

PAUSE 1 minute

That's the end of the test. Please stop now. Your supervisor will collect all the question papers and answer sheets. Goodbye.

TEST 5

First Certificate Practice Test Five. Paper Four. Listening.

Hello. I'm going to give you the instructions for this test. I'll introduce each part of the test and give you time to look at the questions. At the start of each piece you'll hear this sound:

tone

You'll hear each piece twice. Remember, while you're listening, write your answers on the question paper. You'll have time at the end of the test to copy your answers onto the separate answer sheet.

The tape will now be stopped. Please ask any questions now, because you must not speak during the test.

PAUSE 5 seconds

PART 1
Now open your question paper and look at Part One. You will hear people talking in eight different situations. For questions 1–8, choose the best answer, A, B or C.

One
Listen to this conversation between a woman and a man. What does the woman do?

A   She makes an appointment.
B   She makes a suggestion.
C   She offers sympathy.

PAUSE 5 seconds – tone

Question 1

Margaret: George, could I have a word with you, please?

George: Yes, certainly.

Margaret: It's about your meeting with Mr Sharpe tomorrow morning. I've just spoken to his secretary on the phone. She's a friend of mine and she told me that his daughter's in hospital and she's going to have an operation tomorrow afternoon.

George: Nothing serious, I hope.

Margaret: I'm not sure but I don't think it's routine. Obviously, he'll be rather worried, so it might be best if you made it a short meeting. He's a good client, so bear in mind his situation, please.

George: Yes, I'll do that.

Margaret: By the way, don't say anything unless he mentions it because we're not supposed to know.

George: Fine. You can count on me.

PAUSE 2 seconds – tone

Repeat Question 1

PAUSE 2 seconds

Two

Listen to a man talking about his job. Where does he work?

A in an office
B at a port
C in a school

PAUSE 5 seconds – tone

Question 2

Man: I must say that I enjoy my job now, but if you had asked me whether I wanted to work here when I was still at school, I would have laughed. At first, I wanted to work with my father down at the docks. He used to tell me about all the people he met there – people from all over the world. It sounded very exciting, but when I told him I wanted to work with him, he put me off. He said I should do something better like work in an office or a laboratory. That's why he encouraged me to go to university. So, as you can see, coming back here to the place where I was educated was the last thing I expected to do. But I must say I think it's been a good choice if exam results are anything to go by.

PAUSE 2 seconds – tone

Repeat Question 2

PAUSE 2 seconds

Three

Listen to a woman speaking on the phone. Why is she making the call?

A to make some extra changes
B to check that some changes have been made
C to check that the spelling is correct

PAUSE 5 seconds – tone

Question 3

Woman: Hello, Brian. It's Barbara speaking. I hope I've caught you in time. Have you printed the advertising leaflets for the Byzantine music concert yet? [pause] Oh, good. Have you got the master copy in front of you? [pause] Fine. As you may know, I've been away for a few days and I left a message for John to make some changes before I left. I haven't seen him since I got back because he's away at a conference, so I wanted to find out if he's made them. [pause] He did. That's good. Could you read out the... [pause] 7:45-that's right [pause] Town Hall... yes. [pause] Wednesday, 12th March, fine. And the admission charges? [pause] £3.50 and £2 for students. Well, everything seems in or-

der. Thank you, Brian. [pause] Goodbye.

PAUSE 2 seconds – tone

Repeat Question 3

PAUSE 2 seconds

Four

You hear two people talking about a book. What does the man say about it?

A Very few people have read it.
B Very few people can understand it.
C Very few people have bought it.

PAUSE 5 seconds – tone

Question 4

Man: That film reminds me a lot of that book I gave you. You remember... er... *The History...* no... *An Amazing History of Time.* Have you still got it?

Woman: Yes, it's in my bookcase in the living room.

Man: Don't you think the film has a lot in common with it? You have read it, haven't you?

Woman: To be honest, I've only got up to the second chapter.

Man: Didn't you like it then?

Woman: It's interesting, I suppose, but I just haven't had the time.

Man: That's not surprising. Not many people have managed to get to the end. Some haven't even got as far as you. Still, it has sold millions. Anyway, I think you should make time to read it. It's quite easy really...

PAUSE 2 seconds – tone

Repeat Question 4

PAUSE 2 seconds

Five

You hear two people talking about an exhibition they went to. What was their opinion of it?

A It was boring.
B It was interesting.
C It was disappointing.

PAUSE 5 seconds – tone

Question 5

Ron: Have you been to the computer exhibition yet?

Harold: Yes, as a matter of fact I went yesterday afternoon.

Ron: What did you think of it?

Harold: I half expected it to bore me to death. I only agreed to go because Vivian didn't want to go on her own, but I'm glad I did.

Ron: So am I. I went on Saturday with Paul. I must admit I enjoyed it. There was so much I didn't know about this hi-tech stuff. Luckily, Paul was able to explain most of it to me – he does computer studies at school, you know.

Harold: Mmm... How about you and I enrolling for evening classes in computing next term?

PAUSE 2 seconds – tone

Repeat Question 5

PAUSE 2 seconds

Six

Listen to a man talking to a friend about a trip he went on. Why didn't he stay in the town he was visiting?

A   All the hotels were fully booked.
B   The hotels were too expensive.
C   The hotels were terrible.

PAUSE 5 seconds – tone

Question 6

Man: I'd been there several times before, but this was the first time I'd had any difficulties.
Woman: Difficulties? What sort of difficulties?
Man: I'd never been there in March before and I'd completely forgotten about the carnival they have there every year.
Woman: And they'd put up the prices in the hotels.
Man: No, not really. That wasn't the problem. There were simply too many people there and we couldn't find a room for love nor money.
Woman: How terrible! What did you do?
Man: I rang a colleague who lives in a village nearby and fortunately, he put us up for a few days.

PAUSE 2 seconds – tone

Repeat Question 6

PAUSE 2 seconds

Seven

Listen to a woman talking on the phone.   What is the relationship between her and the person she is talking to?

A   They are colleagues.
B   They are friends.
C   They are relatives.

PAUSE 5 seconds – tone

Question 7

Mandy: Hello. It's Mandy here. I was just calling to see how you were. I called you at work yesterday and they told me you were off sick. [pause] Oh, dear! Did you send for the doctor? [pause] Hot drinks and bed, yes. And how long will it last? [pause] You'll be fine by the weekend then? [pause] Good. I'll see you at the party. [pause] Don't tell me you've forgotten! It's Gran's... [pause] Yes, it's this weekend. You haven't made any other plans, have you? The whole family will be there and everyone would be most disappointed if you didn't come [pause] I don't see why not. There'll be so many people there. If you just bring one friend, I don't think anyone will mind. [pause] Right, I'll see you then and I hope you feel better soon. [pause] Bye.

PAUSE 2 seconds – tone

Repeat Question 7

PAUSE 2 seconds

Eight

Listen to two people talking about a man who has been arrested.   What crime did he commit?

A   robbery
B   burglary
C   murder

PAUSE 5 seconds – tone

Question 8

Brenda: Talking about security and burglar alarms, did you hear about that guy who broke into a student's home the other day?
Eric: No, I don't think I did. What happened?
Brenda: He thought she'd be an easy target. There were no alarms and it was quite easy for him to get in, but he didn't realise that she was at home.
Eric: And she was an expert in karate or something.
Brenda: No, nothing like that. She was an art student and she managed to sketch him without him knowing.
Eric: Did he take anything?
Brenda: Not much, but when she took the sketch down to the police station, they recognised him immediately. He'd committed several crimes and was known to the police.
Eric: He wasn't dangerous, was he?
Brenda: No, he'd never been charged for a violent crime like mugging or murder, but she was frightened while she was drawing him in her house. She can't have known he wasn't violent at the time, of course.

PAUSE 2 seconds – tone

Repeat Question 8

PAUSE 2 seconds

That's the end of Part One. Now turn to Part Two.

PART 2

You will hear two people making enquiries about cars for sale.   For questions 9–18, complete the sentences.

You now have forty-five seconds in which to look at Part Two.

PAUSE 45 seconds – tone

Mr Parsons: I see you've had a look through the motoring section.
Mrs Parsons: Yes, I had a look this morning and I found quite a few that sounded interesting. I've marked the best ones in orange.
Mr Parsons: Yes... I see you've chosen three here. Shall we phone now?
Mrs Parsons: Can you do it? You know how I hate talking to strangers on the phone. And here's a piece of paper with the cars written on it, so you can make notes while you're phoning.
Mr Parsons: Thanks. I see you've thought of everything.
[sound of dialling]
Voice 1:   Hello, 229152.
Mr Parsons: Good evening. I'm phoning about the ad I saw in *Change and Mart*...
Voice 1:   Yes, the Honda Accord. What do you want to know?
Mr Parsons: It says in the ad that it's brand new, but the price of £17,950 is well below the list price.
Voice1:   That's right.
Mr Parsons: Well, could you tell me exactly how many miles it's done, please?
Voice 1:   Just over 2,000.
Mr Parsons: ... And it's automatic.
Voice 1:   Yes. All the details in the advertisement are correct.
Mr Parsons: So, it's silver in colour.
Voice 1:   That's right.
Mr Parsons: Does it have air conditioning?
Voice 1:   Yes, it does and it also has a fitted CD stereo and an immobiliser-alarm system, which I'm afraid weren't in the ad.
Mr Parsons: Would it be possible for us to come and see it tomorrow?
Voice 1:   Yes, of course. Tomorrow... that's Wednesday 13th, isn't it? You can come between six and eight in the evening, but give me a ring first. May I have your name, please?
Mr Parsons: It's Parsons – Michael Parsons.
Voice1:   Right. And my address is 24 Forest Drive.
Mr Parsons: Yes, I know it. I'll give you a ring tomorrow then. Goodbye.
[puts phone down]
Mr Parsons: That sounded fine.
Mrs Parsons: [hesitantly] I'm not too keen on automatics.

Mr Parsons:	But it's good value, isn't it? What's next?
Mrs Parsons:	The Alfa. Here's the number.
[sound of dialling]	
Voice 2:	772863
Mr Parsons:	Good evening. I'm phoning about your ad in *Change and Mart.*
Voice 2:	Yes, you're the fifth caller this evening.
Mr Parsons:	Can you give me some details, please. There weren't ···
Voice 2:	It's in superb condition; it's Africa grey; it's got alloy wheels and a manufacturer's warranty and the mileage is about average.
Mr Parsons:	How many miles is that exactly?
Voice 2:	32,000 – that's about standard.
Mr Parsons:	How old is the car?
Voice 2:	About two years old.
Mr Parsons:	You say that you'll accept offers around £13,500. Would you take £13,000?
Voice 2:	Cash? Yes.
Mr Parsons:	Are there any extras?
Voice 2:	Extras? A lot of work has been done on it. You'll have to come and see for yourself.
Mr Parsons:	Would tomorrow – the 13th – be suitable?
Voice 2:	Yes, at any time. Just give me a ring first.
Mr Parsons:	Thank you and goodbye.
Voice 2:	Goodbye.
[puts phone down]	
Mrs Parsons:	You didn't seem to be very keen on that.
Mr Parsons:	The mileage seemed awfully high for such a new car.
Mrs Parsons:	Look, this next ad is quite large. Put in all the details now, so you don't have to rush it while you're on the phone.
Mr Parsons:	Good idea.
Mrs Parsons:	It's a Golf 1.6 HSE Auto... [pause] Oh, never mind. It's done 4,000 miles and it has a host of extras-alloy wheels, air conditioning, an alarm-immobiliser, ABS and 4 air bags. It says here it's in showroom condition – you can put that under "Remarks". And let's see... the price is... er... £15,450.
Mr Parsons:	What's the number?
Mrs Parsons:	478675
[sound of dialling]	
Voice 3:	Hello.
Mr Parsons:	Hello. I'm phoning about your ad in...
Voice 3:	It's been sold, I'm afraid.
Mr Parsons:	Oh, dear! That's a shame. Sorry to have bothered you.
Voice 3:	That's all right. Goodbye.
Mr Parsons:	It's already [fade out]...

PAUSE 10 seconds

Now you will hear Part Two again.

Repeat Part Two

PAUSE 5 seconds

That is the end of Part Two. Now turn to Part Three.

PART 3

You will hear five different people talking about why they were punished while they were at school. For questions 19–23, choose which of the people A–F is speaking. Use the letters only once. There is one extra letter which you do not need to use.

You now have thirty seconds in which to look at Part Three.

PAUSE 30 seconds – tone

Speaker 1

I was only punished once while I was at school and that was only because I was forced to do something I didn't want to do. I got punished because of the class bully, who I was really frightened of. He used to cheat in exams by hiding his crib notes in a toilet paper roll and going to the toilet shortly after the exam had started in order to read them. It was quite a clever idea, but he got caught after some teachers became suspicious. Then he tried writing his notes on the classroom wall but when he moved the desk so that he could read them, a teacher saw him and he had to stop. Then, one day, he told me he'd be sitting behind me and I was to move my paper so that he could read what I'd written. I did as he had said, but a teacher saw us and we were both punished. I had to write a composition about honesty but I think the teacher realized what had happened because she apologised for having to punish me.

Speaker 2

I got into trouble quite often when I was at school. I got up to all sorts of stuff which made the teachers furious. I must have been a right pain in the neck but I didn't care. Probably the worst thing I did was before an exam. We had a teacher who thought he was great. He used to come into class in a white suit, with gel on his hair and his sunglasses on his head. He thought he was so cool and he treated us like dirt. So one day I decided to show him. I wrote a rude word in marker pen on the back of his chair so that when he sat down, it would come off on his white suit. Looking back now, I realise it wasn't nice but I couldn't have cared less at the time. After he'd sat down, he turned round to write something on the board and everyone burst out laughing. When he found out, he threatened to punish the whole class, so I owned up. I got suspended for three days but, at that time, it seemed more of a short holiday than a punishment.

Speaker 3

Do you remember seeing "Kilroy was here" on the toilet walls when you were at school? Well, these words were to be found all over my old school and my teachers were determined to find out who the culprits were. They watched the toilets for a couple of weeks and rounded up some suspects. I was among them but I hadn't done anything wrong. Though I protested my innocence, I was taken to the headmaster's study along with the others. The headmaster didn't really know how to handle the situation so he started being sarcastic. He expected us to listen to his speech and promise to be good. Well, you know how you start thinking about what you'd like to say to someone while they're talking, but you never do? I started thinking about how I'd like to call him and the whole scene ridiculous and guess what? I did – much to the amusement of the other boys. He immediately forgot about the writing on the wall – for which the others were grateful – and gave me a Saturday morning detention for not behaving like a gentleman or showing him respect.

Speaker 4

There weren't many occasions on which I thought I deserved to be punished, but this was certainly one of them. After rugby training, I went back to my classroom to get a book I needed for revision. As I was walking down the corridor, a teacher suddenly came out of the office and bumped into me. We were both given a start and apologised to each other. I explained why I was in school so late and he said goodnight. As he was leaving, I noticed that he'd dropped something. I picked it up and saw that it was a copy of the geography exam we were having the following day. I wanted to run after him, but something held me back. I took it home with the book I'd forgotten so that I could study the exam questions. Of course I got a good mark in geography – far too good for me. This made my teacher suspicious. He remembered that he'd bumped into me and knew he was a copy short, so he put two and two together. I confessed and had to explain why I'd done it to the headmaster and my parents. I also had to do extra homework for a month.

Speaker 5

The first thing you have to do when you go to a new school is confront the class or school bully. When I was in my final year, I transferred to another school where I had to face bullies. There were two of them and their reign of terror caused panic throughout the school. They demanded money with threats of violence and they nearly always got it. One day, they approached me and told me how their system worked. It was simple – pay up, or get beaten up. I immediately told them I didn't want any trouble. By this time a crowd had gathered, watching eagerly. As I was about to walk away, one of them, John Buckney grabbed my jacket. I looked at him for a split second before throwing him to the ground. His friend, Nigel Charles, threw a punch, but I sent him crashing to the ground, too. After I'd thrown a few punches of my own, they gave up but they started cursing and threatening me. I could see that the onlookers were pleased, but they didn't dare express their delight. What I didn't see, however, was a teacher who had seen the whole incident. The three of us got the cane. It hurt but Buckney and Charles never bothered me again.

PAUSE 10 seconds – tone

Now you'll hear Part Three again

Repeat Part Three

PAUSE 5 seconds.

That's the end of Part Three. Now turn to Part Four.

PART 4

You will hear a conversation about predicting the future. For questions 24–30, choose the best answer, A, B or C.

You now have one minute to look at Part Four.

PAUSE I minute – tone

Dave:	You don't believe in that stuff, do you? I mean, it's all nonsense. I remember one programme where they had a Canadian who had predicted a plane crash and there was one. Then he told everyone how he'd made the prediction. It was all based on statistics, Linda. I mean, the man didn't have any special powers.
Linda:	Actually, that was on the programme, too. They also showed how a woman pretended to record a prediction that Ronald Reagan would be shot about a month before it happened when, in fact, she made the recording after the event. So the programme didn't try to cover up the fact that there are fakes.
Dave:	Look! As far as I'm concerned, it's either coincidence or statistics and that's that.
Carol:	I saw the programme as well, Dave, and I don't think it can be explained away so easily.
Dave:	Oh, no – not you, too.
Carol:	OK! Listen to a couple of examples from the programme and see if you think they're just coincidence.
Dave:	Go ahead then, Carol.
Carol:	An American – Booth, I think his name was – had a dream about a plane crash...
Dave:	Not another one...
Linda:	Let her finish, will you?
Carol:	As I was saying, he dreamt that a plane crashed just after take-off and this didn't happen only once. In fact, it became quite a regular occurrence. He described how the plane – a DC-10, I think it was – was making a strange noise just before it turned upside down and crashed.
Linda:	That's right. He got so upset that in the end, he phoned someone in charge of air traffic control and told them in detail about his dream. The day after his call, there was a crash in Chicago.
Dave:	I still don't see...
Linda:	Listen, will you? The plane had lost an engine and that's why it was making a strange noise. But what was really strange was that no jet plane had ever crashed like that before – upside down, I mean.
Dave:	Dreams again. I'm still not convinced.
Linda:	Tell him about the Flixbro prediction, Carol. He's getting on my nerves.
Carol:	OK! This wasn't a dream. A woman was at home watching TV at around midday when she saw a newsflash. In the newsflash she said she saw, there was a report of a huge explosion at a chemical factory in which several people had been killed. Later on, a friend of hers came round for lunch and she asked her friend if she'd heard about the explosion, but she hadn't. Anyway, her friend stayed on after lunch and during the afternoon she spoke to several people on the phone. Every time she mentioned the accident to the people

on the phone, the person she was speaking to said they hadn't heard anything about it. Then, at around five o'clock, while she and her friend were watching a soap opera, there was a newsflash just like the one she said she'd seen five hours earlier, but the reports said that the accident had happened at ten to five in the afternoon. At first they laughed because they thought the reporter had got it wrong, but when they changed channel, they found out it wasn't a mistake.

Linda:	And she was terrified at the time. She had nothing to gain so why should she or her friends lie about it?
Dave:	I must admit that it's really weird.
Linda:	There were also other examples like the one where someone dreamt exactly which horse would win the Grand National in 1965.
Dave:	Er... Foinavon, wasn't it? At 100 – I if I remember correctly.
Linda:	Yes, and he predicted that nearly all the horses would fall at the same fence.
Dave:	I remember. There was a terrible pile-up. (pause) I must admit there may be more to this than I thought, but I'm not saying...
Carol:	And don't forget that Abraham Lincoln foresaw his... [fade out]

PAUSE 10 seconds – tone

Now you will hear Part Four again.

Repeat Part Four

PAUSE 5 seconds

That's the end of Part four.

There'll now be a pause of five minutes for you to copy your answers onto the separate answer sheet. I'll remind you when there is one minute left, so that you're sure to finish in time.

PAUSE 4 minutes

You have one minute left.

PAUSE I minute.
That's the end of the test. Please stop now. Your supervisor will collect all the papers and answer sheets. Goodbye.

TEST 6

First Certificate Practice Test Six. Paper Four. Listening.

Hello. I'm going to give you the instructions for this test. I'll introduce each part of the test and give you time to look at the questions. At the start of each piece you'll hear this sound:

tone

You'll hear each piece twice. Remember, while you're listening, write your answers on the question paper. You'll have time at the end of the test to copy your answers onto the separate answer sheet.

The tape will now be stopped. Please ask any questions now, because you must not speak during the test.

PAUSE 5 seconds

PART 1

Now open your question paper and look at Part One. You will hear people talking in eight different situations. For questions 1–8, choose the best answer, A, B or C.

One
Listen to two people talking about an injury. How did the man burn his hand?

A   There was a fire in his kitchen.
B   He got hot liquid on it.
C   He touched a very hot pan.

PAUSE 5 seconds – tone

Question 1

Woman: What's up! Why have you got that bandage on your hand!
Man: Oh, that. It's nothing really. I burnt my hand over the week-end.
Woman: How on earth did you do that?
Man: I was cooking in the kitchen.   We had visitors on Saturday evening,   so I had to prepare a big meal.   I had vegetables boiling,   sausages frying – you know,   everything was on. Then the phone rang and I forgot about the food that was cooking. It's lucky the oil didn't catch fire! Well, when I went back into the kitchen,   I realised the food was getting over-cooked.   I tried to move the pots and pans off the stove as quickly as possible and accidentally spilt some boiling water on my hand.

PAUSE 2 seconds – tone

Repeat Question 1

PAUSE 2 seconds

Two

Listen to a man talking about a football match. How did he feel immediately afterwards?

A   shocked
B   embarrassed
C   frustrated

PAUSE 5 seconds – tone

Question 2

Man: We didn't even expect to reach the third round,   let alone the final. Anyway, there we were, ready to face one of the best teams in the league. We knew we had nothing to lose so we weren't under pres-sure or anything like that. The other team, though, knew they had to win and I suppose they thought they would quite easily.   I must say we played pretty well and the longer we kept them from scoring, the more frustrated they got. They started fouling us and eventually one of their players was sent off. You know the rest. We scored five min-utes before the end and won one-nil. When we were presented with the cup, I didn't really know what was happening. I was completely stunned. It didn't really sink in till later.

PAUSE 2 seconds – tone

Repeat Question 2

PAUSE 2 seconds

Three

Listen to a man talking to two friends. What is he doing?

A   giving a warning
B   making fun of his friends
C   telling a joke

PAUSE 5 seconds – tone

Question 3

David: So Michael walks down the drive of the third house...
Brenda: Is this the last one?
Margaret: Be quiet, Brenda! Let him finish.
David: Thanks, Margaret. Where was I? Oh, yes ... He rings the bell,   but there's no answer.   Then he hears voices coming from the back garden, so he goes round to have a look. He sees several people round the pool and after finding out who the owner is,   he asks for a job because he needs money desperately.   Eventually the owner tells Michael to get two cans of white paint from the shed and to go and paint the porch.   So off he goes.   After a while he gets back and the owner asks him if he's finished. "Yes, er," says Michael, "but there was one problem."
           "Yes?" says the owner.
           "Well, it wasn't a PORSCHE. It was a FERRARI!"
Brenda: Oh, no. That's awful! It's not funny at all.

PAUSE 2 seconds – tone

Repeat Question 3

PAUSE 2 seconds

Four

You hear this conversation in a restaurant. Why is the man complaining?

A   His food is undercooked.
B   His food is cold.
C   He was given the wrong order.

PAUSE 5 seconds – tone

Question 4

Customer: Waiter!
Waiter: Yes, sir. How may I help you?
Customer: It's the food you brought me.
Waiter: What's wrong with it?
Customer: It's the steak I ordered ...
Waiter: Oh, I see. It's underdone, is it? Sorry, my mistake ...
Customer: No, no. I asked for a medium sirloin steak and that's exactly what I've got.   The problem is that it must have been left on the plate for ages in the kitchen before you brought it to me.
Waiter: I'll get you another one, sir.
Customer: Thank you.   And please don't bring me one that's been re-heated.

PAUSE 2 seconds – tone

Repeat Question 4

PAUSE 2 seconds

Five

Listen to a man telling a woman about a famous person.   Who was the fa-mous person?

A   a business executive
B   a sporting figure
C   an actress

PAUSE 5 seconds – tone

Question 5

Man: And there she was in front of me.   It was the first time I had ever seen such a famous person in the flesh.
Woman: What was she like? I mean, did she ignore everyone and just go about her business?
Man: No,   not at all.   I know she played all those roles where she was wealthy and sophisticated,   but she was really down to earth.   She had time to talk to people who said how much they admired her and she even gave a few autographs.   I've still got mine at home.

PAUSE 2 seconds – tone

Repeat question 5

PAUSE 2 seconds

Six

Listen to a woman who has moved house talking on the phone. Where has she moved to?

A   another country
B   another city
C   a village

PAUSE 5 seconds – tone

Question 6

Woman: Not yet. And I think it'll take quite a long time for us to get settled in. Remember what we used to say about any place north of Watford? [pause] Yes, that's right. It wasn't a joke at all. There are times when I feel as if I've moved abroad. The local accent is hard to get used to. [pause] There are a few. It's not been that bad but there have been times when I haven't been able to understand the locals. [pause] Let me see. Yes, keks. [pause] It means trousers. [pause] Neither did I. Oh, and they say that the people who live out in the countryside are very strange – wary of newcomers and change. [pause] I hope so, too. I'll give you a ring at the weekend then. [pause] Bye and take care!

PAUSE 2 seconds – tone

Repeat question 6

PAUSE 2 seconds

Seven

Listen to a woman talking to a friend about a recent holiday. What was the weather like?

A   wet
B   sunny
C   cold

PAUSE 5 seconds – tone

Question 7

Woman: Yes, I know. I was due back yesterday but I wasn't very well.
Man: You didn't get food poisoning when you went on holiday, did you?
Woman: No. The food was fine.
Man: So, what was your holiday like?
Woman: I took light clothing just as Fran suggested. She went there last year, as you know, and she told me it had been pretty warm. When I arrived, it was drizzling. We thought it would clear up, but it didn't. It was like that all the time.
Man: Did you have to buy warm clothes then?
Woman: No, the weather was pretty mild, but as I said the rain didn't let up at all. Well, that's not quite true. It actually stopped a couple of hours before we left. It's a good thing I'm not the kind of person who spends hours sunbathing every day.

PAUSE 2 seconds – tone

Repeat question 7

PAUSE 2 seconds

Eight

Listen to a radio announcer giving some motoring information. What has blocked the A30?

A   a vehicle
B   a tree
C   floods

PAUSE 5 seconds – tone

Question 8

Announcer: More bad news for you drivers out there, I'm afraid. Last night'

s hurricane force winds have played havoc with our roads and, with fallen trees and flooding blocking most of the minor roads in the region, motorists are advised to stay at home unless their journey is absolutely necessary. Now, reports are coming in of a lorry that has jackknifed and blocked both eastbound lanes of the A30 two miles before the Yeovil turnoff. So there's another stretch of road to avoid. Remember, all you motorists out there – patience saves lives. Drive carefully now and be a passive driver! [Fade out]

PAUSE 2 seconds – tone

Repeat Question 8

PAUSE 2 seconds

That's the end of Part One. Now turn to Part Two.

PART 2

You will hear a radio interview with two experts on keeping unusual pets. For questions 9–18, complete the sentences.

You now have forty-five seconds in which to look at Part Two.

PAUSE 45 seconds – tone

[music fades]

Presenter: Good afternoon and welcome to the third in our series of Unusual Pets. In the studio today, we have Tim Tyde and Daniel Gorman, who will be telling us all about keeping geckos and monitors. Welcome to the show, Tim.
Tim: Thank you.
Presenter: Now, I suppose many of our listeners will be wondering what a gecko is.
Tim: Yes, a gecko is a kind of lizard. I'm going to be talking about *Rhacodactylus auriculatus*, or the gargoyle gecko.
Presenter: Where do these geckos come from?
Tim: There are six species of *Rhacodactylus* and they are all found in New Caledonia, which is an island, or rather a group of islands, 1500 km off the east coast of Australia.
Presenter: You mentioned the gargoyle gecko. What does this kind of lizard look like?
Tim: An adult can reach about 13 cm in length. They have long dark stripes and an orange or red body. They're called gargoyle geckos because of two large bumps on their head.
Presenter: And what about their feeding habits?
Tim: In the wild, they eat flowers, smaller lizards, insects, spiders and pollen.
Presenter: And are they easy to keep?
Tim: Yes. I'd say they would be ideal for a beginner. They're quite tough and they don't really need that much care. A forty-litre tank with an outdoor carpet on the bottom, climbing surfaces and water in a small dish are all they need. Branches of at least 5 cm in diameter make ideal climbing surfaces for them.
Presenter: Where can you get food for them?
Tim: There are specialist shops in most areas. I feed the adults on live crickets dusted in vitamin and mineral powder. For stubborn feeders, I recommend wax worms.
Presenter: So, live prey makes up part of their diet.
Tim: Yes, but you must remember that their appetites vary considerably. They go from having a huge appetite to disregarding their food completely.
Presenter: Thank you, Tim. Now, over to you, Daniel. Your pets aren't so easy to keep, are they?
Daniel: No, not at all. Green tree monitors are definitely not for beginners. Only experienced keepers should have them.
Presenter: Can you tell us something about them?
Daniel: First of all, the green tree monitor, Varanus prasinus, is a truly beautiful lizard, varying in colour from lime green to turquoise with black chevrons on their neck – some have spots, too. With proper care, they can be as tame as a dog,

but they require a lot of maintenance. I spend from two to four hours a day with them. They are from the rainforests of New Guinea, where they eat insects.

Presenter: Where do you keep your monitors?

Daniel: In specially-made tanks, measuring 120 cm × 50 cm × 75 cm. I keep no more than three animals in one tank. There are branches for climbing and plastic leaves. Conditions are important, too. They need to be kept in a climate of 30-33℃ at a humidity of at least 65%. Most of the time I keep the humidity up near 100%. You can do this by steam-cleaning the humidifier daily. Water drains through a hole covered with a screen at the back.

Presenter: Is all this equipment expensive?

Daniel: Not very, but these animals need great care. They're quite nervous by nature and feeding can be a problem. I offer mine crickets with powdered calcium through a hole in the top of the tank. They also get neonate mice every two weeks.

Presenter: You mean you feed them live mice!

Daniel: You can't keep reptiles unless you're prepared to do that.

Presenter: After the break Daniel and Tim will be here ready to take your calls.

[music – fade out]

PAUSE 10 seconds

Now you will hear Part Two again.

Repeat Part Two

PAUSE 5 seconds

That is the end of Part Two. Now turn to Part Three.

PART 3

You'll hear five different people talking about the way they look. For questions 19–23, choose which of the people A–F is speaking. Use the letters only once. There is one extra letter which you do not need to use.

You now have thirty seconds to look at Part Three.

PAUSE 30 seconds – tone

Speaker 1 Julie

I'm quite happy with how I look though I could be a little slimmer. But then everyone thinks that, don't they? I don't weigh myself that often – perhaps once or twice a month but I'd rush off to the scales if someone made a comment like "You've put on weight" or I've overdone the junk food. If I put on a few pounds, I do feel depressed. When that happens, I'd rather eat healthy food than go without food. Junk food like pizza and sweets is a weakness of mine, but I try to eat stuff like fruit and salad, too. I try not to compare myself with slim models, but that's hard because they're everywhere. Sometimes, it does make you feel as if that's what you should look like. But then I remind myself of my perfect role model Kate Tinslett. She's neither skinny nor fat but she's rich, famous, successful and happy.

PAUSE 2 seconds

Speaker 2 Lavon

I'm about a size 20 but I don't have a problem with the way I look. I wouldn't wear short skirts because my legs are too large. But that's nothing to do with weight. I just avoid wearing clothes that don't make me look good. I never worry about putting on or losing weight. When I meet people for the first time, I want them to judge me by who I am. I think looks and personality are as important as each other but I'm not stupid. I know no one wants to hang around with someone who's big and ugly. That's the truth. Friends and family are the biggest influence in telling you how you should look. What the Government says isn't going to make a difference. Friends can help but they can also make things worse. They don't realize that comments made as a joke can be really hurtful. When people have a dig at me, I just try to ignore it. And if I'm ever feeling down, I don't eat to make myself feel better – I put on nail varnish.

PAUSE 2 seconds

Speaker 3 Anna

I think there's an over-reaction to the effect skinny models have on girls. We're not so stupid as to believe every image fed to us. There are many influences at work, like peer-group pressure. It's no coincidence that eating problems are particularly common in high-pressure private schools. I'm not the most attractive girl in the world, but because people judge you by your appearance, I do think it would be nice to be pretty. I'm a size 8-10 now and, apart from my stomach, I am reasonably happy. My weight does sometimes determine the clothes I buy as I tend to choose things that do not draw attention to my stomach. I'm also rather self-conscious when I go out without make-up. Personality is, of course, far more important than looks, but we all know that a man will not usually go up to an ugly girl in a club in the hope that she has a nice personality. It's a shame but it's a fact of life.

PAUSE 2 seconds

Speaker 4 Louise

My friends and I always look at magazines and we have lots of conversations about weight and how skinny models affect us. Even if, like me, you're not that dissatisfied with your body, it's still a big talking point. I know two people who suffered from anorexia – a family friend and a school friend. As a result, I'm determined not to worry too much about putting on weight and I hardly ever weigh myself – maybe once every few months. The only time I get depressed is when I try on clothes while shopping and think: "Why doesn't this fit me?" As far as boys are concerned, I don't really care what they think – if they judge me on my looks, it's their problem, not mine. I won't lose weight just to please them. I eat anything my mum cooks but I never eat snacks. That's not because I want to lose weight but because I want to be healthy. I rarely swim because the thought of getting into a swimming costume around super-fit people is pretty awful. So maybe I'm not as strong on the weight issue as I thought. It's difficult not to equate being thin with being popular.

PAUSE 2 seconds

Speaker 5 Karen

My sister and most of my friends really envy me. I'm the sort of person who can eat anything without putting on weight. There are times when I deliberately wear clothes that make me look a little bigger than I am unless, of course, I'm with a few close friends who look good, too. I feel as if other girls are really jealous of me and dislike me because of how I look. But that's not fair. It's not my fault, is it? The idea that people like me are popular because of the way we look is a myth. There is bitterness on the part of other girls who are influenced by the thin models they see in magazines or on TV. That's why I normally go out with other girls who can wear anything they like and look great.

PAUSE 10 seconds – tone

Now you will hear Part Three again.

Repeat Part Three

That's the end of Part Three. Now turn to Part Four.

PART 4

You will hear part of a conversation in which three people talk about where and how they were brought up. For questions 24–30, choose the best answer, A, B or C. You now have a minute in which to look at Part Four.

PAUSE I minute – tone

Marion: What do you think, Terry? You were brought up in a fairly poor area, weren't you?

Terry: Yes, I lived on a housing estate – our house was owned by the council. Everyone was in the same boat so we didn't know any better. We thought most people were like us. I found out a little more when I went to a grammar school in a rather expensive suburb.

Charles: Yes, I had the same impression, but from a privileged point, of course. I thought everyone had a large house, garden and plenty of money.

Marion: Yes, I had a similar view of the world to Charles. All the books I had portrayed the family with a detached or semi-detached house, two children, a dog and a couple of cars.

Terry: We didn't really read books. Our world was our neighbours and what they got up to.

Marion: What about crime? Did you come from a tough neighbourhood.

Terry: You had to be tough to survive. At first it was gangs. If you didn't join a skinhead gang, they'd attack you in the street. Later on it was pubs. There used to be a couple of bouncers outside and they'd ask you if you had a weapon on you. If you said no, they'd give you one.

Charles: Very good, Terry. I see that you still have the famous Liverpudlian sense of humour. But what do you think of the middle and upper classes? Isn't there a touch of jealousy when you see how comfortable their lives are?

Terry: Some of my friends dislike the idle rich, but I'm not like that. Anyway, don't the upper classes look down on people like me?

Marion: And I think the gap between the classes is getting wider all the time. Now that you have to pay to go to university to get a higher education, many poorer people don't go because they can't afford it.

Terry: That's where I was lucky. I don't think I would be able to go to university now. I got a grant to help me. It seems as if we're moving back to the 1950s, when education was only for those who could afford it.

Charles: But surely working-class children don't really want to go to university. They'd rather go out to work as soon as possible. They're not the kind of people who become ... you know, who enter the medical profession or ...

Marion: (angrily) Oh, come on, Charles! That's the kind of attitude that was fashionable about fifty years ago. And it's an attitude that has prevented many talented people from reaching their peak. I remember the film star, Michael Caine, saying that there was a great waste of talent in the country because of this traditional way of looking at society.

Charles: Look, all I'm trying to say is...

Terry: We know what you're trying to say, Charles, so I think we should stop now before this gets too heated. Why don't we go out for a coffee?

Marion: What a good idea! Coming, Charles?

Charles: Yes, of course. Listen, Terry, I didn't mean to offend you, old chap er...(fade out)

PAUSE 10 seconds – tone

Now you'll hear Part Four again.

Repeat Part Four

PAUSE 5 seconds

That's the end of Part Four.

There'll now be a pause of five minutes for you to copy your answers onto the separate answer sheet. I'll remind you when there is one minute left, so that you're sure to finish in time.

PAUSE 4 minutes

You have one more minute left.

PAUSE I minute

That's the end of the test. Please stop now. Your supervisor will collect all the question papers and answer sheets. Goodbye.

著作权合同登记　图字：01-2008-4807

图书在版编目(CIP)数据

剑桥第一证书英语考试教程2（教师用书)=Cambridge FCE Practice Tests 2 Teacher's Book /（英）斯蒂芬斯 (Stephens, N.)主编. —北京：北京大学出版社，2008.12

（剑桥英语等级考试系列·原版影印）

ISBN 978-7-301-14688-0

Ⅰ.剑… Ⅱ.斯… Ⅲ.英语–水平考试–教学参考资料 Ⅳ.H310.41

中国版本图书馆 CIP 数据核字(2008)第 188323 号

书　　　　名：	剑桥第一证书英语考试教程2（教师用书)
著作责任者：	N.斯蒂芬斯 (Nicholas Stephens)　主编
策　　　划：	刘　强
责 任 编 辑：	宣　瑄
标 准 书 号：	ISBN 978-7-301-14688-0/H·2161
出 版 发 行：	北京大学出版社
地　　　址：	北京市海淀区成府路 205 号　　100871
网　　　址：	http://www.pup.cn
电　　　话：	邮购部 62752015　发行部 62750672　编辑部 62767347　出版部 62754962
电 子 邮 箱：	zbing@pup.pku.edu.cn
印　刷　者：	北京大学印刷厂
经 销 者：	新华书店

889 毫米×1194 毫米　大 16 开　12 印张　386 千字

2008 年 12 月第 1 版　　2008 年 12 月第 1 次印刷

定　　价：28.00 元